Laura Marney was born in Glasgow and currently lives in Barcelona. She is a graduate of the Glasgow and Strathclyde mlitt Creative Writing course. Many of her short stories have been published in magazines and anthologies or broadcast on radio. *No Wonder I Take a Drink* is her first novel.

NO WONDER
I TAKE A DRINK

Laura Marney

BLACK SWAN

NO WONDER I TAKE A DRINK
A BLACK SWAN BOOK : 0 552 77200 3

First publication in Great Britain

PRINTING HISTORY
Black Swan edition published 2004

3 5 7 9 10 8 6 4 2

Copyright © Laura Marney 2004

Set in 11/13pt Melior by
Kestrel Data, Exeter, Devon.

Black Swan Books are published by Transworld Publishers,
61–63 Uxbridge Road, London W5 5SA,
a division of The Random House Group Ltd,
in Australia by Random House Australia (Pty) Ltd,
20 Alfred Street, Milsons Point, Sydney, NSW 2061, Australia,
in New Zealand by Random House New Zealand Ltd,
18 Poland Road, Glenfield, Auckland 10, New Zealand
and in South Africa by Random House (Pty) Ltd,
Endulini, 5a Jubilee Road, Parktown 2193, South Africa.

Printed and bound in Great Britain by
Cox & Wyman Ltd, Reading, Berkshire.

Papers used by Transworld Publishers are natural, recyclable
products made from wood grown in sustainable forests.
The manufacturing processes conform to the environmental
regulations of the country of origin.

This is for Ellen Doyle. And for Holly Marney and Max Marney who gave me permission.

Acknowledgements

Loads of people have given me help, friendship, inspiration and encouragement with my writing. My family, my friends, my colleagues and bosses are all due credit. A big shout out to Zoe, Louise and Zoe, Sadie and Francesca, Jenny, and the loudest shout of all for Colette.

Chapter 1

My lasting memory of Mum is of her standing leaning against her bed, wearing her good pearls, nicely turned out in a peach blouse and lemon cardi, bare naked from the waist down. She was threatening to sign herself out of the hospice for the third time that week. Anticipating this I had sneaked her in a half-bottle of vodka. We both knew it would probably finish her off but that's the way she wanted it. She died three nights later. Before she died and after I'd helped her put her drawers on and poured her a watered-down vodka and Coke, she nearly told me something.

I could see she was struggling and I suppose I should have been more patient or just told her to bloody well spit it out, but at the time I was too busy noticing that my mother had no pubic hair. I couldn't believe that, at age sixty-eight, she would take the trouble to give herself a shaven haven. Where would she have got hold of a razor? And besides, her hands shook most of the time.

At first I thought it was just another of her rants about the Health Service, actually a thinly disguised rant about her own health, but her tone was different, not angry, she seemed frightened. She closed her eyes and shook her head vigorously, the way she did when we argued. And then she went strange. She started rocking back and forth, moaning and shuddering.

'Your dad says I should . . .'

She was scaring me with her amateur dramatics so I decided to nip it in the bud.

'Dad's dead Mum, he died four years ago.'

Slowly she opened her eyes and showed me a thin aggressive smile. In the two years that Mum had lived with me, before she finally agreed to the hospice, our relationship had blossomed. Stuck in the flat together twenty-four hours a day, we flowed through the peaks and troughs of each other's moods. This intimacy had not brought the tolerance and understanding I had expected, but it did give us the ability to have a right good fight and not be embarrassed.

'I know he's dead you eejit, only too well, I'm not senile, and it's four and a half years, actually.'

'Sorry. You said he says.'

'Yes, he says,' she spat, and then she was off on one. 'I meant says. He might have *said* to you Trisha, but he *says* to me, OK?'

'OK.'

'I'm about to pop my clogs and you're pulling me up about grammar!' She was shouting now.

'OK! Sorry!' I was shouting too.

We both sulked for a while. As usual, I was the first to give in.

'So what is it that Dad always "says", then?'

I could see she was swithering whether to fall back in with me or not.

'He always says wash behind your ears . . .'

'Or totties will grow there,' I finished for her.

'He says be true to your teeth . . .'

'Or they'll be false to you.'

We were becoming a double act.

'He knows, he understands. He says I've to explain to you.'

'Explain what Mum?'

'He says to tell you that young women can be daft sometimes.'

'OK Mum.'

I was nearly forty, nobody except Mum thought of me as a young woman.

'Try to understand.'

I knew it was a bad idea to smile so I held it in.

'OK Mum.'

'He says give your mother another vodka.'

'OK!'

'He says d'you think she's daft and can't tell it's watered down?'

I changed the subject, complimenting her on her shampoo and set. Since she'd been ill we bickered freely. At the beginning I bit my tongue and let her get away with it. I didn't want her dying on me after a fallout. She took full advantage of her position but it was no fun for either of us and I think she was relieved when I began to argue back. Now, as time ran out, I was in a sticky position. I hated wasting time on pointless arguments but I couldn't give in too easily. Elsie was a bad-tempered old git towards the end.

I'd rehearsed in my head the deathbed scene loads of times. She would tell me to look after Steven. She would say she loved me, that she was proud of me. She'd only said it twice before, once when her mother died and then again when Dad died. In a sick way I was looking forward to it. I would tell her I loved her, it wasn't a big deal for me to say it, I told Steven I loved him practically every time I saw him but I'd only ever told Mum twice. Tit for tat.

The night she went I sat with her, in what, for the

11

last three weeks, had been Mum's room. There was a coffee table and two big easy chairs on either side, by the window looking onto the garden. All around the room Mum had put her photos of Dad and me and Steven and the plants she'd been encouraged to bring. I brought her a bowl of green grapes and tangerines which she hadn't touched, and there was a telly and a CD player. It was never going to be featured in a lifestyle magazine but it was homely and it suited Elsie.

That night the room looked the same but different. It was the same except her photos had been put on the bedside table beside her where she could see them. Someone had programmed a loop of cheesy New Age music in the CD. A morphine drip was rigged and the bed was jacked up to its full height. It made it easy for the staff to work around her, and when the time came, easier for the nurses to roll her old body onto a trolley and off to the mortuary. The time was coming. Within a few hours the room would be cleaned and cleared, ready to become another terminally ill patient's home from home.

I sat holding her hand for a couple of hours and tried to read *Woman's Own* while she slid in and out of consciousness. Reading was making me sleepy so I gave up and took a tangerine from the fruit bowl. It looked OK when I lifted it but it fell apart in my hand. White mould covered the underside. I'd only bought it three days ago along with the vodka, but the stifling heat of the hospice had turned it to rotten mush.

A couple of times she looked as if she was away. Twice her chest stopped and then started again, sighing a heavy death rattle. I was on my own with her most of the time. About two o'clock she started talking, gibbering in a panicky voice. She shouted 'Hughie!' my dad's name, a few times. I called the nurse but she said it was just the effect of the pain relief, nothing to be distressed about. Three times Mum said, 'It's best all round,' in between making gurgly noises at the back of her throat.

'Mum, shhh now, it's OK.'

She started again but it was the same kind of thing.

'It's as well to let it lie, isn't it? Hughie? Isn't it?'

Every word was an effort for her. I was raging. Two years she'd had to sort things out and now, when she only had a few minutes left with me, she was talking in riddles. I should have got to the bottom of it the other day and then we wouldn't be having all this palaver now. I just wanted her not to fret, to be at peace.

'It doesn't matter, Mum, whatever it is, I'll sort it, I promise.'

She was gripping my hand tightly and when she spoke she spat the words. I tried to ignore the spittle which dribbled between our intertwined hands.

'No!' she gasped. For a second it looked as though she was about to leap out the bed. 'Over my dead body!'

She managed a smile and caught my eye to see if I'd got the joke. I was a bit shocked but I smiled my recognition. She quietened down again for a while and got her breath back. I went back to *Woman's Own*. An hour later a faint movement caught my eye. Mum was weakly flapping her hand, beckoning me to her. I had no idea how long she'd been trying to attract my attention. As I bent over to catch her last words she whispered, 'Turn that bloody music off.'

Steven came to the funeral and looked really smart. Bob, his dad, came too which I thought was a nice gesture, seeing as he and my mother hated each other's guts. She would have been proud of Steven though, as proud as I was. He was desperate to be a pall-bearer as I knew he would be. Mum had said no, worried that

13

he'd drop her. In the end I let him, it was his granny and he had a right. All Mum's pals were amazed. 'Is that your boy? What age is he now? Fifteen? God, look at the height of him! Fifteen and nearly six feet. He's a lovely big lad so he is.'

Mum's elder sister was the living breathing spit of her. They were almost exactly the same height and build. Auntie Nettie had the same hair and the same way of holding her hands across her middle as Mum. They didn't start out that way but as they'd got older the two sisters, Elsie and Nettie, had grown more and more alike. Sometimes when Nettie had been round seeing Mum I was hard pushed to tell one from the other. But while they were physically nearly identical, their personalities were completely different. OK, Mum was a bit cratchety, but she'd been ill, she wasn't always like that. Nettie was. A more self-centred old woman you wouldn't wish to meet.

And now Nettie was in her element. Before we went into the church she was all business, bossing the undertakers about, drilling Bob, Steven and me on funeral protocol. As Mum's only sister and self-appointed Chief Mourner, she formed us into an orderly line and positioned herself at the front. Once we were inside she fell apart and became a bit of an embarrassment, wailing and howling and generally drawing attention to herself. She actually swooned and had to be supported on more than one occasion. What with all the crying and the faces she was pulling, her make-up was halfway down her face, not a good look for a woman in her seventies. As the four of us sat in the front pew I looked down and saw Steven holding Nettie's hand and squeezing it tight. I wasn't sure if he was trying to comfort her or shut her up but I appreciated him trying to help.

It must be said that Bob didn't let me down either.

Even though people knew we'd split up, he did his bit as the devoted husband. He didn't overdo it though. As we walked out the church Bob put his arm around Steven and his hand at my elbow. I let him use my elbow as a rudder to guide us through the mourners. Bob's hair, once a flamboyant red, had paled to a golden blond. He'd kept in shape and the dark suit did his athletic frame justice. I was grateful that he'd made the effort. Auntie Nettie, wanting to spin out the lamenting a wee while longer, insisted we stand and shake hands with everyone coming out. Nettie would only release them from her embrace when she'd left oily deposits of Max Factor's Honey Blush on the men's black suits.

At the cemetery there were a few folk I didn't recognize but I asked the minister to invite everyone to the hotel where I'd arranged refreshments. Mum had insisted on steak pie; she'd had the baker on standby for weeks. After sherry and steak pie and a few vodkas Auntie Nettie announced, without consulting me, that everyone was invited back to the house. I asked Bob if he would come, not because I wanted him to, but because I wanted Steven to come home with me. I knew Steven would come if Bob agreed.

'Nah,' said Bob. 'But you go if you like, I can pick you up later,' he told Steven.

'Steven?' I tried to keep the pleading out of my voice.

'Mum, is it OK if I don't come?' Steven had on this pained expression that made him look the double of his dad. The expression said, *'I'd love to but I really can't be arsed.'*

'Yeah, sure,' I said casually. Steven had been so great all day I didn't want to spoil things. 'You'll be wanting to get back for some of Helga's lovely smorgasbord or pumpernickel or whatever the hell it is and maybe settle down and watch a DBD or something.'

'Nice one Trish,' Bob smirked on his way past, 'and it's DVD.'

'Stick it up your arse,' I snarled.

Nettie organized the funeral party quickly, arranging who was taking who and piling them into cars. They got to the house before me. It was embarrassing, the house was a cowp. With visiting the hospice every day for the last three weeks I had just let everything go to hell. Luckily there was plenty of drink in the house and they didn't seem to notice. I just kept going round filling glasses. Auntie Nettie, from a higher social station than most of Mum's friends, or so she considered herself, tried to dissuade them from getting the karaoke machine out.

'I hardly think it's appropriate,' she said a few times but, knowing her of old, Mum's mates blanked her. To annoy her and to save *me* having to entertain everyone, I went and found it. We hadn't had it out for months. One of her conditions of moving in with me was that Mum was allowed to keep up her regular monthly karaoke nights. Towards the end she just wasn't fit for it. They made room and while they watched I put the plug in the socket and switched the machine on.

'I'm sorry,' I said, 'I think it's chanked, nothing's happening.'

Auntie Nettie sat and smirked but one of Mum's friends' husbands came to the rescue.

'Have you checked the plug?'

'No, but I will,' I told him.

'Get me a screwdriver and I'll do it, it's probably just needing a new fuse.'

I was getting ice for someone so I showed him into the kitchen. He humpfed the machine into the kitchen with him where he had a good rummage in the cupboard under the microwave before he found the screwdriver and a packet of fuses. While I was hitting

16

the ice tray off the edge of the sink I could hear Isa, Madge and the rest of them start a communal version of 'I Ain't No Spring Chicken' as a tribute to Mum.

I'm over twenty-one
Sure know how to have fun

Years before karaoke machines were invented that had been her party piece. 'We don't need the machine!' I heard someone shout. I turned round and smiled an apology at Isa's husband. He smiled too but he carried on fixing the plug.

Don't be so coy
Are you a man or a boy?
Ain't no spring chicken
Ain't no slim pickin',
But I'm finger-lickin' good

I wasn't keen to talk to him, I'd been talking to people all day and anyway I couldn't remember his name. I remembered shaking his hand as we left the church but not what his name was.

'Harry,' he said in a wheezy voice, as if he could read my mind. I nodded hello and continued battering hell out of the ice tray.

'If you run it under the cold tap for a wee minute then it should come out easier,' he suggested.

Again I nodded, I knew it would, but I kept on smashing at the sink.

Ain't no glamorous gal
But I'm an amorous girl

I could hardly hear the women singing above the racket I was making.

Ain't no spring chicken
Ain't no slim pickin'
But I'm finger-lickin' good

I whacked the plastic container until it split right across the middle and the ice cubes slid and plopped into the tea-stained sink.

'There we are!' I said.

Harry quickly gathered the cubes in a pudding plate, took it through to the living room and came straight back.

'May I offer you my deepest sympathy Patricia.'

I nearly burst out laughing at the formality of his asthmatic whisper but the old guy was just trying to be kind. I was still leaning over the sink and when Harry spoke he lightly took hold of my elbow, leaning right into my face, studying me, maybe looking for signs of grief. I couldn't work up a grief face for him or for anybody but I thanked him for his deepest sympathy. Harry was a dapper wee man, he'd probably been quite handsome in his day, his suit looked expensive and his aftershave would have choked a horse.

'I suppose it hasn't sunk in yet,' he said, as if I hadn't heard this fifteen times already.

'No, you're probably right.'

I was getting pissed off with him hanging onto me in the same proprietorial way Bob had at the funeral. Because of where we were, wedged up against the sink, it was hard to break away naturally.

'What will you do now?' he said softly.

'Eh, I don't know, I haven't really thought.'

'Well at least it's over, it can't have been easy, for either of you.'

'No.'

I'd had enough. All day people I hardly knew had been putting their arms around me and telling me what I must be feeling and what I should be doing.

'All on your own in the house now. Must be lonely. Still, you have to look on the bright side. You're a free agent, nothing holding you is there?'

I felt like saying, 'Yeah, you are, get away from me you old bastard!' But I didn't.

'No.'

18

Just for something to do and as a way of getting rid of him, I started cleaning the sink. I gave it my full attention but he was still, with the lightest of touches, hanging onto my elbow. I scrubbed vigorously, my arm sawing forward and back, his hand following as if we were dancing. It would have been funny if it wasn't so creepy. I began to think that if he didn't take the hint I would lash out and punch him.

'Let's go in and join the party,' I said suddenly. I didn't know why I hadn't thought of it before, I'd been too busy fantasizing about pummelling a well-meaning old pensioner.

'No, I'm going to head off now, I think. I fixed the machine. D'you want me to take it in for the ladies?'

'Och no,' I said, relieved now, 'they'll not be looking for it until they run out of old songs.'

I braced myself for a long farewell. With Mum's friends, saying cheerio never took less than half an hour. I expected Harry to go into the living room and gather up his wife. Isa would have to go round the whole company, kissing everyone, chatting and making further social arrangements. But Harry surprised me by walking straight past the living-room door and opening the front door.

'It was great to see you Patricia.'

'Are you not waiting for Isa?'

Harry looked confused. Whatever, he was leaving without fanfare and a half-hour rigmarole.

'Thanks for coming Harry, and for fixing the karaoke machine, that was great.'

'I'd like to do more to help.'

'Thanks Harry, bye now.'

I smiled politely as he slipped out, closing the front door quietly behind him so's not to disturb the sing-song.

Drinks and singing and then tea and sandwiches and

more singing, it went on for hours. Mum hadn't been too specific about who was to get the karaoke machine. I'd got it for her birthday just before she took ill and I'd lived to rue the day. Wanting to avoid favouritism Mum skilfully passed the buck to Muggins, saying only that I was to give it to 'The Lassies'. Auntie Nettie had never been one of The Lassies and had only ever shown her utmost scorn for Mum's wee hobby. I was bloody sure she wasn't getting her hands on it. Luckily The Lassies decided amongst themselves. While Nettie pouted it was amicably agreed that as Isa had the biggest living room and therefore the most space for their monthly singalongs, she should be the custodian.

'That's handy Isa, your man can fix it if it breaks down again,' I said.

Funny looks all round.

'I don't think so hen, my man had a stroke last month, paralysed all down the one side, did your mammy not tell you?'

'I'm awful sorry Isa. I didn't know.'

'Och I suppose Elsie had enough on her plate, God rest her soul.'

So Harry wasn't Isa's husband. That's why he didn't take her when he left. Whatever, they were finally getting their coats on, and as I wound the flex and carted the machine to Isa's car I realized I was actually quite sad to see it go.

All the next week and the week after that when I wasn't sitting stupefied, with my eyes swollen to Barry Norman proportions, I ran around like a blue-arsed fly. Taking great care to avoid my bloated coupon in mirrored surfaces, I was a blur whizzing between the flat, the hospice and the charity shops, sorting, chucking out and giving away all Mum's stuff. It felt great. What wasn't so great was when I had to think about going back to work. Anytime I thought about a job my energy levels plummeted.

And then it was Christmas. I'd done my best to ignore it, I stopped listening to the radio but I couldn't escape the DIY and perfume ads that were on the telly every two minutes.

'You know you're welcome to spend Christmas with us,' Bob said. 'Nothing fancy, Helga's going to do meatballs.'

Of course I declined, and not very politely. I told him to stick his meatballs up his arse. He took it well. Bob had told me, when I'd been ratty with him at the funeral, that anger was part of the grieving process. That was great news, giving me free rein to be as rude to him as I wanted. With Mum gone I didn't have anyone else to be rude to.

I was embarrassed when Steven came round on Christmas Day. I had no tree up, no decorations or crackers, no nuts, no nothing. I'd had a few drinks and I got a bit emotional when he gave me the slippers and the lovely card. He went to the toilet, giving me a chance to quickly improvise a Christmas stocking for him. I didn't have much I could put in the sock except a Penguin biscuit, a packet of crisps, a cheque for two hundred and a satsuma. Steven was delighted.

New Year was slightly better. For once, instead of trying to live up to the traditional Scots stereotypical heuching cheuching Hogmanay, I could do what I liked. What I liked was lying in my bed being miserable. I knew in the long run I'd have to get a grip. I'd have to get a job. I didn't have two hundred to hand out in cheques. For the last two years I'd been on Carer's Allowance; now, without my caree, I was redundant. The prospect of becoming a dole scrounger seemed quite attractive but the money was shit. With a heavy heart I realized I'd have to start selling drugs.

Chapter 2

Luckily the pharmaceutical company I'd worked for were recruiting, so I went back to my previous profession of Medical Sales Rep. I could do the job in my sleep but because I'd been away from it for two years, they made me retrain. I wondered what kind of product I'd get to promote. I hoped for a miracle drug, something new and radical that was pushing back boundaries, something that saved lives, something exciting. I got a product for bladder incontinence.

The other trainees, all women, were new and nervous as we assembled in the hotel suite which was to be our training room for the next few days. I sat beside a nice girl, Becky, who said it was the first time she'd ever left her kids. The first day was Product Knowledge and the company wheeled in Dr Marcus Stevenson, a research scientist from the urology centre of excellence, the foremost bladder man in the country. What this guy didn't know about bladders wasn't worth knowing. Handsomely paid to tell us just how fantastic the product was, we had bladders straight from the horse's mouth. No humble GP would dare contradict Dr Marcus Stevenson.

I'd only skimmed the training manuals I'd been sent so I was having trouble following his lecture. I didn't know my ureter from my urethra. When Dr Stevenson moved on to describing different types of incontinence he breezed through 'stress' and 'giggle' before slowing down to savour the last one.

'And now we come to my own personal favourite,' he boomed confidently, 'coital incontinence: a condition where the sufferer literally doesn't know if they're coming or going.'

That night in the bar I got to know my fellow trainees a bit and found they were an OK bunch of girls. Somebody organized a table for all eight of us for dinner and we had a good laugh drinking wine at the company's expense until the restaurant closed at one thirty. The next morning I felt like death. The rest of the day was a blur of sales training techniques that went in one ear and out the other. We were to be tested on all this rubbish the next day, I knew I should be paying attention. The trainer James Roberts, 'but you can call me Jim Bob!' was a bespectacled lad who considered himself a bit of a comedian/marketing genius. By using different examples Jim Bob never tired of reiterating the theory that *perception is reality*. By afternoon coffee break everyone was complaining about how boring he was.

'He keeps using the same stupid phrases all the time,' Becky groaned. *'Think outside the box, grow the business, perception is reality*, it's crap.'

Everyone agreed. Another girl, Elsbeth, proposed her own theory. 'It's a shame for him really.'

'Why? I don't feel sorry for him,' I said. 'He doesn't have to flog the drugs, just bore the arse off us.'

'Yes, but I think I speak for everyone when I say that we *perceive* Jim Bob as a total wanker.'

That gave me a good idea. Back in my hotel room before we met for dinner I devised a wee game to play during training the next day. This might help us stay awake and have a bit of fun into the bargain. While I'd been job hunting, I saw a daft game on the Internet, 'Wank Bingo'. In place of numbers, a grid was filled with pretentious expressions frequently used in business like 'take ownership' and 'mindset'. This could easily be adapted to accommodate Jim Bob's pompous marketing lexicon. Within ten minutes I scribbled out eight bingo cards each with different layouts of sixteen varied words.

The girls were delighted with them and the next morning, to make it fair, we shuffled them up before they were given out. I knew the rules from when I used to take Mum to the pensioners' bingo on Wednesdays. First game would be a line, then a pyramid and finally a full house. There were no prizes but everyone seemed to be really looking forward to it. Jim Bob was well pleased with the attentive smiles he was getting.

'So ladies, you're all bright-eyed and bushy-tailed this morning, not like yesterday, eh?'

'Well that's your perception Jim Bob,' quipped Elsbeth.

Elsbeth was going in hard right from the start.

'Heh heh, quite right Elsbeth, and as we all know: *perception is reality*.'

Two other heads along with Elsbeth's went down as they scored their cards. I didn't have that one. After such a flying start he disappointed us by not coming up with a single wank word for the next hour and a half but just before coffee he let rip with three brammers, all of which were on my card.

'Our *game plan* has to be to go for a *win win situation*, and we get that when we *think outside the box*.'

Unfortunately they were on three different lines. At lunch Becky was way out in front but by four o'clock it was neck and neck.

'Well done Jan! D'you see what Jan's doing here? She's explaining the product *features and benefits*.'

I didn't have that one.

'Yes exactly Becky, the doctor isn't just asking about contraindications, he's giving you a *buying signal*.'

I had that one. Now I was only waiting for one: *blame culture*. I tried to get him to say it but Jim Bob was being asked questions left and right and he sang like a canary.

'Go get 'em, *close the sale*. Ask him for those scripts.'

Loads of heads went down on that one. It was going to be close. As the excitement mounted girlish tittering went round the room every time he obliged us with a tick for a box.

'Never be afraid to *ask for the business*.'

'Bingo!' Elsbeth yelled.

The outburst of groans and giggling confused poor Jim Bob but we left it to Elsbeth to explain.

'Ask for the business, that's it, spot on Jim Bob!'

'My goodness, such enthusiasm! This is the best class I've ever taught!'

So that was me up to speed as a fully trained medical rep. It was all bollocks. But it paid the bills. At one time there had been four of us in the house, two wages and a pension. Now there was only me. Over a period of fifteen years we'd played musical homes: first Bob got his 'Bachelor Apartment,' in reality a manky student howf. Then I moved in with him whereupon we had Steven, got married and bought the flat, a Victorian tenement in the West End. Then Dad died, Mum got ill and moved in with us, whereupon Bob moved out, this time to an even mankier student howf. Six months later Steven followed him, by which time Bob had taken up with Helga. Bob's howf was bursting at the seams. Then Mum checked out, leaving me rattling around in a three-bedroomed flat I couldn't afford.

Bob was getting impatient. While Steven lived with me Bob was happy for me to have the house. It was a different story when Steven moved in with him and his lady friend. With Mum dead and Steven in the enemy camp I couldn't justify hanging onto the house any longer. Bob was on at me either to buy him out or sell up and split the proceeds.

I had the phone for a fortnight before I worked out that I was able to programme tunes into it. Once I knew what I was doing I was away. For a laugh I got it to play the opening of '*Also Sprach Zarathustra*'. During my presentation to Dr Ross, when I showed him the product, just for a bit of showbiz, I played my little fanfare.

'Well, that's novel,' Dr Ross laughed.

Although the tune was recognizable, it sounded like a drunken ice-cream-van chime. That was my job, to make GPs laugh. It was all bollocks.

The company couldn't know who was prescribing what, so I was measured on how many doctors I visited. It was simple, I didn't actually need to sell, I only had to see doctors. Sometimes I'd barely mention the product, how would the company ever know? The better I got on with doctors the easier it was to see them. Dr Ross nodded his head politely as I did my sales spiel before asking me, 'Got any good freebies today?'

'I've got Post-its, hankies, and soap. Oh, and I've got some nice wee fire extinguishers if you want one.'

'Oh god,' Dr Ross groaned, 'I've got four already, I could start a shop with them.'

'You could have a fire sale.'

I usually saw doctors as they were beginning or

ending their surgery. If they were just starting in the morning they would have their head down in their paperwork. They didn't want me to piss about with sales techniques. They hated all that flimflam, they just wanted information: what was new? What did they need to know? I had to have facts, backed up by clinical evidence. If it was after surgery I stepped into my more usual role of cheerer-upper for burnt-out GPs. Then I had to have jokes, backed up by juicy gossip. Dr Ross had just finished his surgery and was looking scorched.

'I've ended up a fucking pen-pusher,' he wailed as he shoved the stack of records to the side of his desk and lit up the fag I offered him. What with the stress of the new job and missing Mum so badly and all the hassle over the house, I'd taken up smoking again.

'I mean, that methadone clinic out there,' he pointed with his fag towards the waiting room. 'That's not rehab. It's social control, that's what it is. Nobody comes off it, the methadone just stops them breaking into houses.'

I knew he might be on a downer because May the practice manager told me he'd had two deaths this morning. A nice old lady and a wee boy.

'And they all come in here moaning about nothing. "I've got terrible anxiety, Doctor, oh I'm awful fed up!" That's life, that's what they don't get, it happens to all of us.'

'Aye,' I said, exhaling heavily. I could see I was in for a sesh.

'I had a guy in here this morning complaining about hair loss. Nothing wrong with him, classic male pattern baldness, I mean, he's forty-three for fuck sake, what does he expect?'

I could understand Dr Ross's rancour, he looked to be in his mid-thirties and was already a well-

27

established baldyheid. I nearly said *you must be tearing your hair out* but then I thought the better of it.

'Och you're just having an off day.'

'Too right I am, I'm so, so, sick of peering into people's ears, down their throats.'

'Up their bums.'

'I'm especially sick of up their bums.'

We were laughing when May came in with a pile of paperwork. A young mum wanted a house call but May had told her to come into the surgery. By her tone it was clear that May thought the young mum was at it.

'Och you're probably right May but I'd better go out and see her. She's no transport and it's a miserable day to be dragging her kids out. There's always an outside chance that she's actually ill I suppose.'

I didn't only try to cheer up doctors, I also had to feed them. A system of petty bribery had evolved where drug reps were booked into practices and health centres to provide a 'coffee morning'. I was obliged to supply decadently expensive sandwiches and pastries to lure the doctors into the staffroom. There, like a geisha, I'd pour tea and regale them with stories, mentioning only briefly in passing the drugs I was promoting. In some ways this was a cushy number, I was being paid to sit and make pleasant conversation and stuff my face with buns. When the doctors left to do their house calls I took the remaining food home with me. My fridge was permanently filled with high-fat high-calorie irresistible goodies.

It didn't help that I spent all day sitting: either in the car or in the health centres. The biggest health centres, and therefore the ones I visited most frequently, were in the poorest parts of the city: Bridgeton, Maryhill, Springburn. I didn't mind, I could read magazines while I waited for doctors to finish their surgery. The only problem was that the place was full of sick people.

Sick people in sportswear and running shoes. Most of them couldn't run the length of themselves. To avoid catching anything, I was always careful to sit as far away from them as I could but often the waiting rooms were crowded. Amongst the multicoloured jogging clothes I was conspicuous in my sober suit. I would quickly be swamped with screaming snot-nosed toddlers, rattling junkies, pishy old ladies (who were, of course, with my incontinence product, my stock-in-trade) and diseased old codgers expectorating like nobody's business. And they had the cheek to call these places health centres.

It wasn't long before I had a runny nose which turned into a phlegmy chest. The smoking wasn't helping. I was coughing up chunks, laced with white stuff which looked, to me, suspiciously like bits of lung.

Once a month I had to go on a field visit with my boss, Irene, taking her round the practices on my patch. Irene accompanied me while I 'detailed', that is to say told doctors about how wonderful my product was. Each field visit was a test, an ongoing assessment of my selling ability. Irene met me with her usual flood of insincerity.

'You look terrific Trisha, is that a new suit? It's lovely!'

In fact it was a very old suit. Six years ago when I started as a drug rep I bought three Dry Clean Only designer suits that cost more than a month's wages. After only three months in the job, three months of chomping my way through coffee mornings, I was a stone heavier and popping buttons all over the place. I switched to cheap Easy Care polyester suits as a temporary measure until I regained my figure. Four years later I had succeeded only in putting on another stone and buying more polyester, but now with elasticated waists.

'Och Irene, this suit is donkey's years old.'

Two years of nursing Mum had whittled me back into my designer suits. Even if they were six years out of fashion, I was enjoying it while I could. I knew that with a fridge full of sweetmeats my svelte designer look probably wouldn't last. Already the waistbands were beginning to gouge my belly.

'Well you would never know,' gushed Irene. 'Apart from the lapels which are a bit last century right enough but still, where are we off to today then?'

I took her to Archy Marshall, a mate of mine, a tame GP, and went through my sales spiel.

'So, Dr Marshall, as you can see from the data,' here I pointed with my pen to my sales leaflet as I had been trained to do, 'with our product there is no need for you to titrate the dosage, minimizing patient visits to you and therefore saving you precious time.'

Archy nodded, pretending that this was new information.

'No need to titrate, you say?'

'That's correct Dr Marshall.'

I had to remember not to call him Archy.

'Another advantage is that with such a low-side-effect profile, the product is well tolerated, patient compliance is high and therefore outcomes are improved.'

Archy scratched his chin as though considering my argument. 'Well I must say Miss McNicol, you've put up a pretty convincing case for your product.'

It was too easy. I wanted him to pretend that he wasn't going to prescribe and then win him over, demonstrating to my boss my superior sales techniques. He left me no option but to close the sale.

'So, Dr Marshall, can I take it then that you'll prescribe Preventapish for your patients?'

'No.'

Archy was at the wind-up. Out of Irene's line of sight he flashed me a manic grin.

'No?'

'Only the incontinent ones.'

Oh how we all chuckled. As we left Archy pumped my hand vigorously.

'Always a pleasure Miss McNicol, and I'll be pleased to hear of any new products you might be promoting.'

I was worried Irene would catch on. She had been a rep herself until six months ago, she must have been in similar scenarios with her boss, she knew the score. She must have played the same game. It was all bollocks.

Steven came round for his tea on Wednesday night as usual. As usual he looked pale and fed up and wouldn't be drawn when I tried to ask him how he was getting on at school or at the football. His replies were as short and uninformative as he could make them. But things between us had improved a bit since Mum died. Now we sat in the living room with trays on our knees the way Steven preferred and watched *The Weakest Link*. This was much better, cosier. Often when we used to eat in the kitchen the only sound was of the cutlery scraping the plates.

In the living room we interacted with the telly and tried to answer the questions Anne Robinson fired. I was careful not to answer too many or else Steven just stopped playing. He was still a wee boy inside and hated to lose, especially to me. We bet between ourselves which of the contestants was likely to win. The first time we did this I said something like 'I fancy Jim,' meaning I fancied Jim to win. Steven sniggered and teased me for fancying fat baldy Jim. After that I always chose the ugliest competitor, saying I fancied him, but

I could see that as far as Steven was concerned, the joke was wearing thin.

'What d'you want, coronation chicken or Chinese duck?'

'Dunno.'

'Well I've got both, it's up to yourself.'

'Do we have to have sandwiches again?'

'I thought you liked these sandwiches, they're Marks.'

Steven shrugged for a reply.

'I could cook but I've nothing in, I'll have to nip out to Iceland. You can come with me and choose whatever you like. We can make a posh dinner, fajitas or something, whatever you fancy.'

'No, you're all right. I'll take the chicken sandwich.'

He made it sound like eating the best sandwiches money could buy, forcing them down his martyred throat, was an ordeal he would endure rather than cause me the bother of going out to the shops.

'Look, I've got brilliant stuff here.' I opened the fridge and pulled out a bunch of grapes, a four-pack of fromage frais and three fresh cream eclairs. 'A big glass of milk with that and you've got a delicious and nutritious meal,' I said, trying to keep it light. Earlier when buying the spread for the coffee morning I'd shopped with Steven in mind and bought all his favourites.

'Ta,' he said unenthusiastically.

My face flushed with an unexpected rush of shame. What kind of mother was I that I didn't cook for my son and only fed him other people's leavings?

'Why don't we forget this stuff and go out to dinner. Proper nosh-up, there's still time for the Pre-The at the Indian. D'you fancy it?'

'Dunno.'

Dunno could mean anything. He might not want to

go out. He might want to go out but just be too shy to say so. He might not want to hurt my feelings by rejecting my posh sandwiches. He might actually prefer the sandwich option.

I grabbed a promotional pen and an old envelope that was lying on the kitchen table and started scribbling on the back of it.

'Right. I'll write down the choices. A: Have the sandwiches. B: I'll cook. C: Go out to dinner. Take as long as you need to think about it. All you have to do is tick A, B or C, OK?'

I went into the bathroom and stayed ten minutes. When I came out the house was awful quiet. I went into the living room, he wasn't there or the kitchen. He hadn't ticked any of the boxes. He had taken the chicken sandwich and silently let himself out the front door.

I was just leaving Govanhill health centre on the Southside when I spotted the leaflets. On a table full of untidy piles of junk pamphlets about chlamydia, pigeon-fancier's lung, giving up smoking, industrial white finger, haemorrhoids, and breastfeeding, there were flyers advertising half-price entry to the circus. When Bob and I were together we used to go as a family every year. He always moaned, saying it was a rip-off, but Steven loved the circus. The first time we took him he was only five. I asked him afterwards what he'd liked most, was it the flying-trapeze artists or the fire jugglers, although I thought I knew what he was going to say. He'd laughed hysterically at the clowns, as if he was possessed. His mad laughter was so infectious Bob and I giggled with him. But he didn't say the clowns. He said the ladies.

'The ladies?' I asked, thinking this was some kind of kiddie code.

'The nearly naked ladies with no clothes on.'

I phoned Steven as soon as I got home.

'How d'you fancy a wee night out with your old Maw?'

Steven blew out a sigh on the other end of the phone. I knew right away I'd made a mistake using the phrase your old Maw. As a rule I used this when asking him a favour or to elicit sympathy, as in gonnae make your old Maw a cup of tea, son? Or your old Maw's bowly-legged running up and down to the shops. So I was surprised when he seemed quite positive.

'Dunno. Where to?'

'The circus has come to town. All the nearly naked ladies, all the fun of the fair. We could go on Wednesday night, eh?'

There was a lot of activity in the background and Steven seemed to be struggling to give me his attention.

'Eh, dunno. What time is it on?'

'Starts at eight, we could have a nice fish tea in the Ruthven Cafe and after the show I'll drop you off back at your dad's.'

This was another slight diplomatic gaffe. I should have said 'drop you off home', but Steven wasn't listening anyway. He'd tuned into the background noises coming from his end, which were getting louder. A couple of random bangs, a silence, a subdued muttering then somewhere behind Steven a woman's voice shouting.

'I eat you Robbie!'

It didn't sound like the telly.

'Everything all right there? You OK, son?'

It had all gone quiet again. Steven paused before he answered.

'Yeah I'm fine.'

He didn't sound fine.

'Well how about it?'

'Eh, dunno. I don't like fish. That's for old people.'

'Well a sausage supper then. Hey, maybe they have Mars Bar suppers, that would be a laugh, wouldn't it?'

'Am I allowed a Mars Bar supper?'

If sales training had taught me nothing else it had taught me to recognize buying signals when I heard them.

'You can have whatever you like, Steven.'

It was time to close the sale.

'I'll need to get the tickets tomorrow if we're going, it might sell out. What do you say?'

There was another long silence but I held my tongue. I knew how to use silence, to let the customer fill the gap.

'OK,' Steven finally muttered.

'So, who's Robbie then?'

Now that our circus trip was organized I could afford to snoop.

'Who d'you think?'

The utter distaste in Steven's voice told me what I should have easily worked out. I got off the phone as soon as I could. It was all I could do not to laugh and poor Steven was affronted enough as it was.

Pathetic, a grown man going about calling himself Robbie. He'd always been Bob, never anything else. And The Bidie In screaming at him like that within earshot of The Wife. How embarrassing was that for 'Robbie'. But what was she saying? *I eat you.* In front of a fifteen-year-old boy? Surely not. Obscene, but that was Norwegians for you. Maybe it was *I hate you.* Yes, that sounded more like it. Good on you Helga, I thought, a woman after my own heart.

Chapter 3

Before I went to pick Steven up I scrupulously de-fagged. I hadn't smoked since lunchtime. I washed my hair, changed my clothes, scrubbed my teeth and fumigated the car. I went a bit overboard with the Mountain Pine air freshener, giving it another quick scoosh just before he got in.

'Ooof,' he said, waving his hand in front of his face. 'This car is howfing, man.' I only smiled. I knew by this time tomorrow it would be stinking of cigarettes again. I didn't ask for much, just to smoke all day and sit at night with a Marky's chicken sandwich in one hand and a fag in the other.

Steven was disappointed to discover that they didn't do Mars Bar suppers. Ronaldo the owner said he'd read about it in the paper and put them on the menu to see how they'd go. The schoolkids went a bomb on them but after a few weeks it died away. No-one was doing them any more. It was a shortlived craze that had become an urban myth.

Steven plumped for the healthier option of a deep-fried Scotch pie supper. I complimented him on his excellent choice.

'In fact I'll have one as well, I haven't had one for years. Can I have mine in a roll please, Ronaldo?

I'm trying to lay off the chips.'

As Steven's knife cut into his pie, plasma-coloured grease flooded his plate. Scotch pies should have been more properly called 'grey meat' pies as that was the colour of the contents, but even the word 'meat' may have been an inaccuracy. What the hell, they tasted great and we got scoffed in before we had to hurry down to the circus in the park.

When we used to go as a family Bob had always insisted that we get the cheap seats and even then, the cheapest possible seats. Plenty of times I had been ashamed to think of these beautiful highly trained athletes risking life and limb on a high wire for the pittance my husband was prepared to fork out. The wooden planks we sat on were so far back our heads bumped the roof of the big top. Poor wee Steven never had a chance of getting picked when the clowns asked for a volunteer to come into the ring. Although the wee soul shouted at the top of his voice, 'Me! Me! Pick me!' he was always passed over. As the years went by and he still never got picked, he realized the futility of shouting and stopped. I tried to explain that it wasn't personal, it was just that the clown couldn't see him. To the clown he was a colourful dot far beyond a hundred nearer screaming kids, but there was little comfort in my explanation for either of us.

Steven was mortified when the man showed us to our seats.

'No way. I'm not sitting here. It's for weans.'

Encouraged by the half-price deal and as a way of making it up to him for all those years on the very back benches, I'd gone mad and bought the most expensive seats in the place. The man showed us into a box on the ringside. Although there were about ten chairs in the box, it was empty except for us.

'C'mon, the show's about to start, you're blocking people's view.'

I tried to embarrass him into sitting but he was having none of it.

'I'm not sitting here. I'm going home.'

'No, Steven, don't go home. Please.' I panicked. 'I'm sorry, you're right. I'll ask if we can swap.'

I found an usher who waved us generally in the direction of the grandstand seats.

Steven was right. Sitting in the box on our own like that, we would have stuck out like a sore thumb. And the atmosphere in the grandstand was fantastic. There were no animals in the circus any more, the council wouldn't give them a licence. There was no longer the rank smell of the elephants or the cages for the lions. The cages were only for show anyway, Bob always said. Circus lions weren't fierce, they were no more than slightly pissed off at being herded about but they were too pot-bellied and sleepy to rebel. The most they could manage were sullen glances and occasional snarls at the lion tamer.

Without the lions and the manacled elephants the show was even better. Exotic young women with buttocks so developed you could sit a tea tray on them spun painted barrels on their feet while a troupe of young boys formed a human pyramid. When I got a chance to look at them individually, some of the young boys had bald heads and lined faces. A few of them would never see fifty again and yet they jumped and tumbled with the best of them.

As they entered the ring each act was met with warm applause in appreciation of the satiny costumes, feathery headdresses and regal gowns that were dragged across the sawdust. As they left it was always to tumultuous applause and even Steven showed his grudging admiration for their amazing strength and skill. There was a collective gasp of horror when the trapeze man nearly fell to his death. The gasp fragmented into thrilled whispers, squeals and nervous tittering as Steven turned to me and said, 'That's a set-up.' But I could see he was having a good time. When the clowns came on we sat with our heads down, embarrassed by how unfunny they were. Three wee kids in the row in front of us started laughing their heads off and when Steven glanced at me we both smiled.

It was dark when we came out of the big top and we stumbled with everyone else along the muddy path out of the park. I nearly tripped and Steven said, 'Sober up Mum!' and held my arm all the way until we got to the main road. I thought now was as good a time as any to ask him but at the same time I was terrified.

'Are you happy at your dad's, son?'

He might have said 'Dunno' but all I heard was a grunt.

'Would you be happier back home with me d'you think? Now that . . .' I nearly said 'that Granny's dead,' but I didn't want to upset him so I said, 'that there's more room. I'm going to get the place all sorted out, freshen it up a bit. Your room could do with a lick of paint and you could probably do with some new furniture.'

I left it hanging there but he didn't respond. Time for some open questions.

'What d'you think's the best colour for your room?'

'Dunno.'

'Well I was thinking maybe a pale peach or a pink.'

But Steven wasn't that gullible any more.

'Aye, sounds good Mum. And what about a wee frilly duvet cover with roses on it?'

'Well what would you like?'

'I don't mind. Blue. I'm not bothered.'

'Blue. Right.'

After I dropped him at his dad's, all the way home I debated with myself what shade of blue I should get.

The official reason for Steven moving out was that it would make it easier for me to look after Granny. The real reason was that he didn't want to live with an old lady who was slowly dying. Who did? At first I hardly noticed him gone. All his friends lived nearby so he was round almost every night anyway. But after the school holidays and when the dark nights began, he only came on a Wednesday for his tea.

After Mum died the reason I gutted the place so quickly and thoroughly was for Steven. For myself I didn't mind Mum's stuff kicking about the house. In fact it broke my heart to part with her 1960s knitting patterns and her records, *The Sound of Music* and *Calamity Jane*, but I knew Steven found it creepy. Old-lady stuff, especially dead-old-lady stuff, freaked him out. I decided that not only Steven's room but the whole place needed repainting. I couldn't afford to get anyone in so I bought One Coat paint and a roller. It did exactly what it said on the tin and covered the walls in one coat. Even so it took weeks. When I came home from work I was usually too tired for anything but vegging in front of the telly with a bottle of wine and a packet of fags.

I started with Steven's room, evenly applying the paint and taking care around the doors and window. I took down all his old posters, he had probably outgrown them by now, he seemed to have outgrown everything else, but I kept them for him anyway just in case. I must admit that I got bored after that and for the rest of the house I slapped the paint up as fast as I could. I did the living room and the bedrooms as best I could in trendy pastel colours. It was a bit patchy in daylight but it was fresh. The house was now a model of modernity, an Old-Lady-Free Zone. I stashed all my photos of Mum and Dad, Mum's rings and her birth, death, and swimming certificates, in a biscuit tin in the ottoman in my bedroom. I squirmed at such disloyal revisionism of my own mother but I knew Mum would have understood.

I was absolutely raging although I suppose I'd always known it would come to this. In amongst the only mail that I usually ever got, junk mail, for stair lifts, walk-in baths and hydraulic beds, was a letter from a solicitor. The letter asked me to ring the office and arrange an appointment at my convenience. Bob was obviously trying to work a fly one. Too cowardly to come and make a deal with me himself, he'd gone to a lawyer. Bob wanted me out of the house or at least to pay him the highest amount possible for his share. With Mum hardly cold in the ground, he probably thought I'd be a bit disorientated and ready to agree to anything.

The name was Donovan O'Hare and Boyle, a firm I'd never heard of. Bob had recruited a bunch of Murphioso shysters to shaft the mother of his child. Oh, he was a slippery one, this way he could minimize pain (his not mine) and maximize profits (his not mine) without getting his hands dirty. Technically he was entitled. Technically he could move back in tomorrow and there would be nothing I could do about it. I could come home and find him and Helga shagging on the couch. Well that wasn't convenient, not bloody convenient at all.

'Hello, Mr O'Hare?'

'Yes hello Miss McNicol, thank you very much for calling.'

'Well you'll not be thanking me when I tell you I'm not coming in to your poxy office. It's not convenient. It's not convenient this week or next week or the week after that. It's not convenient at all.'

'I'm sorry to hear that, Miss McNicol. Perhaps I could come and visit you at your home?'

'Exactly. It is *my* home and I won't be driven out of it, OK? By you or anybody else.'

I knew I was losing it but in a way I was quite enjoying myself, I had no respect for these sharks anyway.

'Miss McNicol, I fear we may be at cross purposes here. Our client has instructed . . .'

'I don't give a monkey's what your client has instructed, I'm not having that bastard march in and stain my couch.'

'Miss McNicol, our client has passed away. It is the matter of his will that I would like to discuss with you.'

I dropped the phone. Everything jumped into my head at once: Bob was dead. Why was I hearing it from a lawyer? Another horrible funeral. Steven would come back to me. The insurance would pay off the mortgage. Steven didn't have his dad any more. The house would be mine.

It was a bit much to take in all at once and for some reason the whole thing seemed funny.

There was a faint squawk coming from the handset. 'Miss McNicol, Miss McNicol!' I lifted it and was about to replace it on the cradle when I thought the better of it, these guys were only doing their job.

'Miss McNicol. I do apologize for alarming you. Perhaps we could start again.'

'Yeah,' I mumbled. I wanted to hear what he had to say. I wondered if Helga was getting a cut.

'Mr Robertson has made you a bequeath. There are however certain stipulations . . .'

'Wait a minute. Just hold it.' I wasn't following this. 'I thought you said Bob was dead. Who the fuck is Mr Robertson?'

'Oh dear. I'm afraid I don't know who Bob is, Miss McNicol, I'm acting only on behalf of Mr Robertson's estate.'

I was relieved that Bob wasn't dead and this surprised me.

'Mr O'Hare, you've got the wrong Miss McNicol.' I felt embarrassed at having described the poor guy's office as poxy. 'I don't know anyone called Robertson, unfortunately.'

'Mr Robertson is, or was I should more properly say, a second cousin of your mother, Elizabeth McNicol, as I understand recently deceased. Mr Robertson has cited you as his next of kin and chief beneficiary of his estate.'

After hearing this I was gagging to come into his office, but I couldn't. I was about to go away for three days' training in a new product. Nevertheless, Mr O'Hare and I quickly sorted out the next available date.

'I could squeeze you in next Tuesday.'

'Yes, that would be fine.'

He could hardly keep the sarcastic tone out of his voice but I suppose I'd asked for it.

'Now are you sure that's quite convenient Miss McNicol?'

In any other job drunkenness might have been frowned upon, but in the pharmaceutical industry it was an essential requirement. After the first day's training the Project Director closed the session by roaring in a motivational way, 'Are we going to party tonight?'

Nobody answered him. People had travelled from all over the country and sat in a stuffy hotel conference room all day, we were knackered. The Project Director couldn't help but notice this lack of ebullience, this was a sales force giving less than 110 per cent. He rescued the situation by roaring again, this time in a more threateningly motivational way, 'I said, are we going to party tonight!'

'Yeah!' we croaked.

You had to, it was expected. And not only were you expected to get blind drunk and behave outrageously, you were expected to be up and about, fresh as a daisy, next morning.

At dinner I wore a black full-length velvet skirt I'd got in a charity shop with a lovely lemon long-sleeved blouse. Despite having only spent seventeen quid on my entire outfit I thought I looked a million dollars.

'You look terrific Trisha, is that a new skirt?' said Irene.

Did the woman never vary her script? Despite what she'd said, subtle waves of disapproval wafted off Irene. When the rest of the team arrived I understood why. If I'd read the programme contained in the 'welcome pack' I'd have known about the Most Scantily Clad Team at Dinner competition. Management had organized an evening of wacky ice-breakers with games and prizes, designed to loosen everyone up. As I sat there, indecently fully clothed, I was detracting from the team effort. As it turned out, my team won anyway, mostly on the merits of one entrant.

'Well done Alison! You've done the Scottish team proud!' leered the Project Director as he handed over her bottle of Marks and Sparks own brand champagne. Alison was an unattractive girl with heavy glasses and a glaikit expression but she had other attributes. She had a knock-out figure which she'd adorned simply with a nipple-width leather belt across her chest.

'I'm all right as long as I don't breathe!' Alison hissed through a shallow pant.

On her bottom half she wore a leather mini. The mini, which was really what swung it, easily fell into

44

the category of 'fanny pelmet'. Lots of other girls entered into the spirit of things but none were quite so nude as Alison. I thought of Steven and how much he would have enjoyed these nearly naked ladies. Competition was stiff, in more ways than one. A team of lads turned up in only their underpants and dickie bows but they were disqualified on the grounds that boxer shorts were not appropriate dinner attire. 'That's not fair!' they complained, moaning that obviously women's clothes were more suited to brevity. They were missing the point.

These pathetic 18-30-club-type stunts were amusing in their way but what was far more entertaining was the way everyone vied to increase their reputation for scandalous behaviour. Throughout dinner there was the usual unofficial competition as drunk show-offs went to any lengths to 'out mad' each other.

'Oh, there's Margaret at it! That woman is completely bonkers!' squealed Irene. A woman in her late forties, Margaret Pearson, the manager of the north of England team, a person who should have known better, made an early bid for glory. After unsuccessfully throwing herself at the young men under her management, the boys in the boxers and dickies, she used their heads for support and with the slow deliberate movements befitting an older lady, mounted the dinner table. As she'd very publicly failed to mount anything else, she shuffled around the table top proving to them all that she didn't give two hoots. While she shimmied, an unco-ordinated knee action caused her spangly sandals to send red wine pulsing over their melon balls. But it was a poor show.

Gary Cook from the South East team let it be known that he'd run up a hotel phone bill of three hundred pounds calling his girlfriend in Los Angeles. 'Only three hundred Gary?' I tutted, 'you cheapskate.' This was generally held to be more impressive, with high marks for stylish extravagance.

Andrew, a senior rep in my team who was close to retirement, always wore national dress to functions. After dinner and before he was too drunk to stand, he would customarily visit each table lifting his kilt and placing his flaccid member in the prettiest girl's dinner. 'Oh Sally, there's a wee noodle on your plate,' I said while I attempted to prong it. Andrew's old trick was affectionately tolerated but was not of itself particularly noteworthy. In the end, a rank outsider, Evelyn, a New Start, stole the contest when she trashed her hotel toom and was rushed away in an ambulance after slitting her wrists.

On the second day the last session had been scheduled to end at 5 p.m. and went on until after six. Dinner was at eight. Pre-dinner drinks in the foyer were at seven thirty and *pre*-pre-dinner drinks were in Irene's room with the rest of the team at quarter to seven. Attendance was compulsory. There was little time in between for luxuriating in a hot tub in the privacy of my five-star hotel room. It would be a quick dip, a lick and a promise really, and then throwing my kit on and scuttling along to Irene's room. There, through a fixed smile, I'd participate in the corporate hilarity, the hollow jokey mateyness of it all.

As usual I was the last to arrive in Irene's room. Always at the coo's tail, Mum used to say. But they had planned on me being late.

'Surprise!' my team mates shouted as they jumped out from behind the curtains.

'Happy birthday!'

I tried to look pleased. Most of these people I had only met for the first time a few days ago and now they were gathered round me with a cake that was on fire. Everyone was smiling, politely waiting their turn to kiss me while they sang, 'Happy birthday to you'. They even managed the wee harmony bit at the end. I couldn't tell them it wasn't my birthday. But Irene did.

'Now Trisha, we know it's not officially your birthday for another week yet, but seeing as the team aren't all going to be together again for another month we thought we'd have a wee early celebration and give you your prezzie.'

I didn't want my birthday a week early. I'd been holding off my fortieth birthday since my thirtieth. For the last ten years I'd suffered recurring bouts of fortyphobia. When I was a wee girl I would think, 'what will I be, what will I have done by the time I'm forty?' I was going to be a pop star. Like Dana and Lulu before me, I would win the Eurovision Song Contest. After that, with the altruism of youth, I intended turning my back on fame and fortune to become a missionary in Africa. Then marriage, big white wedding, obviously, and kids. Here I was, a sales rep with no husband and a part-time son, in a hotel room with a crowd of strangers. And it wasn't even my birthday yet.

'Trisha, on behalf of the team I'd like to give you this small token of our appreciation and wish you all the very best for your fortieth.'

There was a card signed by all of them and thirty pounds worth of Marks and Spencer vouchers. There was a bottle of champagne and a box of luxury chocolates (both Marks own brand). M and S vouchers were the company's standard giveaway. Not only had she hijacked my birthday to use as a team-bonding exercise, Irene had paid for it from expenses. Manners dictated that I open the chocs and champers. Shared amongst nine people, they were gone in sixty seconds.

'Guys,' said Irene. Including her, six of us were women but Irene called everyone guys. 'Guys, as you know Trisha is new to our team but she brings with her four years of experience in this business. Her experience, skill and professionalism are apparent in the figures she has consistently brought in since she joined us. Now this isn't a blame culture [bingo!] and I'm not being negative when I say that with the piss-poor figures you've brought in lately, without Trisha this team would have gone belly up.'

I was going to be popular. Irene was using me as a stick to beat the rest of them with.

'For the team meeting next month I'd like to ask Trisha to share her experience with us. Trisha, make us a presentation, inspire us, show us how it's done!'

Irene beamed at me as the team dutifully applauded. This was a great honour, she was letting it be known that she was grooming me for stardom. At dinner I asked her exactly what she wanted me to do.

'Oh you know, the usual: facts and figures, case studies, couple of witty anecdotes then finish with the inspirational stuff. About half an hour's worth should do it.'

Half an hour! That would take me months to prepare. I decided to be honest with her, I told her the way I was feeling at the moment, the only thing I could inspire anyone to do was stick their head in the oven. Irene was not sympathetic. She wanted to see it for approval at least two weeks before the meeting. As most of the team were ignoring me after dinner it was easy to slip away. Fags were my only friends so I sneaked back to my room and smoked myself skinny.

The new product was an analgesic and next morning we were given a written exam to see how much we had retained. One of the questions was 'Can you name an instance where pain relief might be required?' What kind of a stupid question was that? I wrote down 'shark attack'. Then we practised our sales pitch.

Two hundred reps sat in long rows. The first row turned and kneeled on their chairs to work with the person sitting behind them. I had the easy job. The man in front of me, Michael from Wales, played the part of the rep. All I had to do was pretend to be the doctor. He sold me the drug and I asked questions. He was a nice old bloke so I gave him an easy time. Then we switched roles. After a few runs through the Project Director clapped his hands above his head. Two hundred reps talking at the same time made a sound like flies trapped in the neck of a bottle. Only those near the front heard him. Unused to being cold-shouldered, the Project Director put two fingers in his mouth and whistled, nearly bursting my eardrum.

'OK people, listen up.'

It was part of a Project Director's remit to talk like an American.

'For the benefit of the new reps, this is a third line product. In GP land you'll only have a few minutes to sell it. So now you know it, let me hear you sell it! But fast, do it in five minutes.'

It was my turn to detail my partner now and he smiled encouragingly as I rattled off the main points about the product.

'Fantastic!' said the Project Director, 'I can hear some really exciting detailing going on out there. Now do it in two minutes.'

Now everyone started screaming at each other. Michael, although he grumbled about having to kneel in his seat, had been sweet and gentle until this point. Bright red from the exertion, he was poised above me spitting in my face while he bawled out the Key Selling Points.

'TWENTY-FIVE MGS THREE TIMES A DAY!'

Despite this he was having difficulty making himself heard above the hellish din. Michael was a heavy man and when he leaned forward he very nearly couped on top of me. As he toppled, instinct made him grab at the air with his pudgy hands. Unfortunately for us both, the air he grabbed was right next to my breasts. I had narrowly missed being squashed and/or publicly groped.

'Trisha, I'm so sorry!'

'Whoa tiger!'

'I didn't mean anything . . .'

'I know. Forget it. Are you OK?'

He nodded but the poor man was suffering. To spare Michael further embarrassment and possibly a heart attack, I excused myself saying I needed to go to the loo. As I fought my way through 200 frenzied reps shrieking their sales mantras, I wondered how it was that I, an ordinary person, had fallen into this huckster's snake pit. Not for the first time I thought that there must be less humiliating ways of making a living.

Chapter 4

I answered the door to someone who had a large gift-wrapped bush for a head.

'Delivery for McNicol,' said a bad American accent.

I recognized the Nike trainers but I entered into the spirit of things.

'Oh! Is it a singing telegram?' I gasped, 'I've always wanted a singing telegram.'

The bush said nothing. I gently pulled leaves and stalks aside to reveal Steven's beetroot-red face.

'D'you want to let me in?' he said in his more usual bored tone as he took a step forward. I stood barring his way.

'I'm sorry I don't think I know that one.'

'Mum!'

'OK, OK, come on in.'

Luckily I wasn't long in myself. I hadn't had a chance to get the fags out of my bag never mind light up yet, so there was no smoke smell. He made the formal presentation of the large house plant in the kitchen.

'Happy birthday Mum.'

It was a beautiful thing with red and yellow, green and orange leaves. The most beautiful plant in the world. I wanted to sit down and cry. I wanted to throw my arms round my son and hear him say, 'It's all right

Mum, let it all out.' I wanted to take the time for a good howl and then gradually, when I was ready, let my crying tail off to the occasional sob. I wanted Steven to rub my back and say, 'You OK now Mum? You sure?' I wanted to blow my nose, crack a silly joke and smile. Pick myself up, dust myself off, start all over again

'Thanks very much son, it's lovely.'

'Sorry it's a day early but I've got training tomorrow night and if I don't go tomorrow I won't get picked for Saturday.'

'I know, I know. I'm pleased to see you, son. Had your dinner yet?'

'No. I'm not hungry.'

'Want chippy chips?'

'Yeah. I'll go.'

The last time we'd eaten together it was from the chippy. I really was going to have to start feeding that boy properly. Or rather when he came back to stay with me I'd have to start cooking proper meals. I just couldn't be arsed cooking for one. I usually just had a sandwich from the fridge. Steven was a growing boy laying down the foundations of his adult frame, he needed proper nutrition, meat, protein, that sort of thing. Not suppers from the chippy.

'What does Helga cook?' I asked when he came back.

'Dunno. A lot of stews.'

'Sounds good.'

'Nah, you get fed up with it, we're sick of it.'

'Are you? What, Dad too? Is Dad sick of Helga's cooking?'

'Hmm, dunno.'

'Yeah, you can't beat a fish supper can you?'

Steven agreed. We sat down to watch *The Weakest Link* with our suppers on our knee.

'I quite fancy Eric,' said Steven.

Eric wasn't fat or bald, he was a pharmaceutical rep.

This was the nicest thing Steven could have said. As it turned out Eric was incredibly lucky. Loads of times he should have been nominated and wasn't. He lasted all the way to the final. In the final his questions were pimps easy but he still got two wrong and it went to a tie-breaker. The other guy got a hard one and got it wrong, letting Eric walk off with nearly three grand. We celebrated his victory as if it were our own, clinking our Irn Bru glasses.

The night just got better and better. I told Steven all about the antics at the training conference, embellishing it here and there to make him laugh. He did laugh, he was in the mood for a good laugh. He threw himself back in the chair at anything mildly amusing and filled the room with his booming laughter. Then we watched a daft teen movie. Although it was mildly sexy and a bit embarrassing for us both, it was hilariously funny. I made myself busy getting us tea and toast at the raunchy bits.

Later on, when I remembered, I showed him his newly painted bedroom. Steven refused to believe I'd done it myself. He inspected the corners and under the window ledges, nodding approval and mumbling 'Respect!'

He noticed with horror that I'd got rid of his *South Park* duvet cover and replaced it with a new blue one. It was from the Men Only range in Marks, bought from my birthday vouchers. The choice was between plain blue on one side or broad blue and white stripes on the other. I pulled the duvet down to demonstrate.

'What side d'you like best?'

'Dunno.'

Steven had slipped his smelly trainers off hours ago in the living room and now he jumped fully clothed under the duvet to test it. He modelled it from every angle. Tossing and turning, kidding on he was asleep, he opened one eye and keeked in the wardrobe mirror. Then he lifted the duvet into the air balanced on his long slender arms and legs. Like the women in the circus he flicked it up into the air and over onto the striped side. He modelled it all over again.

'Plain blue,' he said eventually.

I knew he would choose that.

'Mum, is it OK if I crash here tonight? I'm too knackered to go home, I'm just getting comfy here.'

'Aye, no bother son, what time do you want me to wake you?'

I could hardly believe it would be as straightforward as this. Steven was back home, back in his own room. It was the first night since Mum died that I fell asleep in a good mood.

I woke up the next morning in a good mood too but Steven didn't. I was going about making breakfast, singing along with the radio, when he slouched into the kitchen.

'D'you want to turn that radio down a bit?'

I kidded on I didn't notice his mood.

'Not really, I'm enjoying it thanks.'

I thought if I was as cheeky as he was I might cajole him out of it. I put down a cup of tea by him in the living room where he lay in his shorts and tee shirt, curled up in a ball. His legs seemed to have got even longer. The big knees seemed out of proportion on his coltish legs. Not only were his legs longer, they were hairy. Hair had started to grow up his legs. From ankle to mid-calf he had a thick dark mane. Beyond that point only the blond downy hair of a child. It put me in mind of the fetlocks on a Clydesdale horse or someone wearing moon boots. I brushed his hair off his face so I could see him and said as gently as I could, 'Are you going to get ready for school?'

He pulled away from me, tightening himself into a

smaller ball. When I left for work he was still in the same position. I knew he would be late for school but I didn't say anything.

Steven staying the night buoyed me up all day. I hardly smoked at all. I kept telling everyone it was my birthday, I even told some people I was forty. I was only slightly deflated when I got back from work and there was no mail.

I had another mystery caller with another mystery gift. Bob arrived with a massive bunch of my favourite flowers, flame-orange roses. I didn't know what to say. Bob wasn't exactly dressed up but I could see he'd made an effort. He smelled faintly of Cool Water, aftershave I'd bought him three years ago on holiday in Spain. Surely it must be done by now? Bob wasn't the type to buy himself fancy toiletries. Either it was the stuff I'd bought or Helga had bought him some more.

'Eh, come in *Robbie*.'

I could see by his face that he recognized the jibe and no doubt where I'd heard it.

'Lovely flowers. Valentine's Day is next week.'

His face momentarily became a brighter shade than the roses as he hesitated at the door like a stranger. I could have kicked myself for taking him into the living room. After *The Weakest Link* I'd got out Mum's malt whisky by way of a birthday celebration and tanned three fags one after the other. I moved quickly and just managed to plank the fags and ashtray under the couch before he came in. Bob pretended not to notice the wedge-shaped piece box of Mark's hoy sui duck or the whisky bottle and single glass that sat there giving me a showing up. All I needed to complete the picture was a flickering candle stuck in a wee birthday cake for one.

'Well, how unexpected,' I chirped. 'This is the third birthday party I've had so far. They had a wee bash for me at work and then Steven and I had a good night last night.'

'Yeah, Steven said he had a nice time,' Bob confirmed. He was trying to be nice. He handed me an inoffensive card and he'd brought a cake. Not a wee birthday cake, thank God, a carrot cake. He only took his coat off and sat down after I invited him to. I supposed as he'd brought the cake I should offer him tea but he'd seen the whisky now anyway, the damage was done. I offered him one and to my surprise he was quite happy to take it. I poured large ones for us both.

'Forty eh?' Bob mused as he knocked half of it back. 'I remember when you were twenty.'

I was a bit uncomfortable with this stroll down Memory Lane.

'It puts everything into perspective though, doesn't it?'

Bob had turned forty the year before and I'd sent a sneeringly vindictive card. Perhaps now that I'd joined the ranks of the over-forties he'd come to crow. He could afford to. Bob was bearing up well under the burden of overfortyness. In fact he was flourishing. Playing five-a-sides twice a week and forswearing lager had kept a kyte at bay, or at least down to a mere suggestion of a tummy. Bob had always looked grown-up, even as a teenager he looked mature. Now he'd finally grown into his looks.

'Makes you think. Especially with old Elsie dying and everything, God rest her soul. Makes you realize that life's too short to spend arguing.'

I nodded agreement but now I had an idea what this was about. It was about the house. I was dreading what was coming next and topped up the glasses as quick as they were emptied. Though I tried not to show it, I was massively relieved to hear Bob say that he just wasn't financially in a position to buy me out.

'Not that I would want to,' he added emphatically.

He likewise appreciated that I didn't have the means to buy him out. He said that he hoped I felt as he did, that with the current market slump, selling the flat would be fruitless.

Thank God he's finally seen sense, I thought. He'd refused to see this point of view when we'd discussed it before. In fact we'd never properly discussed it before. In the past, fearful that he would sell the house from under me, I had used diversionary tactics. I referred to Helga as 'that Scandinavian slapper'. Then I got personal. I called Bob everything I could think of including my particular favourite, 'a slut-humping house thief'.

The idea was to make him so angry that he'd start shouting. Then I would know I had him, I could justifiably say in a cold but determined way, 'I think you'd better leave, Bob.'

But I didn't want him to leave now, not when we were on the same wavelength at last. And it got better.

'And we have to think about Steven,' he said. 'He needs a proper home. He should be close to his school and his friends.'

I nodded my head in fervent agreement and poured another. Now we were cooking.

'So, we can't buy each other out, we can't sell, what can we do?'

I knew he didn't expect me to answer.

'It is our home, Trish. We could share it.'

Wow. Share it. Did he mean what I thought he meant? That was a turn-up for the books, the last thing I expected him to say. I noticed he wasn't saying get back together again. He wouldn't dare. 'Robbie' wasn't that brazen. He was the one who left me. But the idea did have a certain appeal. Steven would come home. I wouldn't have to come back to an empty flat every night. Financially things could only get better. Maybe I could go part-time or chuck my job altogether. Now it all fell into place, the orange roses, the aftershave, the cake. Bob must be sick of slumming it with a girl half his age. Like so many married men he'd had his midlife crisis. Now he was fed up with Norwegian stew and wanted to crawl back home to the wife.

I didn't know if I could take him back. Two years was a long time, I might have taken a lover. I could've realized what I'd been missing all these years and taken a succession of lovers. I could've had them lining up in the street for all Bob knew. Things had changed, he'd have to understand that. I wasn't the daft wee house-wife he left two years ago. I was calling the shots now. If Bob wanted back certain demands would have to be met. I couldn't think of them off the top of my head but I was sure they'd come to me. If he came back he'd have to take me as he found me. We'd have separate rooms, there were three bedrooms after all. We could take it a bit at a time.

'I don't know, Bob. I'll have to think about it. It's a bit of a bombshell.'

'I know. Take your time. I realize it's a bit radical but it's the only real solution we have.'

'And what about Helga?'

'Helga understands the situation. She's been really good about it.'

I actually felt a bit sorry for poor wee Helga. I wondered if she'd just pack up her stewpots and head back to Norway. Bob sat there with a nervous begging smile on his face.

'Kiss me,' I dared him.

I would never have believed that asking your husband for a kiss could feel so racy. When had he last kissed Helga? He'd kissed her goodbye now. I moved across the room to sit beside him on the couch and cupped his face in my hands. His eyes kept dancing across my face and I wondered if he was going to take the dare. Bob planted a light kiss on my lips, obeying the letter of the challenge if not the spirit. I grabbed him and snogged the face off him. Like riding a bike, you never forget how to do it. Bob responded and after a long and satisfying winch he came up for air.

This was a very different kiss from our last one. I couldn't even remember our last official kiss. I did remember being worried about Mum and pushing him away a lot. Well, I didn't have to worry about Mum any more. And if kissing was going to be like this I wouldn't be pushing him away. With the passion of the kiss the couch must have moved back slightly. The corner of the fag packet was now just keeking out from under it. I swept my hand across the carpet and tried to push it back under but I'd been rumbled.

'Oh you naughty naughty girl,' Bob laughed. 'It's no use trying to hide it, I smelled the smoke off your breath anyway.'

I laughed as well, it was a fair cop. Bob and I gave up smoking together years ago to pay for Steven's school trip to France. But when we were out with friends we used to sneak fly draws of other people's. I reckoned Bob still did. In a slow tease I took a cigarette from the packet and handed him the lighter.

'Light me.'

I lay down on the couch. As the cigarette smouldered between my lips I sucked the warm smoke down and then seductively blew in Bob's face. I knew he felt the craving as much as me.

'Helga doesn't like smoking.'

I giggled. No doubt there were a lot of things Helga didn't like and I was confident that Bob would dish the dirt. There would be plenty of time for bitching. He put his hand up to his face and waved the smoke away.

'No, seriously. It really upsets her. She's allergic.'

I had another fit of the giggles.

'Well, it's just as well she's not coming too!'

Bob sat up and looked at me as if I was mental.

'What do you mean she's not coming? Of course she's coming, she's my partner, she's coming with me.'

I stopped giggling.

'I said share the house. What did you think I meant? Oh for God's sake Trish, you didn't think . . .'

'Of course I didn't!' I screamed as I jumped away from him. 'I wouldn't have you back in a lucky bag! Not in a million years!'

'Well,' Bob paused. He nodded and smiled. 'That's all right then. Helga is moving in here with me. I'm sure we can sort something out about the smoking.'

He kept smiling as he caught the arm I swung at him.

'No she fucking isn't!' I screamed. 'Why did you do that, why did you kiss me?' I wiped and scrubbed at my mouth as if I might have caught a disease.

'Yes she fucking is,' he said calmly. 'And *I* didn't do anything. You kissed me.'

'But you wanted it, you joined in!'

'I thought you needed it.'

'Well I don't need any favours from you, you fucking bastard! I don't think Helga will be very pleased when she hears about this!'

'I told you, Helga is fine about it. People in Norway do it all the time. Look, what's the problem? Can't we share the house like civilized people?'

'Under my roof with your slut girlfriend?'

'It's my roof too, Trish.'

I had a picture of me sitting in my bedroom in a cloud of smoke while he and Helga went at it in the next room. I'd hear everything, the fighting, the sex. And what would I have? A packet of ten Embassy Regal.

'I think you'd better leave, Bob.'

I kept my voice cold but there wasn't much dignity in it.

'The lease runs out at the end of the month and I'm not renewing. I have a right to live here and I'm bringing Helga. Get over it, Trish.'

As I knelt by the fire I curled and uncurled my toes over and over again. I had my head buried in a cushion so I didn't hear him close the front door on his way out.

Chapter 5

Donovan O'Hare and Boyle were going to be my salvation. The lawyer was going to tell me that my long-lost cousin Mr Robertson, or rather Mum's cousin, had indeed made me the chief beneficiary in his will. There would of course be a substantial sum. At least enough to buy my own house back. Tough if Bob hadn't renewed the lease on his flat, that was his lookout. And with Bob homeless Steven would have to come and live with me. On the other hand, somebody leaving me money just seemed too good to be true. Nobody had ever given me anything for free before. I did the lottery and bought charity raffle tickets but I'd never won anything in my puff. I knew better than to get my hopes up.

The lawyer's office was nothing like I expected it to be. On the outside of the building everything was on a grand scale from when Glasgow had been the second city of the empire. The facade was all Greek columns and ornate statues of women in togas holding banners. Inside, the reception area was plush and recently done out. In the middle of what was really a reception hall, under a garland of tiny bright bulbs, sat a massive blond wood desk cut in a jigsaw shape. The desk was clear but for an outsize vase of white lilies and a

leather-bound visitors' book. The glamorous receptionist, Helen her badge said, snootily insisted that I
sign the book.

When I saw Mr O'Hare's tiny wee back room I
understood why Helen was so superior. The firm
obviously thought more of the receptionist than they
did of the partners. So stuck for space was Mr O'Hare
that on the floor all around his desk were heaps of files
stacked higgledy-piggledy. He had to shift a bundle to
give me a seat. The one narrow window let in hardly
any daylight and although it was only one o'clock he
had all the lights on. The lack of light was caused by
another tenement backing onto this one. The other
building had once been tiled white but now, from
where I was sitting, I could see the yellow stains that
ran down it like diarrhoea.

The airs and graces the receptionist had put on had
given me the impression of a big company, a blue-chip
corporation. The kind of business that might have
had its own subsidized canteen for staff. As she sat
behind her enormous desk I imagined Helen planning
lunch, swithering between the lasagne al forno or the
vegetarian option. By the looks of things beyond
the reception area, the staff facilities would more
probably consist of a kettle and a packet of Nambarrie
teabags. This wee room was not making me feel good.
Everything annoyed me. Three days without fags was
making my skin crawl. Day three was my danger day,
in previous attempts it was always the day I'd fallen off
the wagon.

Mr O'Hare was older than he sounded on the phone.
A tall colourless man in a grey suit, he'd probably
had all the colour sucked out of his life from sitting all
day in this dungeon. I wanted to find out what the deal
was and get out as fast as I could but it wasn't Mr
O'Hare's way. First he offered me tea and hung up

my coat. He was very polite and scrupulous in his explanation of legal terms as they came up. He talked bequests, endowments and annuities.

I couldn't concentrate on what the man was saying, all I could think of was a big fat fag. I imagined lighting up with an expensive Colibri, the kind people used to buy in the Seventies as sentimental gifts. And while I was on that particular train of thought I fancied a cocktail cigarette. A purple one. I was filled with desire for a cigarette. I wanted to let the smoke enter me and curl into every corner of my body. I wanted the rush, I needed that wonderful smogasmic sensation.

Next thing I knew Mr O'Hare was asking me to sign for keys for a business in the West Highlands.

'So, no cash then?'

Mr O'Hare looked confused.

'There is, as I've set out, Miss McNicol, an annuity more than sufficient to cover the running costs of the business but this is dependent on your taking up residence.'

'Residence?'

What the hell was he talking about? There and then Mr O'Hare stopped being a kindly old gentleman and became a mean keen legal machine. This was more like it.

'Mr Robertson has left you his home and business,' said Mr O'Hare as he rummaged in the file. 'Yes, Harrosie in Inverfaughie on the west coast north of Inverness, which until Mr Robertson's recent death has been operated as a bed and breakfast. This he has bequeathed to you, Miss McNicol, on condition that you live there. Under the terms of the endowment you are unable to realize capital by selling it. Neither are you obliged to operate a bed and breakfast business from the premises, Mr Robertson having made generous provision in the form of an allowance, paid monthly, which should comfortably cover all living expenses.'

'So no cash then?' I asked again.

Mr O'Hare shook his head sadly.

'No cash I'm afraid, Miss McNicol.'

'No, don't get me wrong, I mean it's a brilliant deal. If I'm understanding you properly then it's a house by the sea in the Highlands, a business if I want it and enough money to live on if I don't.'

Mr O'Hare nodded this time.

'It is and you have.'

But there was no substantial lump sum. I wasn't going to be able to pay Bob off. He was going to walk in and set up his harem under my nose. I'd have to bunk up and shut up. There was another option, I could always kill myself.

Auntie Nettie took Mum's death worse than anyone. Since Mum died Nettie phoned me every week, sometimes several times a week. She came round to the flat a few times but mostly I was away on training or I didn't answer the buzzer. Just when I thought she'd given up, she caught me. I picked up the phone thinking it would be Steven. Oh she was wondering if there was anything wrong, she hadn't seen me since the funeral, she hadn't set eyes on a living soul for ages, she was missing Elsie and her ears were giving her gyp. Sick of her moaning at me and just to get her off the phone, I agreed to visit.

I knew the first thing she would say. She would start on about the damp in the house. Nettie had been singing the same song for over thirty years. The damp was running down the walls and growing in dark moulds and mushrooms in corners of the rooms. Over the years the council had tried everything to get rid of it, every kind of damp-proofing there was. They even built false walls inside the house but still it seeped through. Tommy, Nettie's husband, had died years before, officially of a heart attack, but Nettie argued his death was damp-related. There was probably some truth in this but the more likely cause was that it was Nettie-related. She worked the man to death. But, I reminded myself, Nettie was family. She looked so much like Mum that when she opened the door I found that I was pleased to see her.

'Come away in love, och it's nice to see you, it's just nice to have a visitor.'

She fussed about and brought through a tray with sandwiches and biscuits she'd already prepared. It wasn't long before she got onto her favourite subject.

'I'd love to get out of this house, the damp is running down the walls, that's what killed my Tommy, but the council say I havnae enough points.' And there she went on, bumping her gums about her housing problem.

Nettie had lived here for thirty-four years. If Tommy hadn't indulged his wife so much in her hunger for all things expensive – holidays, clothes, soft furnishings, designer kitchen utensils and festoon blinds that eventually became tinged with the grey-green mould that permeated everything – they could have bought their own house. A substantial damp-proof property in a nice area would have been bought and paid for by the time Tommy retired. Instead he slogged every day in the shipyards working overtime and extra shifts to pay for Nettie's fripperies until his poor heart gave out and he keeled over.

Tommy ran about daft after her. He called her 'Princess' and there was nothing he wouldn't do for her. They never had kids, she didn't want them, so that when Tommy died, reality hit Nettie like a sledgehammer. All on her lonesome, she inflicted her self-pity on Mum, and Mum, being a good sister, put up with it. Nettie got a good deal of mileage out of the situation, turning Mum's illness into her drama. 'Naebody understands how painful it is for me to watch my own sister dying in front of my eyes,' was a favourite refrain.

While her own sister stoically suffered in silence, Nettie squealed like a pig about her tinnitus and expected sympathy. She'd seen a specialist and been told there was nothing wrong with her ears but still she complained. A couple of times I could have cheerfully rattled her ears for her just to give her something to moan about. Eventually, Mum and I hit on a good way of getting rid of Nettie when she became a pain in the arse as she so frequently did. Mum would fake a bad turn. I helped her to her bedroom and we both sat, stifling giggles until Nettie got fed up and left.

As she boffed on about the council's latest dampness-eradication scheme I suppose Nettie must have thought me a poor replacement for Mum. I wasn't paying enough attention to her egocentric bleatings, not making sympathetic enough noises, so she gave up and changed tack.

'Och I'm missing my wee sister Elsie awful bad, I've been that lonely without her. I suppose you'll be pleased to have Steven back,' she said in an accusatory tone. Her loss was my gain, she seemed to be implying. As if I was glad that Mum was gone and she was lonely.

'Well, he's still at his dad's for the moment,' I said, trying to take the heat off, but this was a mistake.

'Oh, I'm surprised at that. I thought he'd want to come back to you.'

My face flushed in anger and shame.

'He does,' I snipped, 'we've just got to sort things out yet.'

'Of course you have, dear.'

Nettie put her head down and picked imaginary

crumbs off her lap as if there was some reason to be embarrassed. I decided then that some day I'd get the vicious old bitch back. When the time came, Mum's sister or not, I wouldn't show up for her funeral. For the meantime I had to get her off the subject before I lost the rag.

'I've come into a bit of an inheritance, Auntie Nettie,' I said.

That would put her gas at a peep.

'It seems I've inherited a house in the Highlands, in Inverfaughie.'

I told her all about it, about Mum's cousin and the lawyer, rubbing it in, making it sound wonderful. Nettie was in a quandary, she was too jealous to want to hear about it and too nosey not to. She couldn't stop herself asking questions.

'Fancy,' was all she could say.

'Yes, on the west coast, totally unspoilt and fabulous sunsets they say.'

'Fancy.'

Once the fly old bugger had established the facts she said, 'You know, I've never heard of a Robertson in the family.'

'Yes, Henry Robertson, Mum's second cousin apparently.'

'And who did you say the lawyers were again?'

'Donovan O'Hare and Boyle,' I chirped.

I was quite enjoying myself now.

'Now,' Nettie said, moving forward in her chair, holding her hand to her throat exactly the way Mum used to, 'don't take this the wrong way Trisha, but do you think you could ask them to look into it for me, love? I think there's been a mistake.'

'What d'you mean, Auntie Nettie?'

'Well, no harm to you hen, you weren't to know, but being the older sister I'm actually Elsie's next of kin.'

'I'm sorry, I don't get you.'

I got her all right but I could hardly believe it, and I wanted to hear her say it.

'Oh God love you Trisha, I hate to let you down, but you have to see it from my point of view hen. I've got to get out of this house, the damp'll kill me. And with Elsie away there's nothing for me here any more.'

'Uh huh?'

'Och, try to be happy for me hen, a wee house by the seaside is just what I'm needing. I've not got long now, God knows, I'm not long for this world. And you'll be next in line. Tommy and me wernae blessed with kiddies so you'll be my next of kin, it'll come to you in good time hen.'

Fuck! Talk about shooting yourself in the foot? I'd just blasted my leg off! Or rather Nettie had, and by telling her about the cousin and the lawyers I'd given her all the ammunition she needed. Not long for this world? She was only seventy, technically she could last another thirty years, the Queen Mother had. In thirty years' time *I'd* be seventy. Nettie would probably see me out just for spite. If I was right it was going to be a long hard thirty years. I'd have to seriously start looking after myself, the fags would have to go for a start.

I'd already talked to Steven and written the outline of my presentation for Irene. I just had to finish off the bedroom for Bob and Helga.

Steven had talked incessantly with a sincerity and intensity that was unnerving. In the last two days I'd learned more about my son's life, his friends, the girls he fancied and the teachers he hated, than I had in the previous fifteen years. I discovered why Nike was cool and Kappa wasn't. This kind of previously classified information came tumbling out of him in a torrent of confession and getting-to-know-you fervour. He also asked me lots of questions. It was as though he was five again. Steven had suddenly discovered an interest in and total respect for my personal tastes in everything from my political views to which kind of dogs I preferred. He was my constant companion. He came with me and pushed the trolley round Asda. When I cooked dinner he kept me company, even volunteering to peel the potatoes. I ran a bath and the water was nearly cold before he got the message and left the room. In the end I more or less insisted that he go and help his dad with the packing. I needed a break and I was gasping for a fag.

The presentation had been fairly straightforward. I'd sat looking at a blank piece of paper for hours before it came to me. It came in a sudden exciting inspirational flash. It took no time at all, needed virtually no editing and when it was finished I knew it was perfect. I emailed it, not just to Irene but to the whole team. I couldn't in all honesty call it a presentation. It was really more of a statement. In fact it was a resignation. Dear Team mates, it read, Grow the Business has been our watchword. But when shall we stop growing? When we explode? Dear Irene, I added as a footnote, stick your job up your arse.

I chuckled away, impressed by my own effrontery, as I scraped at the wallpaper. This room, the biggest of the bedrooms, with its built-in double wardrobes and king-size bed, was the obvious choice for Bob and Helga. This had been our bedroom, the room in which Steven had been conceived. The room where we'd had our muted arguments after Mum moved in.

I knew how much Bob hated scraping wallpaper, we'd had enough fights about it over the years. He'd worked at a rate of about a square foot a week and I'd always ended up finishing it myself. Bob would be severely pissed off if he had to scrape these walls, and bare walls wouldn't be very welcoming for Helga.

In between fag breaks, I pulled the bed away from the wall and had almost finished that side of the room when I noticed my mistake. I was obviously getting too good at this decorating carry-on. All the way along the wall I had removed a thick horizontal slice from each strip of wallpaper. The problem was that I was so used to making a neat job of it that I'd scraped it at the same height all the way along. This was no use. Bob would just slap up a border, in fact it would probably improve the look of the room. With the wall opposite the bed, the one they would spend most time looking at, I decided to be a bit more inventive. This wall had a stubborn orange and green paper underneath, which had been there since before we moved in, and as I scraped I created a kind of batik effect. It was harder and took longer but the overall effect was worth it. I got the camera and took a picture of it. In tidy letters eight feet tall I had chiselled out the words 'FUCK YOU'.

Chapter 6

The Highlands were a foreign country to me. The only words I knew in Gaelic were *uisge-beatha* for whisky and *slainte* for cheers. The important ones. Like most Glaswegians I'd been to Spain, even as far south as Agadir in Africa on a package deal, but the furthest north I'd ever been was Loch Lomond. On summer Saturdays the lochside rang with the sound of schemey Glaswegian Neds playing ghetto blasters and arguing over who drank the carry-out. And so I found myself an official resident of the Highlands with a proper Highland address and postcode, ready to start living la vida Scotia.

The drive up was a dawdle, including two stops it only took six hours and the scenery was brilliant. It was tea time when I arrived and despite it being only March, the sun was still in the sky, blindingly bright when the clouds rolled off it.

The map Mr O'Hare had marked for me was pretty straightforward and I found Harrosie without any bother. It wasn't actually in Inverfaughie; it was about ten minutes along on the road north of the town. Harrosie was middle in a row of three cottages, the only one advertising Bed and Breakfast. The other cottages looked deserted with all their curtains closed. So, it was going to be solitary confinement, I thought. It was hard to imagine living so removed from human contact. I'd always been intimate with my neighbours, at least in terms of space. They were always just a few feet away; above, below and through the wall. Sometimes they were a bloody nuisance but at least they were there. I was going to be out on this country road all on my own. Harrosie's red and yellow painted wooden sign boasted of the facilities on offer: B. and B., TV, sea view, ensuite b and sh, h and c. It felt like a lonely hearts ad and I was going to need a GSOH.

From the outside Harrosie looked small, hardly big enough for a house, but inside it was a Tardis. There were five bedrooms, three with their own bathrooms, another bathroom and toilet, a big kitchen, a wee back room and a long lounge facing the front. The bedrooms had brass plaques on the doors and they were each named after a different famous whisky. The cottages were at the top of the hill before the road swung back down the other side and from the lounge the view was spectacular: to the left the moody purple and grey mountains stood guard around the loch, shiny as a fish scale when the sun hit it. To the right I looked out to sea at the islands, swathed in mist, like tropical islands, but with a subtropical climate no doubt, sub zero more like. There was a musty smell so I opened all the windows to air the place while I explored the garden.

Having grown up in tenements a garden was a new concept to me, an expensive time-consuming waste of space, something for posh people. This was huge, you could have put two tenements, living space for a hundred people, in the area I had for a garden. There were bushes and beds and trees and grass, a parkload of brown and green. It made me nervous, especially when I opened the hut at the back. Rusting tools that looked more like medieval weapons of torture were stacked around the walls. I'd never cope with this.

Think positively. How do you eat an elephant? One bite at a time. The journey of a thousand miles begins with one step. These and other *Woman's World* gems fought for dominance over panic in my head. The tool nearest the door was a spiky thing with three corroded prongs. Merely looking at it caused it to fall off its peg and out the door. I picked it up and placed it gently against the next one. Years of playing Jenga and Buckaroo with Steven had given me the lightest touch and the thing behaved itself. Until I tried to shut the door. Closing the door was enough to bring the whole lot down. Spades, hoes, rakes, crumbling poles and spiky things fell out the door in an orange cloud of rust. Think positively. One step at a time I stacked the tools back in the shed. With my Buckaroo deftness it was going well, only three more to go when the first one, the spiky bugger, couped again causing a domino effect. Now I tried to shove them in any old way but as panic took hold I ran back to the house leaving the rotting tools splayed out on the ground.

I found the central heating, put it on easy enough, thank God, shut all the windows and then chose a bedroom. I settled on Glenmorangie, the front-facing bedroom with the best views, and unpacked methodically. The drawers felt damp, not just in Glenmorangie but in all the rooms. Maybe it was just cold, I told myself, the place had lain empty, it would be all right once I got the house warmed up. The drawers smelled of wintergreen. I wrapped all my clothes in poly bags so the smell and the damp wouldn't get to them. Then I sat on the bed and looked out the window for ages before I could stir myself to phone home. Home. It wasn't my home now, this was.

Amazingly the house phone worked and I didn't need to use my mobile.

'Steven?'

'Oh hi Mum.'

Thank God Steven picked it up.

'Right I'm here son, safe and sound, just to let you know.'

'So what's it like?'

'Aye it's great. Fantastic. Lovely views. Have you got a pen?'

'Eh . . .'

I could hear him fumbling about the hall table.

'Top drawer left-hand side, beside the tin, there's stacks of pens.'

The familiarity of our hall table was already making me homesick and I'd only been here an hour.

'Yeah, got one.'

I gave him the number, speaking slowly and repeating it, and then I made him read it back to me.

'Yes, that's it, but you've got my mobile number if you need me son, just phone any time you like.'

'Hey Mum, don't go away yet! Tell me about your new house.'

'I told you, it's fine.'

'Heh, heh, I saw what you did to the bedroom. Heh, respect. Dad went off his head.'

'Is he there? Can he hear you?'

'Nah, chill out man, he's in the kitchen. He's cooking tonight.'

Steven had never called me man before, he only used that with his pals. Would he have called me man if I was standing in the hall next to him?

'Look, I'll need to get off Steven, the bills'll be horrendous, but you phone me.'

'Heh, heh. So Dad pays. Good one.'

'I'll have to go son, and remember, if Auntie Nettie phones . . .'

'I know nothing!' Steven said, mimicking an Italian gangster.

Terrified that Bob would discover me on the line and start shouting at me, I got off as quick as I could. I was too fragile to be shouted at. I wasn't coping with the thought of him and her in my house while I was here, in a pongy cottage in the middle of nowhere.

I woke up the next morning absolutely starving. I'd noticed a wee shop in the village yesterday as I passed through, I could go down there and stock up. As I came out of Harrosie I was caught completely by surprise by the view. Nothing had changed, the loch and the sea and the islands were still in the same place, but they were different. The sky was cloudy but the sun hadn't reached above the clouds yet, and the strong yellow light overwhelmed everything and made it look brand new. The two other cottages were still dark, not a soul anywhere, but this time I was glad.

I made all kinds of healthy resolutions there and then. Stop smoking, that was the first priority. Healthy eating, long walks, early nights, get my head sorted out. I thought about giving up drinking as well but maybe that was taking it a bit far. Forget the B. and B. business for the moment, one step at a time. It would be ages before there were any tourists anyway and it wasn't as if I needed the money. Recently I'd systematically waded my way through the top five stress factors: bereavement, new job, family split-up, leaving job, moving house. Enough was enough. Think positively, I didn't need to worry about it any longer, I didn't have to look after Mum, or flog drugs, or worry about money. All I had to do was enjoy the view.

The shop was a branch of McSpor, proprietor and licensee Jennifer L. Robertson, the sign above the door said. Probably related to Mum's uncle Henry, I thought. The selection inside was disappointing to say the least and the old lady who ran it was hard work. By the look of her she was in her early sixties, a bit on the fat side but you could see she had been a good-looking woman in her day. Right away she told me to call her Jenny and asked me my name.

'Trixie? That's a nice name.'

Maybe she was deaf.

'Eh, no, it's Trisha,' I said, enunciating clearly this time.

She seemed to ignore my correction and carried on asking me questions. I told her about the cottage, that I'd inherited Harrosie from my mother's cousin. I remarked that she shared his name, Robertson.

'Och, along with everyone else in this town!'

So we weren't related, I was a wee bit disappointed with that. I could be doing with some family, however distantly connected. She continued quizzing me, replying 'uh huh' to everything I said, as if she already knew the answers, as if she was checking that I did.

'And what about your family Trixie?' she said in her sing-song Highland accent that implied a weird mixture of sympathy and glee.

If I'd had time to think about it I'd have been offended by the bloody nosiness of the woman, but instead I fudged.

'No brothers or sisters, there's only me. I'm actually in for a packet of muesli, d'you have any Jenny?'

I looked her straight in the eye. If she could ask such personal questions I could change the subject. After all, she was the shop assistant and I was seeking assistance. She took ages to answer, drawing her eyes across me. No she didn't have any. Well did she have porridge? Yes she had porridge, McSpor Porridge. Oh, not Scott's Porridge Oats then?

'Well you see Trixie, this is a McSpor retail outlet and as such only really carries McSpor lines.'

I couldn't work out if she was boasting or apologizing. For McSpor read limited choice and damned expensive. She only had one wee tray of knackered old carrots and turnips, and she was charging an arm and a leg for them. I had expected there to be more local produce available. It was mad, the fields around the village were chock-full of fresh lamb and beef and pork and venison and eggs and grains and veg and berries. I'd seen them on my way up here yesterday. But Jenny explained in her sarcastic patronizing Highland lilt that these weren't available from McSpor, the farms were all contracted to Asdi and if I wanted Asdi I'd have to drive to Inverness. Although her face was straight, the accent was baffling me. Was she genuine or was she taking the piss? It was more than just the hissy pronunciation. She spoke so slowly and gently and her inflection was so random that you could read almost anything into it. I was being paranoid, I decided, I hadn't got a handle on her accent, the old lady was just trying to be helpful. Or was she? With her voice rising and falling as if to mock me she said she had a special offer on toilet roll. What did she mean by that?

'You'll not get a deal as good as this at Asdi,' she sang to me.

I relaxed, she wasn't having a go, she was simply giving me her sales pitch. I could see how the accent was an asset in retailing. Entranced by her melodic spiel I stuck the toilet roll in my basket along with a few frozen dinners and everything else she recommended. We were getting on like a house on fire now and I was relieved. If I was going to live here I was going to have to make friends.

An old boy from the village, introduced by Jenny as Walter, came in. A tall skinny old bloke, Walter was dignified without being unfriendly. He was a bit unsteady on his feet and allowed Jenny to lead him to an old chair parked in a corner of the shop. Above the chair a sign said 'We Care with a Chair'. Walter wouldn't sit down however, he didn't care for the chair, and extended his hand to me.

'Trixie is it? Pleased to meet you dear.'

'It's actually Trisha, bit of a mix-up earlier I think.'

But poor old Walter had other things on his mind.

'I've to go in this afternoon, Dr Robertson booked a bed and they're sending an ambulance,' he said quietly as he nodded his head at the floor.

The man was embarrassed so I turned away and pretended to be looking for something on the shelves. Which was just as well because Jenny immediately dropped what she was doing, i.e. serving me, and spent the next twenty minutes huddled with Walter while I was left standing about.

After a while, Walter's dog, which he had tied up outside, became bored and started to whine. Deep in conversation with Jenny, Walter didn't notice. The dog did what dogs always do but in a more organized way than I'd ever seen before. It whined and leapt in the air, its head and shoulders visible through the shop window. As the dog landed it rested for a beat and then whined and leapt again. Tirelessly the poor mutt trampolined up and down, in and out of my peripheral vision, each jump the same height, each whine the same pitch. The rhythm set up by the unvarying noise and the piston-like jumping was at first impressive, then comical and eventually irritating.

'Bouncer!' Jenny shouted without a trace of Highland liltyness.

Bouncer stopped. After about five seconds, he started again.

As Walter went out and untied the dog, Jenny, without asking him, packed a bag of messages: toiletries, Lucozade, mints and a newspaper. He brought Bouncer in and said cheerio but Jenny wouldn't let them leave until she'd gone into the back shop (which seemed to be where she lived) and come out with a Tupperware dish of home-made soup for Walter and a bone for Bouncer. As Walter left the shop no money changed hands. Her kindness towards the old man touched me until I reached the till. Then I realized that the exorbitant prices I was being charged were subsidizing the old guy.

The shop doubled, or more correctly quadrupled, as grocer, post office, video library and off-licence. There was a telly and video in the wee back room in Harrosie, I'd spotted it the night before. The films she had out on display weren't the latest releases, some were years old but there were a few that I hadn't seen. I asked Jenny about hiring.

'Well you'd have to be a member of the I.R.V.C. Trixie dear, the Inverfaughie Residents Video Club. I could enroll you but it will require me asking a few details if you don't mind.'

She was getting me back for wriggling out of her earlier interrogation.

'What kind of details?'

'Och y'know, your name and address, date of birth, marital status and income, just the usual kind of thing.'

She was a nosey old cow but I knew I'd get bored without videos. Lured by her kindly intonation I told her everything. Jenny had worn me down. I would have told her my National Insurance number and distinguishing birth marks if she'd asked. She didn't make a note of anything but after staring at me hard up and down for moment, she decided I could join. I took a psychological thriller on overnight hire although Jenny did kind of spoil it for me.

'And you'll hardly believe it, but it's the young girl, Beth, her with the lovely red hair. It turns out she's one of those psychopaths.'

The off-licence part of the shop was remarkably well stocked for a small village, but there were only a few wines to choose from. I couldn't make up my mind.

'Well, what do you like, vin blank?' Jenny pronounced vin to rhyme with tin, 'or would you prefer the vin rough?'

'I'll take the vin rough thanks,' I said with a straight face, 'and twenty Silk Cut please Jenny.'

From the upstairs window I watched a man cycle up from Inverfaughie. He pedalled effortlessly up the steep hill. I was looking forward to seeing him skite down the other side but instead he got off the bike and chapped my door. I think I actually gasped when I saw how handsome he was. He wasn't far off six feet and as broad as a house. Not fat, muscly. Going by his face he must have been in his late forties but going by the shape of him you would have taken him for a young man.

'Good morning Trixie.'

This sex god knew my name!

'I'm here to do the garden?'

Was he telling me or asking permission?

'Oh, right.'

'Sorry. I'm Jackie,' he said, offering me his big warm dry hand. 'Jack Robertson, call me Jackie.'

Another Robertson, the place was full of them.

'My mum's uncle Henry, Henry Robertson, left her this place, are you any relation?'

'We're all Jock Tamson's bairns.'

Although I'd seen it written down, I'd never actually heard anyone use that expression. It sounded couthy, kind of warm and inclusive. I decided I liked it.

'Well it seems we're all Robertsons in Inverfaughie. Everyone I've met so far is called Robertson.'

He laughed at that.

'Never a truer word.'

He had a lovely laugh, it seemed to just burst out of him naturally and had the effect of instantly cheering me up. I couldn't believe this guy was here to do the garden. Thank you, thank you God, I thought, not only have you sent me someone to tame the jungle behind the house but he laughs at my jokes and he's beautiful!

Jackie didn't look like a gardener. I'd never actually met a gardener before but I'd seen them on the telly and they were usually scraggy wee chaps. Jackie looked like a movie star. Not in a fussy way, but a down and dirty, manly way. I invited him in and led him through to the lounge. I offered him a seat but he didn't want to sit down, hovering about just inside the door. It took a minute for it to dawn on me that he was being polite. He didn't want to stain the chair with his working clothes and he was happier when we moved outside, happier, that is, until he saw the garden.

'Och, look at this mess.'

The more he saw the more annoyed he got. He strode around the garden pulling bushes apart and wrenching dead wood from the trees. I could hardly keep up with him and I wasn't sure if I wanted to, his strength and his temper were fearful. He was taking his job too seriously, what the hell was wrong with this guy?

'Aww!'

He stood looking at the tools lying rusting outside the hut.

'They're ruined. Wasted. A bloody waste.'

'I'm awful sorry, it's my fault. They fell out and I couldn't get the door closed.'

'This didn't happen overnight, it's years of neglect. The old bastard just let them go to rack and ruin. Look at these tools, they're done. There was a good business in this lot, a good few hundred pounds' worth if he'd only looked after them. A bit of grease on the blades through the winter and they'd have been fine.'

'I'm sorry it offends you Jackie.'

The 'old bastard' he was referring to was my uncle Henry. I could agree that the garden needed tidying up but there was no call to insult my family, however distant. I must have scowled because he quickly changed his tune.

'I'm the one who should be sorry. Sorry for getting so steamed up. Sorry for the state of this garden.'

His easy apology made me feel I'd taken the huff too quickly. I was relieved we weren't going to fall out before we'd become friends. It would have been a cruel twist of fate if my newly discovered male-model gardener turned out to be a nutcase.

'It's a pity you didn't work for Mr Robertson.'

Jackie smiled and nodded his head when I said that. I was waiting for him to say 'never a truer word,' again but he didn't.

I invited him back into the house but this time I took him into the kitchen and he seemed comfortable enough there. I made a pot of tea and we had a good blether about my moving to the village. He was interested to hear about Steven and was surprised that I'd left him in Glasgow.

'Oh it's only until he sits his standard grades. This is an important year for him at school and we, my ex and me, didn't want him changing schools in the middle of things. But he'll come the minute his exams are over.'

He was the first person that I'd told and it didn't

83

sound so bad once it was out. Jackie accepted it easily enough, but then again, he was a man.

Jackie said he'd be able to get started on the garden tomorrow with his own tools, but in the long run the tools would need to be replaced.

'Now the best place for this kind of thing is Inverness. We could go together sometime and I could show you what you need.'

I readily agreed. Jackie was nearly out the door before I could bring myself to ask him how much he charged. This was going to be sore, but what the hell.

'Och, a couple of pounds an hour. Whatever you think.'

Jackie seemed embarrassed talking about money but surely this couldn't be right. A couple of pounds an hour? It was too good to be true. I didn't say anything to him at the time but I decided that I'd pay him a fair rate, the official minimum wage at least. We agreed on two days a week. I got the impression he'd be happy to come every day but I couldn't afford it. Although Jackie was gagging to get the garden into shape I was in no hurry. This way would give me something to look forward to two days a week. That would only leave the other five to take care of. When he left I began to think that maybe Inverfaughie wasn't going to be so bad after all.

Chapter 7

Steven phoned me as usual that night. We were just chatting away, chewing the fat, when Bob must have realized who was on the phone and grabbed the receiver.

'You've ruined that bedroom. You should get help. You're a sick twisted woman.'

'It's only a bit of wallpaper for God's sake, there's no need to get so excited.'

'No it's not. It's an expression of your nasty evil venomous nature, that's what it is, a constant fucking reminder of you.'

'Well you can always redecorate, Bob, it's not the end of the world.'

'That's not the point. The point is that we agreed amicably that Helga and I get the house. Amicably, didn't we? But no, you don't know the meaning of the word. You've wilfully vandalized my home.'

'So sue me!'

'It's a good thing you're so fucking far away because if you were here Trish, I'd rip your fucking head off.'

'Oh that's nice. Offer me violence why don't you, are you sure Steven got all that? Get a hold of yourself and stop swearing for fuck's sake.'

'You're swearing at me!'

'Yeah, but Steven can't hear me, I'm allowed. OK, enough, calm down, don't shout like that in front of him.'

'Oh you and Steven are getting helluva cosy aren't you, on the phone every bloody night. On my fucking bill. Having a good chat were you? I bet he didn't tell you his prelim results, did he? He fucking crashed maths! Forty-two per cent! I've been up at the school today trying to rescue his ungrateful arse. They're trying to bump him. Mr Gozie sys he's taking him out of credit maths. No maths, no university, but d'you think Steven is bothering his arse? Not one bit!'

'I am bothering my arse!' I heard Steven remonstrate.

'Just you mind your language!'

'Bob, we'll need to do something. What about a maths tutor?'

'Yeah and who's going to pay for it? D'you know how much it costs. Twenty-five quid an hour. I don't have that kind of money, I'm too busy paying McKay and Son to redecorate the bedroom you destroyed.'

'Oh for Christ's sake Bob. You don't need a decorator. Just peel it off and slap up more paper, it's easy.'

'Get off my fucking phone, you're costing me money.'

'Let me speak to Steven.'

'You spoke to him, you were on for fifteen minutes, long distance.'

'I just want to say goodnight.'

'Yeah. Goodnight!'

Bob slammed the phone down with such force it hurt my ear.

I tried calling Steven back but it was the answering machine. Bob had obviously forbidden Steven to pick up, either that or they were having such a big row that they hadn't heard it ring. Bob hadn't changed the outgoing message and I listened to my own voice tell me that I would return the call as soon as possible.

*   *   *

Jackie came and started on the garden before I was even out of my bed. By the time I was up and respectably dressed, he had chopped and cleared masses of it. The garden looked even bigger now. I took him out a cup of tea.

'It looks naked.'

'Och, you have to get rid of the dead wood. To let the new growth through. It'll look a lot better in a few weeks.'

I went back into the house and let him get on with it but I could see him from the kitchen window. By lunchtime he had taken off his sweatshirt and was down to his vest. I called him in for a plate of soup. It was just tinned soup from Jenny's but he was grateful.

'Aye Trixie, that was grand.'

I had to set the record straight.

'My name isn't actually Trixie. It was a bit of a misunderstanding with Jenny in the shop. I should have sorted it out at the time.'

'Aye, that Jenny has a habit of misunderstanding to suit herself.'

'Och I don't know about that. Anyway, that's not my real name.'

'What is your real name then?'

'It's Trisha, bit of a let-down after Trixie I suppose.'

'And which would you prefer?'

'I don't know, I hadn't thought about it. I've always just been Trisha.'

'Aye but you haven't always lived in Inverfaughie.'

That was true, I could be Esmerelda for all anyone in Inverfaughie knew.

'Well I won't tell anyone if you don't.'

'OK then.'

We shook on it and this time Jackie put both of his lovely warm strong hands round mine.

*   *   *

I did have neighbours after all. One morning I heard noise through the wall and spotted a people carrier parked outside. I didn't do anything about it but a couple of hours later they came to the door. Two sweet little girls with a bunch of flowers for me, to welcome me to Inverfaughie, their mum Polly said. I introduced myself as Trixie without as much as a blush and seemed to get away with it. Then I put my foot in it by asking if the girls were twins.

'No,' said Polly, 'Michaela is six and Rebecca is eight.'

'Eight and a half,' said Rebecca.

'Oh you're quite right darling, eight and a half.'

The kids had gorgeous cute little English accents and they called their mum 'Mummy'. Polly passed on her husband Roger's apologies but he was at his desk in the middle of a videoconference. They were just back from visiting his mother in London, she explained.

'It took fifteen hours to get back. Makes you realize how far away we are.'

Polly was beautiful, all delicate cheekbones and soft hair, but she was nervous. I tried to put her at her ease, offering her wine but she said she didn't drink. I told her the vin rough story, thinking we could have a laugh, but Polly was disappointingly shy of gossip.

'I try to get on with everyone in the village.'

The pitch of Polly's voice had got a bit higher.

'It might be easier for you Trixie, being Scottish.'

To change the subject I asked her about the house next door.

'It's owned by Clive and Helen, good friends of ours.'

Oh well, I thought, things are looking up.

'They let it out in the summer to tourists. Roger keeps an eye on it for them, burst pipes, all that sort of thing. They used to live here. We used to come and visit them, that's really why we moved here. It's funny, Clive and Helen back in Sussex and us up here now.'

She sounded as if she'd been abandoned.

'They say that if you last two years in the Highlands you're going to make it.'

'And how long has it been?'

'Three months.'

My only female neighbour didn't drink, didn't gossip and I could see it was only a matter of time before she started telling me how lonely she was. The kids were great though. They dragged me into their garden to meet Smidgy Rabbit. I'd never touched a rabbit before but Rebecca thrust him into my arms before I got a chance to think about it. I could feel his little bones shaking inside his gorgeously soft fur. He was fragile and vulnerable and suddenly I understood why children loved pets.

'Polly, I'd be happy to look after the girls any night you and Roger want to go out on the town.'

'Can she Mummy, oh please? Can Trixie babysit for us? Please?'

'We'll see.'

But later when the kids were putting Smidgy back in his hutch Polly said, 'Thank you for offering, it was very kind Trixie, but I don't know if Roger would be keen. We haven't been out since we moved here.'

Polly's perfect bone structure wobbled a bit when she said that.

I discovered that Harrosie was hoaching with beasties. The bath panel was loose so I pulled it back and keeked in but I wished I hadn't. There were loads of grey-coloured creepy-crawlies writhing around in the damp darkness. It was disgusting and every time I thought of them my lips and my spine curled. The house was clean enough but I found spiders, moths, beetles, wee red ants and the grey things. I was scared to open cupboards and drawers for fear of what was in there. I told Steven about it when he phoned but it was all a big joke to him.

Any time I encountered beasties I'd completely freak before spraying them with something, anything, just to stop them crawling. Knowing how fast these things can move I would never contemplate baring my arse in the presence of a beastie. But there were so many of them. After a week of freaking and spraying, I was exhausted. Eventually I gave up and just tried to avoid them.

I concentrated on getting the house sorted out. One step at a time. Nothing major, no decorating, I'd had enough of decorating. I just wanted it to feel homey. I wanted to stop waking up wondering where the hell I was.

I put my photos up on the mantelpiece in the lounge and all my wee knick-knacks and ornaments around the furniture. The middle of the altar was reserved for my favourite photo of Steven. At age sixteen months, his tear-stained baby face girning behind the bars of his cot, he stood with his arms outstretched, knackered, refusing to lie down and sleep. That seemed like a long time ago, it was hard to imagine it was the same person. But even my most recent photo of him, taken last Christmas, was out of date. Steven had changed so much since Christmas, his face lengthening and becoming more angular, he was changing all the time now. Even when he became an old man I'd always think of him as that wee tyke banged up in his cot.

The cupboards in the kitchen had a horrible smell in them, like antique rich tea biscuits. No amount of scrubbing with Zoflora would get rid of it. The shelves were lined with ancient sticky-back plastic that was curling up at the edges and had some sort of organic grey stuff worked into the creases. It was a pity because the design on the plastic was beautiful, teensy wee pink and red roses, really old-fashioned. I caught myself thinking what a gorgeous floral pattren it was. I was turning into my mother, that had been one of her linguistic foibles. Anything that ended in 'ern' she pronounced as 'ren'. She didn't seem to be aware of the correct pronunciation. When she used to knit she'd phone and tell me about the lovely modren knitting pattren she'd got from the wool shop.

I stacked all the dishes, and there were hundreds of them, on the sideboard and started howking out the shelves. Under the bottom shelf there was a certain amount of dusty fluff amidst mystery objects, one of which turned out to be a chip. It was black and solid, petrified, the only way I could tell it was a chip was that I could see the potato eye on the top edge. Another was a photograph which I very nearly threw out. I hadn't noticed it while I was sweeping up, trying not to look too closely after the unpleasantness with the chip. As I was tipping the rubbish from the shovel into the bin, the photo stuck on the edge of the shovel. I shoogled it about but it was stuck firm. I wouldn't be able to use the shovel until I got rid of it so I gritted my teeth and yanked it off. When I wiped it the dirt came off easy. It was a picture of a child. A wee one, a girl. It was a cute photo, she had on a yellow dress and a green ribbon in her hair. The colours were enhanced and made her cheeks a bit too rosy, or maybe she was teething. She didn't look too happy anyway. She was so cute and comical I felt rotten throwing her in the bin so I stuck her up on the mantelpiece beside baby Steven, propping her up against the wall. They were about the same age, they could keep each other company.

It wasn't until I ran out of cigarettes that I realized how late it was. I'd fiddle-faddled about that much I'd lost all track of time. The Calley hotel, which was nearer than Jenny's, didn't sell cigarettes, not even in the bar, due to a high-minded decision by Ali the owner, a born again non-smoker with an evangelical streak. I was too tired to give up smoking tonight, I didn't have the emotional strength. I was weak and feeble and if I was going to make the shop before Jenny shut up for the night I'd have to bomb it down to the village.

When I turned the ignition the radio came on playing the local station. It was the evening request show, I'd caught it the last few nights while I unpacked and pottered about the house. I didn't know why Inverfaughie fm bothered taking requests because they only seemed to have about three records they played in rotation. As I turned it on I heard Andy Robertson, the presenter, say,

'Colin, the barman from the Caledonia hotel wants, I think it's some Dutch fella, Van Morrison, to sing "Have I Told You Lately That I Love You" for Chillian, the new waitress at the Seaward. Chillian is all the way from Glasgow and is here for the season. Unfortunately we don't have that particular record tonight, but I'm sure neither of the lovebirds will mind if we play for everyone's enchoyment: a strathspey from the marvellous Chimmy Shand!'

Coming down the hill into the village, I lost the signal. I twiddled the knobs and it came and went and then nothing, white noise. I suppose I wasn't giving my full attention to the road.

I recognized Walter's dog Bouncer as it crashed onto the bonnet and bounced over the car. When I got out all I could see was a heap lying between the wheels. I leaned down to comfort the dog and blood seeped onto the edge of my new waxed jacket. He lifted his head and whined; he must be in terrible pain, I thought.

Walter was in hospital, how would he take this news? It might kill him. How could I tell him? And what kind of future did Bouncer have? It was pitiful to listen to him. I could only hope that he'd die quickly. The shop was closing in fifteen minutes and I was gagging for a fag. As I stroked his matted fur there was no recrimination in Bouncer's eyes, only resignation. Again and again he lifted his head and whimpered as if begging for an end to the suffering until I could bear it no longer. I got a shovel from the boot and whacked him over the head. He never saw it coming, now at last the pain was over for Bouncer. I lifted his poor broken body out from under the car and threw it in the ditch. There was no-one around, nobody need ever know and Walter would be spared the news of his faithful companion's death.

Jenny's was shut by the time I got there. At thirty seconds past seven o'clock the door was locked and bolted. Hanging about the Calley car park until I could bum a smoke from foreign backpackers was humiliating and the roll-up they made me was so loose I was spitting tobacco all the way home. It was time to quit.

Chapter 8

I looked at catalogues and picked out furniture I could've ordered if I wasn't paying twenty-five quid a week for Steven's maths tutor.

'How did you get on with Mr Lennox then Steven?' I asked when he phoned.

'Tam? Aye, he's OK, quite a good guy. He's going to Europe for the semis if Celtic go all the way. He said I can come with him and his mates if I want.'

'Well you don't want. Forget it. And I'm not paying "Tam" twenty-five quid an hour to discuss Celtic's European chances.'

'But you and Dad agreed that if I pass my exams I've to get a present, and that's what I want.'

'Within reason Steven, and you haven't passed them yet.'

'It's not fair, that's exactly what Dad said.'

'Well for once I agree with your dad. You need to get the head down now and get on with studying.'

'I hate that big bastard.'

'Steven. Stop it.'

'He grounded me, for nothing. He's just acting the big man in front of Helga, trying to boss me about all the time, it's embarrassing.'

'If he grounded you it must be for a reason.'

The phone went quiet.

'For swearing,' he said eventually.

That did seem a bit harsh. I bit my tongue and waited.

'But he swore at me first. He shouts at me all the time. I was home late on Wednesday and he cracked up. He didn't like it when I answered him back. It's his fault I can't study, I'm sick of him on my back.'

'Let me speak to him.'

'He's not in. And anyway, he said he's never speaking to you again. He says you're an evil bitch. I told him he'd better shut it and he went, "Or you'll what?" I hate him.'

I felt the heat in my face. Not with anger at Bob for name-calling, or with pride for Steven defending my honour, but with the burning shame of what we were doing to our son.

'I'm sorry, Steven. Dad loves you. He's just angry with me and he wants you to do well in the exams.'

'Helga says he's hurting because everything's changed, you're so far away and the family's broken up.'

I cleared my throat so that my voice wouldn't sound soppy.

'I never thought I'd say this, Steven, but Helga's right.'

Thank God we weren't the only dysfunctional family I knew. I saw Roger put the girls on the school bus and came out to introduce myself. Roger wasn't good-looking like his wife, he was balding and had a thick black moustache. We quickly ran out of things to talk about so I asked after Polly.

'I'm afraid Polly isn't feeling too clever this morning.'

'I'm sorry to hear that.'

'Oh it's nothing serious. She just can't seem to get out of bed. I don't mind, I enjoy the air in the morning. If Polly has a lie-in it means I can work undisturbed.'

I hung out a washing on the line and noticed there were curtains drawn all day in the back bedroom, all day every day.

I could always tell when Rebecca and Michaela were home from school. I could hear the telly and hear them on the stairs, but through the day the house was as quiet as the grave. If Polly was quiet during the day she made up for it at night. It'd sometimes start about ten o'clock, probably when they thought the girls were asleep.

They weren't really arguments, more like a ritual. Polly howled and Roger shouted at her to pull herself together. She'd start screaming, he'd clatter up the stairs slamming doors and then it'd all go quiet again. Polly was depressed. Lying in her bed all day and howling all night, the selfish cow was going to be no company for me at all.

Steven's phone calls were getting shorter and terser. Things between him and his dad weren't getting any better. I'd tried to apologize but Bob refused to even speak to me. I was wary of putting pen to paper, Bob might use it against me at some later date, but I couldn't get through to him any other way. Choosing my words carefully, I wrote that it was regrettable the bedroom wallpaper had been damaged. I acknowledged the pain that this may have caused him. (I stopped short of offering to pay for the repair. He should have been man enough to fix it himself and anyway, I was already shelling out plenty for Steven's maths tutor.) I begged him to consider Steven's feelings during this dispute and I assured him that we shared common objectives, i.e. for Steven to be happy and pass his exams. Not even pass the exams, just be happy.

I thought it was a pretty good letter and it did seem to do the trick. Bob phoned me three days later.

'You really know how to apologize.'

'Thanks.'

'I was being sarcastic.'

'I know.'

'Anyway. It doesn't matter. I've rung to tell you that I've forgiven you.'

This was the first time Bob had been civil to me since he came round on my birthday. It was a great relief.

'Thanks Bob. I really am sorry. I didn't mean to cause all this trouble.'

'I can hear apology now. I can hear it in your voice.'

'It's all my fault. I feel really terrible . . .'

'It's OK, it's gone. I've released it.'

'What do you mean, Bob?'

'Well, I've freed myself of the anger, for my own sake, and I'm feeling the benefits.'

'That's great, Bob.'

I had no idea what he was talking about.

'When I think about that bedroom wallpaper I say to myself, *I release, I let go and let God.*'

'Are you OK Bob?'

He laughed at that.

'You think because I've mentioned the word God there's something wrong? Actually something's right for a change. Helga lent me a book and I discovered that by staying angry with you I was only making myself miserable. So, I let it go.'

'So Helga, a mere woman, is actually cleverer than you? Surely not.'

Bob laughed again and he wasn't forcing it.

'I think you're right Trisha.'

'Anyway, I'm sorry for causing an atmosphere

between you and Steven. I'm worried about how much you two are fighting. I feel responsible.'

'No. Steven and I aren't fighting, we're working things through. He's made life difficult here, Trisha, let me tell you, but I'm learning to release.'

He boffed on for another twenty minutes about God and letting go and all that shit. I just let him get it off his chest. The main thing was we were talking again, this would maybe take the heat off Steven.

'Anyway, I'm glad we're friends again but Bob, just to set the record straight, remember? It was me who wrote to you. I released before you did.'

Steven phoned the next night full of the joys of springtime. He got 63 per cent in a maths exam. Bob was delighted, Steven and Bob were getting on great.

'Sixty-three per cent? That's fantastic, son.'

'Second top mark in the class. Chris Henderson got 87 per cent but he's a maths genius. The guy's a total boffin.'

'With results like that your maths tutor is earning his money.'

'Hey, it was me that sat the exam!'

'I know, I know. Credit where credit's due, you did well Steven.'

'Well Helga helped as well.'

'Helga?'

'Yeah, have you ever heard of mind maps, Mum?'

No, I had never heard of mind maps. Some kind of memory tool. Helga had shown him how to make a map of his knowledge of maths. He was now making maps, with Helga's help, for all his subjects.

'It's mad, Mum. It doesn't feel like homework, it's like primary two. We're colouring them in. I put a swastika on my history map and I've designed the chemistry one to look like an experiment, I just keep extending it. Helga's hung them up in the kitchen, it looks really cool.'

Steven said he'd send me one of his mind maps to let me see the concept. I think he thought I was somehow jealous of Helga. I got the impression he thought I was annoyed at her being there with him, helping him with his schoolwork, colouring in and having fun. He more or less said so.

'You're still my mum,' he said.

The next day the weather looked all right for a change. I walked to the top of the big hill behind the house without stopping once. I didn't even walk really, stride or *yomp* would be a better description. Every time I thought of Helga and her mind maps I yomped a bit harder. What if the maths teacher had made a mistake and misread Steven's result? Or it was just a lucky fluke? What if, after all the colouring in, all the sticking up round the kitchen, what if after all that the mind maps turned out to be useless? Hah! That would settle her Norwegian hash. I was dizzy when I got to the top.

I had to lean forward and rest my hands on my knees while I heched and peched to get my breath back. I was a bad person. I was wishing exam failure on my son.

The view was amazing. The sea and sky and mountains and the lochs looked the way they look on brochures for Bonnie Scotland, humming with colour and life. The clouds scudded across the sky above me as though they were racing each other, the jaggy mountains only briefly snagging them as they passed. I felt like Julie Andrews in *The Sound of Music*.

But Julie Andrews was a nice person, she taught the Von Trapp children. By comparison Helga was more like Julie Andrews than me. Thinking about how Helga was taking over my son and how I wasn't there for him and how Steven was feeling guilty and caught in the middle, was doing my head in. It was ruining the view. Oh fuck it, I thought. Maybe Bob had a point with his releasing.

Chapter 9

The weather was changeable. It would rain and dry up and then rain and dry up again. It was wet then dry, warm then cold, windy then calm, bright then cloudy. Eight variables, endless permutations, four seasons a day, every day.

Jackie was good though, rain or shine he worked hard on my garden. I always felt I had to be matching his efforts. I never smoked in front of him and never missed it. I began to save up the washing and cleaning for the days he came so that I was as industrious as he was. We worked like bees, me in the kitchen and him in the garden. It was difficult to find enough things to do in the house. When I ran out of stuff to scrub I dug out the old cookbooks I'd found and experimented with baking.

I had to admit that Jenny's shop was a lifeline. Although her stock was crap, if you placed an order with her, given enough time there was nothing that Jenny couldn't get. To test her I started asking for fancy ingredients for baking: rice paper, fresh nutmeg, lemon grass. She never let me down. If I'd asked her to get me a kilo of heroin and an Uzi machine gun she would've asked what colour did I want the Uzi. Yes, it was expensive, but I was getting used to paying a higher premium for all things Highland.

My cooking and baking were coming on a treat. I'd take Jackie out a cup of tea and casually pop a home-made ginger snap on the saucer. When it was too wet to work he came in and hung about in the kitchen while I put the kettle on. The rain gave us both a break. When we stopped for a cuppa it gave me a rest and blether although Jackie wasn't much of a one for idle chit-chat. Maybe he was shy, I thought, but how could a man who was so handsome be that shy? Did I intimidate him in some way, perhaps because I was from Glasgow, the big city?

'Smells good.'

'Och, it's only a curry. Chicken jalfrezi. I don't usually bother.'

'I know. Not worth it, cooking for one.'

'Are you the same as me then Jackie, on your own?'

'Aye, the same as yourself.'

Aha! As I suspected. He had never mentioned a wife or family. Married men always mention their wife.

'I've made plenty and the meat is as tender as anything, would you like to try it?'

'It smells good all right. I've my wee flask with me.'

'It's not ready yet, it'll be done in an hour. Why don't you stay for your tea? It's daft you sitting on your own in your house and me sitting here. Stay for your tea, you're more than welcome.'

'Och that's kind Trixie but I'm . . .'

Jackie pointed to his mud-stained jeans and dirty boots.

'Don't be daft. There's no dress code in this house.'

If that was his only objection it was a pretty weak one. Jackie wanted coaxed.

'I'm only sitting here in the kitchen anyway. The same chair as you sat on for your soup at lunchtime. It's nothing fancy. Just stay for your tea Jackie, it'll be good to get some feedback on my curry, I need a second opinion.'

There was a fine line between coaxing and grovelling and I wasn't sure if I'd crossed it.

'I'd appreciate the company.'

I had now.

'Aye OK then. It smells grand. Ready in an hour you say? I'd better get that back hedge finished.'

Jackie sprinted out the kitchen and away to the back hedge which he attacked with renewed vigour. He was embarrassed. My cunning plan had worked but now I began to wonder if I'd bullied him. Maybe because I was paying him a few pounds an hour he felt obliged.

The curry was just about ready but I needed some time. Jackie being all shy about his working clothes had thrown a spanner in the works of my plan. It meant I couldn't change into my new skirt and top, it would be too obvious. I wouldn't be able to put on my full face either. I could probably risk a bit of eyeliner and lipstick, men were daft, they didn't spot the details. He would just think I was a bit flushed, in an attractive way, from my exertions in the kitchen.

I cracked open a bottle of red wine to let it breathe before I went upstairs to get washed. It had been a long time since I had seduced a man unless I counted that horrible embarrassment with Bob. Thinking of that really did make me flush, not in an attractive way. I decided a wee steadier was in order and poured myself a glass of wine.

I couldn't risk a shower, Jackie might hear the water running, so I made do with a silent stand-up wash at the sink. I picked out a matching bra and pants, the only matching set I had, newly bought for coming north. During Mum's illness, co-ordinated underwear had been low priority. The undies weren't very sexy, yellow with a lilac trim, but with Easter approaching at least they were seasonal. At least they weren't thousand-wash grey like the rest of my scants. Outwardly I'd have to keep on the blouse and jeans I'd had on all day.

I turned up the radiators to make the place cosy. With the house a bit warmer my baggy old cardi could go and I undid the top button of my blouse. I undid the next button as well. Hadn't I been working all day in a hot kitchen, what was wrong with cooling off a little? I put a 40-watt bulb in the standard lamp. Likewise with the music. The only thing I had was Barry White but that was too obvious. What was required was something a little less smoochy, more comforting and familiar. Inverfaughie fm would have to do.

I caught sight of myself in the kitchen mirror. I was looking good. Mature men appreciate an hourglass figure, I told myself. Rehearsing a Marilyn Monroe-type giggle, I leaned forward slightly and realized I'd have to rethink the second button. Two buttons was a button too far. With this kind of cleavage, when I bent over to take the bhajis out of the oven Jackie could lose an eye. I did up the second button again.

If Jackie was interested he'd let me know and that would be fine. And if he wasn't, that would be fine too. We would still be friends. He was the only friend I had here, I wasn't going to blow it by throwing myself at him. A wee dab of perfume, there was no law against it. He'd be lucky to get a whiff of it anyway amongst the garlic and onions of the jalfrezi.

Everything was ready. I put the lipstick on and carefully blotted it off again, three or four times. A professional beautician would've had trouble spotting it, never mind a man. It just looked like I had naturally tinted lips. I set the table, drained my wine glass, poured another wee one, downed it, then I called him in.

Chapter 10

Ten minutes into the chicken jalfrezi the phone rang. The first phone call wasn't too bad. I was pretty focused on entertaining Jackie so I didn't think anything of it. Bob asked me for the phone number of Steven's pal. I didn't know it off the top of my head but I told him Gerry's second name and where he lived. He could get the number out of the book. At that point I was more bothered by the fact that Jackie didn't want wine.

'I could nip down to Jenny's and get some beer if you like Jackie, I'll just catch her if I go now.'

'Och no, don't be silly. You have your wine, I'm happy with a drink of water.'

I set out a jug of water and he filled his glass frequently. The jalfrezi was a lot hotter than I'd intended it to be. There was no conversation, only the noises of us carefully negotiating the blistering curry, Jackie gulping water and me gulping wine. Then the phone rang again.

'Steven didn't come home from school. I finally got a hold of Gerry Thompson and he says Steven wasn't at school today.'

'Phone the police Bob, right now.'

'I have. I phoned them before I phoned you.'

'Have you tried his other pals? What about James and Christopher? And Paul, maybe he's at Paul's.'

'I've phoned all of them. And the Biggins and the Mcleans. Nobody's seen him. Can you think of anywhere else he might have gone? Any pals I've missed? You two have been pretty thick these days on the phone, has he told you something?'

I racked my brains.

'If he's dogging school he might have gone swimming or to that new pool hall. Maybe the park, or the pictures, have you tried the library?'

'He's not in any of those places.'

'What about the hospitals, oh my God, what if he's had an accident?'

'He's definitely not in hospital. I've tried them all and they haven't admitted anyone fitting Steven's description.'

'Go out and scour the streets! You have to find him, Bob!'

'I'm trying! What do you think I've been doing? I've been driving around since five o'clock. Helga is out now. Someone has to be here in case he comes back. I need to stay here for the police. Helga has her mobile, if she finds him she'll phone. I'll let you know right away.'

'Why didn't you tell me right away!'

'I didn't want to panic you. I knew how you'd react. There's nothing more we can do.'

I burst out wailing. 'Well where is he?'

'Calm down Trisha. I have to get off the phone. I have to keep this line clear. I'll let you know the minute I hear anything.'

'I'm coming. I'll be there as quick as I can.'

'No, don't. Trisha don't be ridiculous. You must be at least five hours from Glasgow.'

'I'm on my way. Phone me on the mobile if you hear anything, *anything*. D'you promise, Bob?'

'Look, I said I'd phone you, now just sit tight.'

Sit tight. That was the last thing I was going to do. I ran upstairs and got my fleece and ran back down again pulling it over my head. On the way down I tripped on the last stair but two hands caught me.

'Oh Jackie!'

I had forgotten all about him.

'I'm really sorry Jackie but I have to go out. I have to go to Glasgow.'

'I know. I heard you, is it your boy?'

'Yes, he didn't go to school and Bob can't find him anywhere. He's called the police. I have to find him. Maybe he's been knocked down or mugged or something. He needs me, he could be lying bleeding somewhere . . .'

I found myself babbling and crying and it was the most natural thing in the world when Jackie put his arms around me. He hugged me tight as if he was trying to protect me. It felt good but I was in a hurry, I had no time for tears. With Jackie trailing behind me I rushed through to the kitchen to search out my car keys and handbag.

'Finish your curry Jackie and help yourself to pudding. Is it all right if you let yourself out?'

'You're not thinking of driving are you?'

'Yes. Sorry Jackie, I'll have to go right away.'

'How much of that wine have you had? You must have had half the bottle.'

I hadn't thought about that. We both looked towards the wine bottle on the table. There was less than a quarter of it left.

'I'll be fine Jackie. The shock has sobered me up.'

Jackie saw the car keys before I did and his big hand closed over them.

'Ah now Trixie, I know it's urgent. But think for a minute. You feel sober but the wine is still in your system. You don't know that Inverness road very well. It's a cold and lonely place to have an accident. And that'll not do Steven any good, you in hospital or worse.'

I knew he was trying to be kind and what he was saying probably made sense but it was none of his business. He was only the fucking gardener, part-time at that, and he was withholding my car keys.

'Give me the keys Jackie.'

I think Jackie surprised us both.

'No! You're not driving that car!'

It was too much for me, I started greeting again. I approached him and tried to take the keys out of his hand. He held his closed fist up high where I couldn't reach. I pushed myself at him, trying to reach the keys, and when I couldn't I punched his chest.

'I'll drive,' he said quietly.

Jackie was right about the road. I hadn't remembered it being so twisty. But then it was daylight when I had driven up here. Now it was pitch black. The only light came from the dashboard and I could see the concentration on Jackie's face as he swivelled the steering wheel into the frequent bends. It was as if he was playing an arcade game. I didn't speak to him, that might slow him down.

I phoned Bob to make sure he had my correct mobile number and told him I was on the road. He hadn't heard from Steven or Helga or the police. I phoned again ten minutes later but still there was no news. Fifteen minutes later I called again and when I asked, Bob just went, 'No!' and slammed the phone down. A wee while later, another fifteen minutes, I started to dial again. Without taking his eyes off the road Jackie put his hand over mine and said, 'Leave it a while yet Trixie, he'll phone when he hears.'

I was getting a bit sick of Jackie bossing me around. I had agreed to let him drive me, but only as far as the A9. It was a straight road from there and he'd be able to hitch a lift back. When I thought of him standing by the road thumbing a lift back to Inverfaughie at night I was filled with gratitude that he would do this for me. Jackie hardly knew me. If I'd asked my neighbours in Glasgow if they'd take me to the West Highlands in the middle of the night, even with this emergency, I knew the kind of response I would've got.

Bob phoned.

'The police have just left. I gave them a photo of Steven. One from Christmas. It's the most recent.'

The word *photo* made me retch. Jackie immediately slowed the car down and pulled over. He reached across me to open the door. I put my feet outside the car and chucked up my curry onto the gravel. I held the phone away from the horrible plopping sound it made. I'd never felt so frightened. I had the image of the children's photos you see on the news behind the newsreader, that you tut over and hope will turn up safe. The photo they show again three or four nights later when they find the body. And they keep on showing it, every time new evidence comes to light or they have a suspect. A picture of a smiling innocent kid, taken when they were safe, before the sickening thing happened to them. I didn't want the police to have a photo of Steven.

'The police asked me if there was anything I needed to tell them about Steven. *This is not a time for secrets Mr Hanlon*, the sergeant said to me. The bastard was trying to make out it was my fault that Steven's missing.'

'It's not your fault. They have to ask stuff like that, that's their job. You want them to find him, don't you? We need to co-operate.'

'I did fucking co-operate! I'm not a fucking kiddie-fiddler!'

'OK. I know, Bob. No-one's saying that you are.'

'They wanted a description of what he's wearing but I didn't see him this morning. We left before he did. Helga checked his jackets, they're all there except the green one, he must be wearing that. But there's a lot of other stuff missing. He must have packed a bag. It's a good sign, they said. It means he planned to leave. He hasn't had an accident or anything. They asked if he took drugs.'

'Oh my God.'

I retched again but it was a dry boak.

'Is he taking drugs, Bob?'

'I don't know. I told them that. But I think I'd know if he was on heroin. His behaviour would be different.'

Behaviour like running away, I thought.

'Has he told you anything about drugs?'

'Bob. Don't go mad.'

'What is it? Just fucking tell me.'

'He told me that they smoked hash, Gerry and him. They bought it off someone and took it to a party. He didn't even like it, he said Gerry gave the rest of it away.'

'He's smoking hash?'

'He tried it, Bob. As you did yourself once.'

'Yes but what about heroin? The police said it's rife. They caught a dealer who was supplying kids at Steven's school. He could be on heroin.'

'If he is we'll get him off it. We need to find him first.'

Bob was crying now and he made me start again.

'Bob, it'll be OK.'

But he had put the phone down.

When I'd been a drugs rep I'd often see junkies creep into the health centres for the methadone clinics. I could still hear their thin self-pitying braying in my head. They affected a weak vibrato as if their addiction had damaged their vocal cords. Although most of them were only teenagers they had none of the cocky arrogance of youth. Dependent on getting their script, they were on their best behaviour. They treated all staff members with an exaggerated respect, giving everyone a title: Doctor, Nurse, Miss, Sir. They tried to be, if not lovable, then at least agreeable. They would have doffed their caps if they'd worn any. Occasionally one of them would make the mistake of turning up after a heroin hit. Gouching, bent double, their eyes loose in their head, even if they could formulate the words and ask to be seen, they were refused. They were right to pity themselves.

Some of the young girls looked like hags, stick-thin, dirty and smelly. I remembered waiting to see a doctor and hearing three girls, who couldn't have been older than about seventeen, discuss the death of their pal. Their whiny voices communicated no horror. They spoke about it with acceptance and inevitability, as if she had been an old woman at the end of her days.

I would know if Steven was on heroin, I thought. I'd watched and heard enough junkies to know the signs. But I hadn't seen Steven for weeks now. It was possible that he'd kept it from me. I wasn't there to see if he was withdrawn or having mood swings. I didn't know if his face was pale or there were tracks on his arms. But I just couldn't believe it, Steven wasn't daft, although I knew from all the leaflets I'd read in waiting rooms that it wasn't only daft people who ended up on heroin.

Maybe Steven saw this as a form of revenge. Bob and I had messed him about so much with our fighting and splitting up. Maybe he wanted attention. I was hundreds of miles away and Bob was loved up with Helga. Maybe we had put too much pressure on him over the exams. If he was on heroin he'd start stealing from the house. I decided to phone Bob and ask him if anything valuable was missing. I went to dial the number and remembered Jackie beside me. I was sick of his disapproval, it was my son and it was important.

'I'm going to phone Bob again Jackie, just so's you know. I need to speak to him about something.'

He never took his eyes off the road.

'You're building his hopes every time he answers the phone.'

I ignored him and carried on dialling. Bob said no, nothing had been taken from the house and would I please stop calling so often, I was just building his hopes up every time the phone rang. He slammed it down on me again, but I kidded on he hadn't and said cheerio as if he was still there. I turned my attention back to Jackie.

'I don't need your fucking advice so would you please butt out and just drive.'

'I'm sorry.'

'No.' I'd have to get a grip. 'I'm sorry, Jackie. I'm really sorry for speaking to you like that.'

Jackie took his left hand off the wheel and held mine in my lap.

'It's all right. You can say what you like to me.'

We sat like that in silence for the next hour until I phoned Bob again. Steven had now been officially missing for fourteen hours.

It started raining heavily, Jackie was having to drive slower. The windscreen wipers calmed me, the rhythm hypnotizing me for a while. Jackie didn't speak and that was the way I liked it. We were clear of Inverness now, we had been on the A9 for ages. I didn't want to drive to Glasgow alone and although I was annoyed with his interfering, I was glad to have Jackie with me. I might need a tight hug again. I prayed that I wouldn't. It was selfish of me to drag him all the way to Glasgow, but when we had reached the A9 Jackie hadn't said anything about stopping and neither had I. When we got to Glasgow I'd see him all right. I'd get him a good hotel and pay his train fare back home.

We stopped for petrol at Aviemore. The needle was only just touching the red. That meant we had another fifty miles or so in the tank but I needed to go to the toilet and Jackie probably did too. While he went to the toilet I got us paper cups of tea. When we set off again I poured in the milk and sugar for him and held his cup. I passed it to him every so often. Jackie turned the radio on. He looked at me for permission and I nodded. Not playing the radio wasn't going to get us to Glasgow any quicker. I wanted the comfort of Inverfaughie fm but we were well out of range by now. Jackie tuned into Radio Two, a late night easy listening show. He hummed along with the old records, some from the Sixties and even the Fifties.

'You're giving your age away,' I said to him. Someone so handsome was bound to be vain and I wanted to annoy him. He had annoyed me plenty. But he just smiled.

'I'm older than I look.'

'Well you must be very clean-living.'

'Och I can't say that.'

By the time we got to Perth the rain had tailed off. I knew by my thumping hangover that I had sobered up. I scrambled about in the glove compartment for paracetamol but I couldn't find any. Still no word about Steven, my sore head was the least of my worries.

Just outside of Stirling we passed the Wallace Monument sticking up through the trees like someone had dropped it there.

'Have you been up it?' Jackie asked me.

'No. I went on a school trip once but I was sick so I had to wait on the coach.'

'Aye you're an awful woman for being sick!'

Now he was trying to annoy me. I had to laugh. He was trying to take my mind off Steven.

The phone rang. I had put it on the floor and now I was scrabbling around in the dark trying to find it. It would only give two and a half rings before it automatically went to the answering service. The phone stopped ringing.

'Oh FUCK!'

We were on the motorway but Jackie pulled over onto the hard shoulder and rummaged under my seat before howking it out. I grabbed it from him and redialled Bob's number. It was engaged. He would be talking to my answering service. I phoned it but there were no messages. I phoned Bob again.

'He's fine. He's at your Auntie Nettie's.'

'He's at Nettie's?'

'Yeah, Helga had a brainwave and tried Nettie's place and sure enough there he was, quite the thing, sitting there eating tea and toast.'

'Thank God he's safe. You'll have to call off the police.'

'I know, I'm just about to, how embarrassing is that? Where are you Trish?'

'Eh, I'm not sure. Where are we?'

'Who's that you're talking to?'

'A friend. He drove me. We're just passing Bannockburn, not far.'

'Well it looks like you've had a wasted journey. I told you not to come.'

'I'm nearly here now. I want to see him, just to make sure he's OK. I've come this far.'

'Suit yourself but I'm going to fucking kill him when I get him.'

114

Chapter 11

Jackie's congratulatory hug was nowhere near as intense as the comfort hug he gave me in Inverfaughie. I moved to kiss him on the lips but he turned away a fraction and I missed, resulting in an embarrassing teeth clash. I laughed it off, I was so excited, Steven was safe. Jackie patted my back as if to say that was enough hugging now. Maybe I was a bit over-enthusiastic.

'Thanks Jackie for driving me all this way, thanks a million. Bob is really pissed off. Steven was hiding out at my auntie's house all along. You've driven all this way for nothing.'

'I'm glad it was for nothing.'

'You're right. I'm dying to see him.'

'No doubt.'

'So how would it be if we drove into the city and found you a nice hotel? You can get the train back tomorrow. I'll pay. Or hang around Glasgow if you like, whatever you want. I'm very grateful to you.'

'Och there's no occasion for that.'

'You've been so good to me.'

'What are you going to do, Trixie?'

'I haven't really thought beyond seeing Steven. I'm not bloody staying with Bob and Helga, that's for sure.'

'Well why don't you go and see your boy and then we'll drive back to Inverfaughie tonight? I'm not much of a one for hotels or sightseeing. I prefer my own bed.'

'Oh come on Jackie, we've come two hundred and fifty miles, you can't just turn round and go back again.'

'Well if you're not coming I'll hitch, but I won't stay here. I've no time for the city.'

Jackie adopted the same tone as he had in Inverfaughie when he wouldn't let me drive. He was a big intractable Highland man, a big wean.

'Jackie, you were good enough to bring me here. Of course I'll take you back. I just want to clap eyes on Steven, it'll only take about an hour.'

'Of course you do, take as long as you like.'

Thirty minutes later we were entering my home town. As we passed the gasworks off the M8 I exhaled heavily, but there was none of the usual feeling of homecoming. I hadn't a home to come to. The famous Helga, that I had so far avoided ever meeting, was now sitting in my living room. Any wee free samples of shampoo or face cream delivered by the paper boy and addressed to The Lady of the House would now be Helga's. Even although it was now one o'clock in the morning I wasn't setting foot in the house. I'd call Steven out to the car, no, not the car, Jackie would be in the car. Oh well, Steven and I would have to go for a walk. I gave Jackie directions to the house and as we came onto the slip-road exit from the motorway Bob phoned again.

'Now the wee bastard is refusing to come home.'

'What d'you expect, Bob? The last I heard you were going to kill him.'

'He says he's staying there with Nettie, she's agreed apparently, he's staying there until his exams and then

116

he's going to Inverfaughie. I can't win with that boy, I've only tried to instil a bit of discipline in him.'

'He doesn't really want to stay with Nettie, Bob, you know that. He's angry, he's only trying to hurt you.'

'Well it's worked. He has my heart roasted, and that old bitch is only encouraging him. *Oh*, she says, *the boy's welcome here any time, he's the only bit family I have left.*'

'Och maybe it's for the best, Bob. Just for a while. Give you both a bit of time out from each other. And d'you not want to spend some time alone with the lovely Helga?'

'Just keep Helga out of this. She's the one who found him, remember? And yes, actually, Helga and I would very much appreciate some quality time, especially as we have to finish off decorating the bedroom that you trashed.'

'Bob,' I said gently, 'release, let go and let God.'

'Oh fuck off!'

'Hello? Hello Bob? . . . Change of plan I'm afraid, Jackie, we're going to my Auntie Nettie's.'

Nettie stood waiting for me at the front door in her housecoat.

'Who is that man in your car?'

Nettie didn't miss a trick. I saw her curtains twitch as we turned into the street.

'A friend. He drove me here.'

'Well bring him in for goodness' sake, it's two o'clock in the morning.'

'He's quite happy out in the car, Nettie.'

'You'll panic the neighbours, they'll think it's a police stake-out. I'll go and get him myself.'

Steven came to the door and hugged me. With his usual distaste for making physical contact with his

117

mother's front bits, my son grabbed me round the neck while he bowed out the rest of his body. You could have driven a double-decker bus through the space between us. It had been a night for strange hugs.

Nettie succeeded where I had failed and managed to winkle Jackie out of the car and into the house. She was all made up with him, all fluttery and girlie at how tall and handsome he was.

'I've put the kettle on. You'll take a wee sandwich?'

Nettie bustled away into the kitchen with a coy backward smile for Jackie.

'Steven, this is Jackie. He's a friend of mine from Inverfaughie.'

That sounded like I had loads of friends in Inverfaughie.

'Aye.'

Steven nodded a suspicious acknowledgement to Jackie.

'Aye.'

Jackie returned the nod, neither friendly or unfriendly but respectful.

'Steven, I've got something out in the car. Will you give me a hand in with it please?'

It was a bit obvious. Jackie, having just come from the car, was better placed to help me. Steven didn't even have his shoes on but we all pretended while he forced his feet into his trainers. We didn't speak until we were in the car.

'Steven, thank God you're safe, son. You had us worried sick.'

'I'm sorry Mum, really sorry, it was stupid.'

'Are you all right? Let me look at you.'

'D'you want to check in between my toes as well?'

I didn't have a clue what he was talking about and it must have showed on my face.

'I'm not shooting up, Mum. I saw you checking out

118

my arms for tracks, I haven't got any. Dad was the same, he openly accused me of doing heroin.'

'Your dad is frightened for you Steven, that's all. The police put the idea in his head.'

'I'm not a junkie, OK, do you believe me Mum?'

'Yes. I believe you.'

And I did. You know your own son and you know when he's telling the truth, sometimes, but I was sure this was one of the times.

'Well what the bloody hell were you playing at? Why didn't you phone me? That's all you had to do, one wee phone call.'

'Oh Mum, don't start. I've just had Dad round giving me the same shit.'

'The same shit! I drove two hundred and fifty miles!'

'You didn't drive, your old boyfriend did!'

We were shouting at each other now. A few lights had come on in Nettie's close. A few curtains twitched. I made an effort to speak quietly, I didn't want our voices carrying to the house and into Jackie's hearing.

'I told you, he's a friend.'

'And I told you I'm sorry.'

'So you did.'

'If I'd told you, you would have told Dad, wouldn't you? Wouldn't you?'

'Yes. I suppose I would.'

'And anyway, how else could I get you to come and see me?'

I looked at him sharply but a mischievous grin had spread across Steven's face.

'Well you could have got me to come during the hours of daylight, that would have been a help.' I shook my fist and in an American gangster accent I said, 'Why, I oughta . . .'

When he was a wee lad and had been naughty I used to say that and Steven would kid on he was scared.

119

Now he grabbed my fist and play-wrestled me. I was squealing and laughing but I sobered up. We had serious stuff to discuss.

'You're not really going to stay here with Nettie?'

'Why not? I'm not staying with Dad, no danger. He grounds me for being late, for swearing, for not studying. He even grounded me for farting in front of Helga.'

'Why, was it her turn?'

'Very funny. Helga's OK actually. If you knew her you'd like her. She doesn't try and be my mum or anything, she doesn't even try and be my pal, she's just quiet, gets on with her own stuff. It's him that does my head in.'

'I thought you didn't like living with old ladies.'

'That was different. Gran was sick. I was in the way.'

'You were never in the way, Steven.'

'Well I felt as if I was.'

'But you can't stay here! Nettie's house is rotten with damp.'

'Och, she says that but it's fine. Have you seen the rooms? The council have spent a fortune doing the place up. It's fine.'

'Right that's it. You've had your fun, Steven. You're coming back to Inverfaughie with me. Get your bag.'

'Mum. Newsflash. I haven't lived with you for more than two years. The days of you telling me what to do are over.'

I started greeting again at that. It had been a strange day for greeting. Steven was right. I couldn't force him and anyway, he needed to be here for his exams. As I sat sniffling Steven put his arm around me but he didn't take back what he had said.

'You're still coming up for the Easter holidays though, aren't you?'

'Of course I am. It'll be great. I've invited Gerry, if that's OK.'

I'd been looking forward to spending two weeks with him. His friend Gerry coming would mean I wouldn't have time alone with Steven but I supposed it would be OK, what choice did I have?

Jackie came out and politely chapped the car window.

'Nettie says you've to come in, your tea's getting cold.'

Nettie had made a mountain of sandwiches and gave us proper teacups and saucers. She was tickled pink to have so many visitors in her house all at once. She spoiled us rotten with Tunnock's teacakes and caramel logs. I'd forgotten how good caramel logs were and made a mental note to order some from Jenny. To Nettie's delight Jackie and I demolished all of her sandwiches, and when we were finished I helped her clear off the tea things into the kitchen. I wanted a word with her about Steven's keep.

'It's a pleasure to have him, Trisha love. He'll be great company for me.'

I could see that there would be a few advantages for Steven. So besotted was she with her only great-nephew, and so grateful for his company, that Nettie would run after him hand and foot. She'd clean up his mess, wash his clothes, bring him his tea by the fire where her work-weary husband Tommy used to sit, and feed him unlimited amounts of sandwiches and Tunnock's teacakes. Nettie would train him to be a good old-fashioned West of Scotland man. A man handless and unable to look after himself in the real world. Bob and I would have to work together for damage limitation on this one.

'Well if you insist Trisha, what about, say, thirty pounds a week?'

Little did she know that Steven could eat thirty quids' worth of biscuits a week, never mind everything else. But Nettie didn't want to waste time discussing it. She wanted to talk about something else.

'Oh he's a lovely big man you've brought, Jackie, isn't it? And he's a Robertson too apparently?'

'Yes, Inverfaughie's full of Robertsons.'

'But apparently no relation to me or your mum. How are you getting on up there in your wee Heilan hame then Trisha?'

'Aye fine thanks Nettie.'

'Och you're so lucky. I wish I was in your shoes, hen. And Jackie says it's lovely up there apparently.'

Mr O'Hare my lawyer had officially put it in writing that Nettie had no claim on Harrosie. I knew she had a copy of the letter, Mr O'Hare told me he'd sent it recorded delivery. But she wasn't going to let it go.

'I've looked out all the old papers but I cannae find a Robertson in our family. Now I know I'm no going to be popular when I say this, but I think there's something funny going on.'

'What do you mean Nettie?'

'I mean there's jiggery-pokery has went on here.'

It was half two in the morning and I had a five-hour drive ahead of me, I couldn't expect Jackie to drive any longer. I was anxious to get started although if I'd known then what was going to happen between me and Jackie, I wouldn't have been so keen.

'Thanks for looking after Steven, Nettie, I really appreciate it. I'll have to go, it's a long drive back.'

'Och you're not wise driving all that way in the middle of the night. Apparently it's hundreds of miles.'

'Yes, apparently.'

Chapter 12

Jackie didn't want me to drive but it wasn't fair on him, so I finally talked him round. We agreed that we'd spell each other, an hour at a time. I took the first shift while he got his head down. The only other traffic on the motorway were delivery trucks which trundled along in the slow lane. I expected to be exhausted with all the drama Steven had caused and I was surprised by how awake I felt once we were back out in the cold night air.

Jackie conked out right away. He looked absolutely knackered. The stubble on his cheek was coming in white and with his face relaxed in sleep, he seemed much older. He snored in steady little piggy grunts but instead of it annoying me the way it did with Bob, I found it quite sweet. Jackie was nowhere near as handsome when he was asleep. He looked kind of sleazy. I could easily imagine him with a fag in one hand and a whisky in the other, maybe a *Racing Post* stuck under his arm. He looked like the kind of guy who liked the bookies and the ladies. He looked sexy. When I pulled out to overtake his head slid around on the headrest, and his mouth fell open. I could feel his rhythmic breath on my arm and I liked it.

It was strange just how comfortable I'd become with

Jackie. The crisis had accelerated our relationship. In the space of a few hours we'd kissed, hugged and argued. He'd seen me being sick and I'd heard him snore. He'd met my family and we had spent the night together. We were practically engaged.

I would have let him sleep on, but Jackie woke after exactly an hour, as if he'd set an alarm clock. I wanted to keep driving but he made me pull in at the next service station. In the shop I bought us coffees, cans of Coke, a packet of barley-sugar sweets and loads of chocolate. I was supposed to take my turn sleeping but the caffeine and chocolate kicked in and made me a bit high and giggly.

'What a mental night! I've had more excitement tonight than I've had in the whole time I've been in Inverfaughie. In some ways it's been great.'

'Great?'

Jackie looked at me as if I was daft.

'Sorry. I was forgetting it probably hasn't been much fun for you.'

'It's been fine for me. It's yourself I was thinking of, you were awful upset.'

'Och yeah but he's safe now, I knew it would be all right in the end. I had a feeling about it, a mother's instinct.'

I flapped my hands around casually as I told this whopper.

'At least I got to see Steven and I think it did Bob good to sweat a little.'

'I seem to remember you were doing a fair bit of sweating yourself, my girl, in betwen crying and chucking up, that is.'

That made me laugh. Jackie laughed too, nodding his head, forcing me to admit it. The other thing that made me laugh, made me hug myself inside, was the fact that he'd called me *my girl*.

'Well, that's weans for you. Troublesome, ungrateful gits.'

Jackie smiled and grunted.

It occurred to me that I didn't know if Jackie had any kids. I didn't know very much about him at all and I wanted to know everything.

'Tell me your life story, Jackie.'

'Och, away you go!'

'Oh come on, tell me, it'll make the time go faster and it'll keep you awake. You can miss out the boring bits if you want but tell me everything else.'

'It's all boring bits.'

'It can't be.'

'Well, I'll tell you mine if you tell me yours.'

'It's a deal.'

'You have to go first.'

'But you already know everything about me! You know about Steven and Bob and you've met the lovely Nettie. There's not much more to tell.'

'Tell it.'

'Well, I was born at a very young age . . .'

I went on in that flippant vein, skimming over my lack of academic achievement, embellishing my career in medical sales and giving him the gory details of my marriage breakdown. Jackie was very interested in my childhood and asked loads of questions about Mum and Dad. I answered him as honestly as I could, I wanted him to know me. Yes, they were happily married, and yes, definitely, my dad was a great dad. As an only child I'd had a lot of my parents' time and attention. I told him about our holidays to the caravan site and the way Dad always let me bury him in the sand, even though he was freezing. I talked on and on about Mum. I explained that being with her through her illness wasn't as depressing as it sounded, a lot of the time it was good fun. Of course I missed her but I was glad it was over. He asked me lots of daft things too, like was I musical and did I have any interesting moles. That was a bit saucy but I rolled up my jeans and showed him the one behind my knee. Then it was his turn.

We had a lot of things in common. He also was born at a very young age, also an only child and useless at school.

'I didn't get on with my father. He kicked me out of the house when I was sixteen. I wanted out of the village anyway, I went into the Navy. Signed on for nine years.'

'My dad was in the Navy, the Merchant Navy, but it was before I was born. Did you ever meet a Hughie McNicol?'

'There were a lot of Hughies in the Navy, especially the first day we sailed. Everyone was leaning over the side and shouting *Hughie*!'

'Jackie, that joke is nearly as old as you are.'

'Anyway, it was the *Royal* Navy I was in.'

'Oh excuse me! What as, a cabin boy?'

Picturing Jackie in a uniform struck me as funny.

'Sort of. I was a steward in the officers' mess, but I saw the world: America, the Gulf, Africa, all over. It was a great life.'

'Why did you leave?'

'For love. I had a girl in Plymouth. We got married and came back to Inverfaughie. We opened a restaurant, La Belle Dame. There were a few in the town who thought I had a cheek coming back with enough money behind me to open a restaurant and call it a fancy French name. I put all my severance money into it, but it didn't work out.

'We were in a car crash, stupid accident. I don't really remember what happened but we ended up in a field. We were lucky to get out alive. That's why I didn't want you to drive that road on your own with a drink in you. It was bad, we were both smashed up, Marie worse than me, she broke both legs. She was never the same after that. Her family interfered, they took her back to Plymouth, to look after her. I don't blame her. I know she missed them. My father, like everyone else in the town, never accepted Marie. She was a white settler, an incomer, but worst of all she was English. I struggled on with the restaurant but it was no use. There were a few who must have laughed up their sleeves.'

'Did you and Marie divorce?'

Just checking.

'Och aye, her family saw to that.'

'And you never remarried?'

Just checking.

'Not at all.'

That was another thing we had in common.

Jackie had obviously been uncomfortable telling me this. Swapping life stories had been a bad idea. Revisiting the past had put us both in a melancholy mood, or maybe it was just tiredness. To perk him up I asked him about life in the Navy.

'I was the youngest on board and that made me a kind of mascot. I was involved in the ceremony as we sailed across the equatorial line. Here, these services are open. Will we stop?'

We stopped for a pee and petrol. Jackie got more chocolate and coffee and he refused to let me pay for them. When we got back in the car I wanted him to continue talking. I was enjoying the sound of his voice.

'Och, no more stories now. Lie back and close your eyes. If you're going to be driving you'll need to get some sleep.'

I did as I was told. I was getting to like the way Jackie bossed me about.

I woke up as we were leaving the A9, out the other side of Inverness. I'd slept for two hours.

'Jackie, you should have wakened me!'

I drew my hand across my wet chin. I must have been slebbering in my sleep, how attractive was that?

'Och you're all right, I need to drive this last bit anyway. From here to Inverfaughie is the tricky bit but we'll just take it easy. There's no hurry.'

Jackie opened the window to liven himself up. It let in a cold blast but I got used to it quickly. The road was deserted.

'Keep me company. Put the radio on.'

We were in close enough range for Inverfaughie fm and this time he didn't hum, he sang. He had a great voice and he seemed to know the words to every record. A Burns ballad 'Green Grow the Rushes O' came on and he sang sweet and clear:

> Green grow the rushes O
> Green grow the rushes O
> The sweetest hours that e'er I spend
> Are spent among the lasses O.

We curved round the lochs and up over the hills as if we were in a car advert. With every song the sky was getting lighter and lighter and we were getting nearer to Inverfaughie. Sleep deprivation had made me light-headed. I was enjoying myself so much I didn't want us ever to get there. But all good things must come to an end and inevitably we saw the town in the distance.

My house was roasting hot when we went in. I was in such a rush to leave I'd forgotten to turn the heating off.

'Oh my God! The radiators have been on all night!'

'Your heating bill is going to be sky-high.'

'Och well, at least it's nice and welcoming. Sit yourself down Jackie and I'll stick the kettle on.'

'Don't be daft lassie, I'll get away and let you get to your bed.'

'Let me get to my bed nothing. You've just driven a five-hundred-mile mercy mission. The least I can offer you is a cup of tea. And we're not sitting on these hard kitchen chairs. Take a saft seat through in the parlour and I'll bring you in your tea. Could you manage a wee roll and bacon?'

Jackie was too tired to put up an argument and went as meek as a lamb into the parlour. As I defrosted the rolls and got the bacon on, a line from the Burns song kept running through my head.

> The sweetest hours that e'er I spend
> Are spent among the lasses O.

While I buttered the rolls I chuckled to myself, remembering the elaborate preparations I'd made for the great seduction last night. Last night seemed a million miles away now. Funny how things turn out, I thought. I'd got my wish, to spend the night with Jackie. Not the way I'd intended but, despite the fortune I'd shelled out in petrol and the heating bill, I was glad. I'd slept alone for years now and hardly noticed, but if Jackie had got on his bike and gone home I'd have been gutted.

I carried a tray through to the parlour with the cutlery and condiments and was pleased to see he'd taken my advice. He was lying on the couch with his eyes shut and his arms folded. I was so busy looking at him that I tripped over something and the tray went flying. The tomato-sauce bottle fell and scooshed out onto the carpet and over Jackie's boots.

That's what I had tripped over, Jackie's big black gardening boots. They were no longer attached to Jackie's legs and lay slap bang in the middle of the floor. He had taken them off so's not to dirty my couch.

It was sweet that he felt comfortable enough to take his boots off. I took them back into the kitchen and cleaned them out as best I could. Jackie was sound asleep so the bacon could wait a minute.

The right boot only had sauce on the outside so that was easily wiped clean. Unfortunately the sauce bottle had exploded all over the inside of the left one. I mopped out the blood-red gunge with kitchen roll but the instep still felt greasy. Now I squirted washing-up liquid in to it and attacked it with a cloth soaked in boiling water.

The boots were huge, size twelve or thirteen, if they made such a size, and my mind slid momentarily into the gutter as I wondered if the rest of Jackie was of similar proportions. Not that it mattered, Jackie could have been endowed with a button mushroom for all the difference it would have made to me.

Too tired to think straight, I was making an arse of cleaning the boot. The more I tried the worse I made it, the boot becoming soapier and wetter. I tried to dry it off with an old towel but by this time the leather was soaking. The only way I'd get it dry quickly was if I blow-dried it with my hairdryer and there was no way I was attempting that at this time, the bacon would be getting cold. The best thing to do was to turn the heating on again and hang the boot over the kitchen radiator.

When I went back into the parlour Jackie was still fast asleep with his outsize feet hanging off the end of the couch. I sat on the floor leaning against him while I half-heartedly dabbed at the tomato sauce on the carpet. A teaspoon had fallen onto Jackie's chest. As I reached over to pick it off him I grazed my lips, faintly, hardly at all, against his. It was nice to have him on my couch, my sleeping beauty, unaware that I was taking liberties.

I poked him and he woke up with a start, a bit embarrassed, I think, that he had fallen asleep. He budged up to let me sit down beside him, wiping his eyes and taking the plate from my hand. Too tired for conversation we scoffed our bacon rolls and tea in silence. When we finished I didn't even clear the plates away, I just dumped them on the tray on the floor. I fancied a smoke and then realized that I hadn't even thought of smoking for the last twenty-four hours.

As I sat beside him I could feel the heat of Jackie's arm against mine. My eyes were dropping and without even thinking about it, I half turned and snuggled into him. I hoped he would take this as some kind of signal but he made no move. I opened one eye and keeked at him. His eyes were closed, surely he hadn't fallen asleep again as quick as that? Maybe he was shy, maybe, like when I'd asked him to stay for dinner, he wanted coaxed. I decided I would try the old brushing-my-lips-against-his trick again. If he was awake he could respond without having to open his eyes, and if he was asleep I could have my evil way with him again. It took me a minute to build up the courage. The smell of his clothes and the heat off him, his nearness, were making my heart thump and my breath quicken.

I went forward and as I leaned in towards him, quarter of an inch from making contact with his lips, he woke up with a violent snort. He had been asleep after all. Or if not asleep then dozing, not fully conscious at any rate. Jackie yawned deep and long, pulling a gargoyle face and holding it so long that I began to worry that his own beautiful face would never come back. He stretched his arms out, creating a distance between us. The moment was gone. The first kiss was going to be an awkward one, there was no getting away from it. Then

131

again, Jackie was an awkward kind of guy, it was probably just the way he did things.

'Oh well, time's getting on. I'd better be getting home.'

I couldn't believe it, he was going to cycle back down into Inverfaughie, he was going home and leaving me.

'Oh Jackie don't go. You're too tired, it's ridiculous, you'll fall asleep at the handlebars.'

'No I'm fine. The breath of air will do me good going down the hill. I'll away and let you get to your bed.'

He affected a cheeriness but underneath I sensed he was nervous. I was going to have to put my cards on the table.

'Jackie, you can stay here if you want to. I want you to.'

'No. I'll have to get home, where did I put my boots?'

Jackie started scrabbling around the floor looking for his boots. I couldn't let him go. I couldn't stay here alone, without him.

'There's a great sea view.'

I'd meant that as a joke, I expected him to laugh but his face was like fizz. I was confused and tired and I suddenly felt terribly lonely, being left alone in this house so far away from everything.

'Please, Jackie?'

He ignored me and carried on searching for his boots. I lifted a cushion and buried my head. This was not the way things were supposed to have gone. I didn't get it, I thought he liked me. Why did he drive me to Glasgow if he didn't like me?

'Look, just keep the fucking boots, OK? I'm away!'

He went through the kitchen and slammed the back door. I took the pillow away from my face. Surely the stupid bastard wasn't going to cycle to Inverfaughie with no boots on his feet?

132

Yes indeed, that was exactly what he was going to do. I got to the front window just in time to witness Jackie hirple along the gravel path before mounting the bike and skiting down into Inverfaughie in his stocking soles.

Chapter 13

The next morning I tried my best to put the whole sorry incident out of my mind. I didn't last very long. As soon as I saw Jackie's boot hanging on the kitchen radiator I burst into tears. Look on the bright side, I tried to tell myself over a breakfast of four cigarettes, but there was no bright side as far as I could see. Once again I had made a total fool of myself. Worse than that, much worse than that, I had fucked up the only friendship that I had so far made in this godforsaken hellhole of loneliness. What had I done? Had I broken some unspoken Highland code of etiquette? Maybe I should ask him. Or maybe not. But I kept thinking of the fun we'd had singing in the car.

I would return his boots. This was obviously a silly misunderstanding, we'd probably end up having a laugh about it. Then it occurred to me that I didn't actually know where Jackie lived. I looked in the phone book but he wasn't there. I knew it was Inverfaughie somewhere, I could ask Jenny in the shop. I'd take him a present, a thank-you present for driving me to Glasgow and to say sorry for whatever the hell it was I'd done.

Jenny was always desperate for gossip and I knew that my story – driven by the gardener to Glasgow in the middle of the night and mysteriously retaining his boots – was going to be meat and drink to her. To put her off the scent I told her about the request I'd heard on the radio the other night.

'I think Colin from the Calley must be stepping out with the new girl from the Seaward,' I said.

It was lucky I'd remembered it and I was pleased to be bringing her this titbit.

'Stepping out?' she replied, 'I heard he was fucking her.'

Oh Christ, I thought, if that was the kind of conclusion she was jumping to, what was she going to make of me with Jackie's boots?

'Oh, eh, is that right?' was the best response I could make.

'Just as well if you ask me, that Colin is very nearly twenty-four now, and he's never had his hole. I was beginning to think he was a bent shot.'

My romantic notion that Highland folk were somehow sheltered from the vulgar realities of life was instantly shattered. I concentrated on buying a present.

'What's the nicest bottle of malt you carry, Jenny?'

'Oh, having a party are you?'

I thought it best to ignore her prying. Get the stuff and get out of there as quickly as possible. Never mind asking her about Jackie's address. I'd get it somewhere else. I took the most expensive malt she had, and a big box of Roses chocolates. That was *thank you* and *sorry* covered, and I wondered what kind of gift would I need for *please be my friend again*.

As I packed my bag, I heard the bell on the door of the shop ring as someone else came in. I turned and who should I see staggering towards me, with a white crêpe bandage piled on top of his head like a turban, but Bouncer the dog.

'Trixie, you're awful pale. Are you not sleeping?' said Jenny.

'No, no, I'm er . . .'

Actually I was lost for words.

'Oh poor old Bouncer eh? The minister brought him in last night. Found him out on the main road all battered and covered in blood. I'm looking after him while Walter is in the hospital but I'm not fit for it. I had to sit up with him whining and moaning all night. I took him to the vet and I had to pay thirty-four pounds for the stitches and the bandaging! Who's going to reimburse me? I'm not fit for a dog, I can't be running to the vet every five minutes, I have the shop. If someone could take him off my hands . . . Now you Trixie, you must be lonely out at that cottage all on your own, you could take him. It would only be for a wee while until Walter gets back, they say he'll be back on his feet in a few days.'

'I don't think so Jenny, the cottage next door, they keep a rabbit. It wouldn't be suitable.'

'Ach, the minister, he was out on the hill, he couldn't just see properly for the mist but he thought he saw someone hit the dog. Aye, hit the dog! Can you imagine anyone doing a thing like that?'

Jenny busied herself giving me my change.

'What's that on your jacket there Trixie?' she said, 'have you been having an accident?'

'What? Oh that, eh yes, I cut my finger on the . . .'

'Och poor Bouncer is awful lonely without Walter you know. It's a terrible thing for a dog to be lonely, and him getting his head bashed in as well.'

I looked down at the pathetic figure of Bouncer with his bandage falling into his eyes.

'OK, OK, I'll take him.'

'Och well done that woman! Walter will be fair pleased.'

Jenny was absolutely delighted, and before I had the chance to reflect on the wisdom of such a rash offer she'd rushed into the back shop. She returned and slapped on the counter: Bouncer's basket, his Kennomeat and dry meal, his leads (various), his wee tartan waterproof coat and all his rubber toys. It took several trips to load up the car. After talking me through Bouncer's feeding and exercise regimes Jenny walked us to the door.

'Now remember Trixie, you've not to let him out on his own. I don't want that nutcase beating him up again. Och I'll miss the wee chap, so I will, but at least I know he'll come to no harm with you.'

As with everything Jenny said in her soft accent, it was possible to put more than one interpretation on it. Was she onto me, warning me not to do it again? Or was she just a daft and kindly old lady? As we left she called something to me that I didn't properly hear. It sounded like, 'And Jackie Robertson is Wee Free!'

Bouncer wouldn't get in the car. I instructed him to sit on the floor in the back. I didn't have anything to protect the back seat and I didn't want dog hairs all over the place. There was plenty of room but he refused.

Yes, I told Bouncer, regrettably it was true that I'd mowed him down and then hit him with a shovel and thrown him in a ditch, but I meant no harm. I explained in an urgent whisper that I wasn't trying to bump him off, I thought I was putting him out of his misery. From what I could see of his face beneath his dressings, Bouncer looked confused. He seemed to be having trouble distinguishing between kindness and murder when the net result was the same. I had trouble making a distinction myself. The whole business was taking too long and finally in desperation I grabbed him by the collar and yanked him into the back.

As I drove off Bouncer jumped up onto the back seat and barked at everything we passed: other cars, houses, farms, horses. That was fine while he was seeing things from the side window. I had to stop and let a farmer take a flock of sheep across the road in front of me and Bouncer tried to jump into my lap to get a better view.

I found Jackie myself. With Bouncer barking enthusiastically in the back, I drove through the village looking for his house. By an amazing stroke of luck or, as I thought at the time, serendipity, I spotted Jackie on his bike, fully shod, turning into a street on the edge of the village. Even better, he hadn't seen me. I planned to catch up with him and accidentally bump into him in the street. The car was facing the wrong way and by the time I found a place on the road where I could safely turn, Jackie had disappeared into one of the houses. Luckily his bike parked against the wall gave it away. I would have known it was his house anyway by the garden, the most looked-after garden in the street. The house itself looked a bit ramshackle, like the house of a man who lived alone.

The street was deserted. If Jenny was anything to go by, others in the village might be intrigued to see me approach Jackie's door. I wasn't going to give them anything to gossip about, I would be discreet. There was no such word in Bouncer's vocabulary. He went mad when I tried to leave him in the car. He yelped and did what he did so well, in fact what he had been named for: he bounced. Like a clock ticking, on the up stroke he rhythmically banged his swaddled head against the car roof. He only stopped when I put the lead on him.

I gave Jackie's door a loud confident chap, a friend-popping-round-to-visit type of knock. It felt like a long time Bouncer and I stood waiting. Bouncer got bored before I did, peering up at me and whining. Surely

Jackie would have heard that knock? Or maybe he was working in his back garden. We went round there but there was no sign of Jackie. I chapped the back door, maybe he was in a room at the back and hadn't heard us at the front. No reply. I chapped again, trying not to convey my desperation to see him, to sort things out. It started to spit rain which gathered momentum into a full-scale shower. I'd left my jacket in the car.

Earlier, when I gave myself the positive thinking, one step at a time, look on the bright side pep talk, I had imagined how it would go. Jackie would be pleased to see me, he'd look a bit sheepish and to spare him embarrassment, I'd pretend not to notice. He'd apologize repeatedly for storming out and give a brilliant reason (although I couldn't imagine what it might be). After subtly letting him understand how hurtful and confusing it had been for me, I'd tell him to forget it.

The rain was getting heavier. He knows I'm standing here, I thought. When he sees that I'm not giving up, sooner or later he must come to the door.

I was having difficulty seeing as the rain dripped from my sodden eyebrows. The boots that I had so thoroughly dried out were taking on water and the chocs were beginning to get damp. My jaw tightened and although the rain was cool I felt hot. I imagined the raindrops evaporating as steam as they hit my bare arms. And I felt reckless; fuck discretion, fuck the nosy neighbours, I wanted to shout his name, force him to acknowledge my presence. I was making an arse of myself, again. The man obviously didn't want to see me. I couldn't bully him into opening the door. Holding him under siege was only making things worse. I put the boots in Jackie's coal bunker with the whisky in one and the chocolates in the other, at least they would be dry there.

*　　　*　　　*

I knew taking Bouncer was a bad idea from the word go. As soon as I brought him out of the car Roger from next door was over quizzing me. The two wee girls, especially Rebecca, took an instant shine to Bouncer but Roger wasn't so sure.

'It's Smidgy Rabbit we have to think about, Trixie. It's a dog's instinct to hunt, not the dog's fault of course, but I'm worried that Bouncer might attack him. The children would be devastated if anything happened to Smidgy.'

I knew all that, I didn't need that patronizing bastard to tell me, but I just smiled. I couldn't afford to fall out with my only neighbour even if he was a dickhead. Obviously I wouldn't be able to let Bouncer out alone, the stupid mutt had no road sense and if I didn't knock him down someone else surely would. I wouldn't even be able to let him run around the garden in case he ate Smidgy Bloody Rabbit. The full impact of taking the dog was only now beginning to hit me. I'd have to take him out for walkies, every day, several times a day, even when it was raining.

A while later, Rebecca, the older girl, chapped my door.

'Can I take Bouncer out for a walk please Mrs Trixie?'

I ushered her in straight away. Bouncer was already doing my head in. After my humiliation and our drenching outside Jackie's house, Bouncer was keen to get in the car. He obviously wasn't used to exposure to the elements without his wee red tartan coat. Although I shouted at him to sit on the floor, Bouncer drew me a look and leapt onto the seat. I'd only had the dog an hour and I'd already given up hope of keeping the seats clean, it was easier that way. We were both soaking but I just quietly dripped. As the superior species I had the sense not to try to shake myself dry in a confined space while someone else was driving.

Since we'd come into the house Bouncer had sniffed every corner. He'd climbed up onto everything, and where he couldn't reach he rested his two paws and snuffled and peered. I had to follow him round in case he tried to mark out his territory by pissing on the furniture or whatever it was that dogs did. When Rebecca came in Bouncer turned his attention to her. She thought he was great. She clapped his head, a bit vigorously I thought. With every enthusiastic stroke Rebecca pulled Bouncer's eyelids up to an unnatural angle, exposing the whites of his eyes and making him look surprised. She roughly scratched his back and then his belly. I wondered if it was decent. Bouncer lay on his back, his eyes closed and one of his back legs trembling. Rebecca was only eight, she didn't understand the kind of ecstasy the dog was apparently experiencing. She was a chubby-faced wee girl, no cheekbones to speak of, she was never going to be as pretty as her mother. I knew that feeling.

'Does your mummy know that you're taking the dog out, Rebecca?'

'Mummy's tired, she's sleeping today.'

Rebecca looked at the floor as she said it.

'Well did you ask your dad?'

'Yes.'

I bustled about getting Bouncer's stuff.

'Here's his lead. D'you think it'll rain again? You can put his wee coat on him if you like.'

'Oh cool!'

Rebecca grabbed Bouncer's tartan raincoat from me and tried to fasten it under him. Bouncer, hoping for more sexy scratching, avoided the Velcro and lay on his back rolling around playfully until his excitement became obvious.

'Och just leave the coat off him pet, he doesn't want it.'

I saw her to the door, asking her not to go far and be back in half an hour. I'll give her a pound, I decided, although the wee soul hadn't asked for any money. We could make it a regular thing, Rebecca could walk the dog twice a day and I'd pay her. Twice a day at a pound a time would be two pounds a day. Depending on how long I'd have to keep the dog until Walter got out of hospital, it was working out at fourteen quid a week, nearly sixty quid a month. I could just give her a flat rate of a tenner a week, or even a fiver, a fiver was a lot of money to an eight-year-old.

Twenty minutes later I heard the front door. Rebecca hadn't done the full half-hour, if she was going to be working for me she'd have to appreciate that half an hour meant thirty minutes.

Roger stood at the door with his face like fizz. No sign of Rebecca or Bouncer.

'Michaela has just told me that she saw my daughter out on the road with your dog, is this true?'

He never gave me a chance to answer.

'What the bloody hell do you think you're doing sending a child out alone on an isolated road? How dare you exploit my children! I'm going to find her and if any harm has come to my girl so help me God I'll kill you, d'you understand?'

And with that he stomped off.

'Get off your fat arse and take your own bloody dog out!' Roger yelled back at me as I hurried to close the door.

I heard him rev up his car and drive away. A few minutes later the door went again. As I cowered behind it I could hear Bouncer whining.

'Rebecca?'

'Yes it's me Mrs Trixie, we're back!'

I opened the door a crack and let them in. They were both in top form. Bouncer bounced around while

Rebecca, with her cheeks rosy and eyes bright, chattered away.

'We had a great time didn't we Bouncer? We walked right down to the loch . . .'

'Rebecca, I thought you said you'd asked your dad if it was all right to take Bouncer out?'

I didn't mean to accuse but it came out that way.

'I did ask Daddy. I shouted upstairs to him. He was on his computer and he said I could.'

'What did he say exactly?'

'He said yes darling.'

I could see she was telling the truth. She looked frightened and close to tears. Roger probably wasn't listening when she asked him. He obviously wasn't aware that he had agreed. I should go back next door with her and make sure he believed her.

As we walked across the garden his car drew up. Michaela, the six-year-old, the one who had dubbed us in, jumped out of the car with a big smile on her face.

'Daddy says he's going to kill you!'

She addressed this to her sister. Aye, he's a great man for the death threats is old Roger, I thought, a great one for killing women and children. Roger got out of the car looking shattered but relieved. The fight had gone out of him. The whole scenario reminded me of my own frantic search for Steven the other night, and now I felt for Roger.

'Roger, I'm sorry. Please don't be annoyed with Rebecca, she says she asked you when you were working at your computer.'

He didn't own up but it was written all over his face, he remembered.

'I should have checked with you. I'm sorry for the worry you've had. It won't happen again,' I said as gently as I could.

Again Roger didn't say anything, only nodded and looked embarrassed.

'But Daddy I want to take Bouncer out, he's my friend. I haven't got any other friends.'

Rebecca put her hand to her eye and began wailing.

'Maybe Rebecca can come with me when I take Bouncer out? I'll take good care of her.'

'Can I Daddy, please, can I?'

Rebecca clawed at his jumper as she begged. Roger lifted his head and nodded his permission before walking off into his house. Rebecca picked up Bouncer's front paws and danced with him in jubilation.

'And besides,' I said to no-one in particular, 'it'll be good for my fat arse.'

Chapter 14

I thought the whisky and chocs would have softened
him, but no. Tuesday came and went, as did Thursday,
and not a dickie bird from Jackie. A week went by and
I realized he wasn't coming back.

With the slightly warmer weather I kept finding
more creepy-crawlies. I'd put my hand in the cupboard
under the sink to get the scrubbing brush and there
they'd be, creeping and crawling. I thought about pouring the scouring powder over them but something
stopped me. The beasties had lived here far longer than
me. Really it was more their house than it was mine, I
was only a visitor. Harrosie was teeming with life.
There were hundreds of us here, maybe thousands.
And what the beasties lacked in social skills they made
up for in numbers.

I was fed up with the amount of money I was
spending on cigarettes. I bought a packet of Silk Cut
and smoked eight in a row, eventually gagging as I lit
one from the stub of the fag before. I kept imagining
my blackened lungs, dry and inflexible as popadoms.
The remaining twelve I put in the kitchen drawer. The
packet had cost me nearly five pounds, I wasn't going
to chuck it away, some other smoker could get the good
of them.

Five hours later I was gasping again. I wasn't throwing the towel in, I told myself, I wasn't giving up giving up. It was all part of the process. Just like the peace process, it wouldn't happen overnight. And I was right, I did make progress. I saw a marked improvement in the aversion therapy – this time I only smoked six.

This time I took a more scientific approach and noted that with the first cigarette the impressions were all positive. Sensations of relaxation, well-being and relief were the principal effects. With ciggies two and three I felt a light-headedness that wasn't entirely unpleasant. Number four was neither one thing nor the other and I smoked on. I gave myself the dry boak on fag five but between retches I managed to light up the next one. I observed that my actual smoking technique had altered and was in direct relation to how many I smoked. On the first couple I had taken deep lungfuls at a time. Now I was only able to withstand short sharp draws. The light-headedness had burgeoned into room-spinning dizziness and nausea. The inside of my mouth was so hot that I swallowed a whole glass of water in a oner. The water was no sooner down than it was up again, albeit this time by a diverse route as I discharged thick clear slime from my nose and mouth. Never again, I thought, that was it, I was *so over*, as they said on American TV shows. I was dizzy and sick and couldn't contemplate smoking another cigarette for as long as I lived. As I lay on the birling couch, enveloped in thick smoke with the basin by my side, I smiled. It had all gone rather well, I thought.

When Steven phoned I made out that everything was fine with me. I told him about the dog, not about the accident, just that I was looking after an old man's dog while he was in hospital, being a good neighbour. As directed by Jenny, I had taken Bouncer's bandages off that day. Apart from a shovel-shaped scar on top of his head, he was absolutely fine. Steven could hardly contain his delight, we'd never had a family pet. He asked me to bring Bouncer to the phone. I tried to get him to bark, swishing the dishcloth I was holding in front of his face, but he thought it was a game and tried to catch it in his teeth. Bouncer would consent only to breathing and slebbering over the receiver. Steven *couldn't wait* for the Easter holidays when he would get to see Bouncer. I tried to stay upbeat, not wanting to spoil his elated mood. He told me he was *loving life* with Nettie looking after him *twenty-four seven*. I nearly phoned Bob just for the company, but with Steven at Nettie's there was no good reason.

I read all the Victoria Holt novels in the bookcase. Jenny told me the mobile library wasn't due for another two weeks so I was forced to start on the dusty old hardbacks. I picked one up and had to laugh. It was about a guy who turned into a beetle. Where do these people get their ideas, I thought, are they on drugs or what? The guy who wrote it was called Kafka, a made-up name if ever I heard one.

But I found I was really enjoying the book. I could hardly wait to find out what happened to Gregor in the end. It was only a wee short book so I had to spin it out. I could demolish a Catherine Cookson in a day but I wanted to savour this *Metamorphosis*. If I only allowed myself seven pages a day it would last until the mobile library came. Then I could ask for other books by the Kafka guy.

I was smoking again but this time it was different. I wasn't inhaling. This way I wouldn't get hooked like before. It was quite nice lighting a cigarette and just blowing the smoke straight out. I experimented with blowing it through my nose, and as I watched the nine o'clock news I played at framing the newsreader's face in wispy smoke rings. Over the next hour I smoked, without inhaling, another two recreational cigarettes, safe in the knowledge that this way I wasn't harming my health. At last I had found a solution.

I was down to my last two cigs. Not inhaling was going well except that I was missing the nicotine hit. In fact I was craving it. As I lit up I realized I was going to have to buy another packet. Another five quid and I wasn't even getting the buzz. Not inhaling didn't make smoking any cheaper, there wasn't a discount for partial use. It didn't reduce the smell. I'd still have to use smoker's toothpaste and mouthwash that tasted like bleach and loads of perfume. Unless I wanted to smell like a bookie's shop I'd still have to wash my clothes after one wear. Neither did not inhaling make the house any cleaner. I'd still have to scrub ashtrays and keep a window open in below-zero temperatures. The paintwork and ceilings would still yellow. And still I wouldn't get the hit. This was no use, with not inhaling I was getting all of the disadvantages of smoking and none of the advantages. I'd have to reconsider my strategy.

The fag suddenly tasted so much better when I inhaled. I hadn't meant to but then I just continued sucking it in, until I got the hit.

Rebecca was away so Bouncer and I took a new route and had what turned out to be a very long and very boggy walk. As soon as we came in I put on the immersion heater for a bath. After that walk I needed one, my clothes were manky and I knew my muscles would seize unless I had a good hot soak. I fed the dog, had my tea and watched the news. The next thing I knew it was ten o'clock.

I'd fallen asleep in the chair, bog-manky trousers and all, and left the water heater on for four hours. If I didn't run a bath quick I was scared the bloody thing would blow up. While Bouncer was out for the count in front of the telly I brought in my book, my fags and ashtray and my wine glass, and balanced them all on the corner of the bath for easy access. Then I noticed the beetle. This was happening all the time at Harrosie. There was always some beastie in the bath when I wanted in. Generally I just left it a while and when I came back it would be gone. Tonight I didn't have time for bathroom etiquette. The boiler was making a bumping noise, she could blow at any minute.

The last time I'd had a beetle in the bath in Glasgow, which was a long time ago, I used the shower head and cannoned it down the plughole. Clean, fast, efficient, I'd quite enjoyed it. But this time I couldn't do it.

The beetle was trying to climb up the side of the bath. Maybe it heard the boiler whining and banging and was trying to escape an explosion. Instinct was telling it to get out. It would get so far up and then when the sides got too steep, slide down again. I sat on the pan watching the beetle try and try again. I decided to give it a leg-up with a hairbrush. I was trying to be encouraging, holding the hairbrush below it, but it just kept tumbling down. Once as it fell it brushed my arm and I got the fright of my life. I gave it chance after chance. Then the beetle stopped. I didn't know if it was hurt or whether it was just getting its breath back. It started climbing again but I think it was getting pissed off with the hairbrush because now when I tried to help, the beetle just turned and walked down the hill again in protest.

'Och c'mon now, you can do it, you know you can!' I said.

Those few words of encouragement seemed to rally him because this time he really gave it his best shot. Hunching his body forward, his wee legs were going

149

like billy-o as he took a runney at it. The momentum did carry him a bit further up but again he fell. The sides of the bath were too sheer, the surface was too slippy; he wasn't getting enough purchase. What he needed was a ladder.

I had a couple of pairs of tights hanging on the pulley and I wasn't long in pleating the legs together to make a kind of ladder. At first he blanked the tights, crawling round them, but after a bit of persuasion with the hairbrush he got the idea. It wasn't easy for him, each bumfled braid of nylon was a mountain to climb. I knew the feeling. Earlier when I'd been out on the hill, I thought I was nearly at the top only to find another peak and another peak ahead. The wee soul worked like a Trojan and his wee black head and legs, finally and triumphantly, came into view over the lip of the bath.

As soon as he got to the top he started running along the lip. I thought he was doing some kind of victory lap but he was probably looking for a way off the bath. Whether he slipped or just chucked himself off the side I don't know, but he ended up on the floor on his back with his legs flailing.

He needed flicked over but the hairbrush handle was too thick to slide beneath him. In a panic that he might die like that, I did something that I'd never ever done before. I touched an insect.

As soon as his feet hit the floor he was off. No doubt that would be a story for his grandchildren, casting himself as the Indiana Jones of beetles. Not a word of thanks, not even a backward glance. I laughed when I imagined him turn towards me and briefly touch a front limb to his wee antennae by way of a salute.

I just wanted a wash. Not only was I honking of bog water but now my hands were covered in beetle germs. I turned on the taps, quickly pulling my arm away from the scalding water. My elbow caught the edge of my book and it clattered to the floor. The wine glass went the same way. Worried that the red wine would stain the book, I kicked it away from the spreading pool. It took ages to mop it up and get myself sorted with another glass. I poured in half a bottle of aromatherapy bubble bath and dropped my clothes where I stood before finally stepping into the bath.

It was filled to the brim with deliciously smelly bubbly hot water. I made a mental note to leave the heater on for four hours in future. Lying back and shutting my eyes, I let the aroma do its therapy and the hot water seep into my skin. After a few sips of wine I reached across to get my book. The fact that I was only allowing myself seven pages made it all the more luxurious. Stuck on the back cover there was what looked like a squashed currant. Surprised, I studied it closely and was horrified to discover that it wasn't a currant, it was a beetle. Most likely my beetle. As I lunged forward the flattened body of the creature and its internal organs landed between my breasts. I freaked. Frenzied splashing turned the bath into a jacuzzi. In my hysteria I flicked the body off my chest and ran screaming from the bathroom.

When I calmed down I realized that there was a perfectly good hot bath going to waste. I knocked back the wine, a send-off toast, before scooping and pouring him down the toilet. Naked, I hugged the toilet bowl and cried more at that beetle's funeral than I had at Mum's. It made me think of her body, a poor wee empty shell. I dried my eyes and sat back in the bath until gradually the hot water and the wine kicked in.

Jenny was the only one who noticed my growing depression. Reassured that Bouncer was doing fine, she asked about me.

151

'Och you're looking awful down in the mouth Trixie, are you all right?'

This was the last thing I needed, somebody being nice to me. To my mortification, as I fumbled in my purse to pay for my honey-roast ham, I started to bubble. A tear plopped onto the ten-pound note I was handing her.

'I'm sorry Jenny.'

I was angry with myself for this display.

'Don't be silly, there's nothing wrong with crying, it's a woman's prerogative.'

It was the sort of thing women say to each other in the powder room, making light of my outburst to save me embarrassment. Jenny was trying to cheer me up with a bit of girl power. I felt a flood of affection for this old lady who, until now, I had treated with deep suspicion.

'My mum died.'

'Oh my God! Sit down lassie.'

Jenny took my elbow the way Bob had at the funeral and sat me down in the armchair in the corner. She disappeared into the back shop and for the first time I wondered who the *we* referred to in the '*We Care with a Chair*' sign. It had only ever been Jenny in the shop any time I'd been in. As far as I could make out, Jenny was like me, on her own. I heard her moving about and then she emerged through the plastic fringed curtain that separated the shop from her living space. Both fists held steaming mugs of tea. After milk and sugar were sorted out Jenny dragged over the chair she kept behind the till and sat beside me.

'When did you find out, Trixie love?'

'Oh months ago, she died months ago.'

Jenny looked confused.

'I'm sorry Jenny, I've given you the impression that it's only just happened.'

'It doesn't matter when it happened!'

She reached over and rubbed my arm vigorously, as if she was trying to revive me from a bad dose of hypothermia. I looked up at her, wishing I could gather and rechannel the kinetic energy she was expending.

'It's still sore isn't it Trixie?'

At which point I started howling again. Jenny pulled a packet of man-size Kleenex off the shelf, burst it open and handed me a hanky. I blurted out loads of stuff, a litany of self-pity really, about missing Mum, and Steven, and Glasgow, my lack of friends in Inverfaughie etc., although I was fly enough not to mention Jackie. After a while I ran out of things to whine about and ground to a snivelling halt.

'I nursed my mother too,' Jenny said.

I stopped mid-sniff, delighted, in a perverse way, that we had this in common.

'We've always had this shop,' she said.

There was the *we* again.

'The building has been here for over a hundred years. I feel as if I've been here a hundred years as well. I've worked in this shop since I was a child. The minute I left school I got as far away from Inverfaughie as I could. London. It was great, and when the Sixties came, och we had a ball! There were tons of Highlanders in London if you knew where to find them, and Irish and Australian, American, you name it. Musicians, actors, painters, London was full of them. I met them all you know, Mick Jagger, Mary Quant, I even knew Jimi Hendrix. Aye, all you see is a wee Highland spinster but let me tell you Trixie, I won't die wondering.'

'What was Jimi Hendrix like?'

'He was American, black fella, fantastic on the guitar.'

'Yeah but, you know. Sex with a rock star, what was that like?'

'I'm sure I don't know!'

'But when you said you knew him I thought you meant . . .'

'Aye well, when I said I knew him, I saw him at a party once, but he was sound asleep on the couch the whole time. He was wasted but I sat on the edge of the couch for a good half-hour, right beside his head.'

There was nothing I could say in response to that and so we both sat quiet for a minute.

'I was in Woolworth's on Regent Street for twelve years, assistant manageress. I know that doesn't sound very grand but that was in the days before women were managers. Then they offered me my own shop out in Kent. I took it of course but it wasn't the same, I missed London. I would have went back to Regent Street like a shot, even as a junior. No doubt you're wondering how the hell I ended up back here?'

I wasn't, I hadn't got that far, I was still thinking about her and Jimi Hendrix, but I nodded to encourage her.

'I came home every year, Christmas and that kind of thing. You'll maybe not remember the power cuts and three-day weeks at that time. My father was ill and Mum was trying to look after him and run the shop. I stayed on, just until Dad got better. The thing was, he died, of the flu. It was so stupid. I didn't *have* to stay, Mum wanted me to go back, but how was she going to cope on her own? We were running the business by candlelight for God's sake. Ach, I never liked Kent anyway, too many English.'

'When did your mum die?'

'Fifteen years ago now. I was glad to see her off. She was in a lot of pain at the end.'

I thought of that last night with Mum, she'd been so

brave. This had the effect of nearly starting me off again, I had to change the subject.

'And you, Jenny? Did you never want to get married?'

'You don't always get what you want in this life, Trixie. I've a good business and good neighbours, I've no regrets, what's the point? When I was living the high life in London I never dreamt I'd come home but nearly everybody does. It's the ones that don't go home that I feel sorry for, they're not happy. No matter who you are or where you are, instinct tells you to go home.'

I nodded my head in recognition and agreement. Ever since I'd arrived in Inverfaughie, instinct had been telling me, bawling at me, to go back to Glasgow.

'Marriage? For why would I do that? No man's going to come in here and tell me how to run my business and take half my profits. Mind you I wouldn't say no to a wee toy boy maybe. Toy boys are thin on the ground in Inverfaughie but a girl can dream.'

Jenny was giggling, I was too. I liked the idea of a woman of sixty plus referring to herself as a girl. It meant there was hope for me yet.

As the talk turned to men I thought of Jackie. Jenny must know that I'd met him, why else would she mention him to me when I left the shop the other day? And what had she meant? She'd said something about the Wee Free, I seemed to remember. Had he spoken to her about me? I was dying to know what she knew.

A good way to broach the subject, I thought, was to talk, or rather moan, about the garden. I told her about the rotting tools in the shed and the wilderness behind the house. My distress was genuine enough even if my motives weren't, it really was more than I could cope with. I expected Jenny to bring up Jackie, but she didn't.

'I've never had a garden before,' I bleated. 'I wouldn't

know where to start and I think the grass is needing cut.'

It was pathetic, I was disgusted with myself. I was trying to use Jenny, who I now regarded as my friend, as a conduit to Jackie.

'Och that's easy done, just run over it with the mower.'

'I've been out and looked at the mower and I don't think it'll work. It's awful stiff and I don't know if I've the strength to push it round that massive garden.'

'What you need is a hover. Walter has one.'

Jenny stared at me and waited. I would've liked to oblige but I wasn't sure what kind of reaction she was looking for.

'With the hover you'll have it done in jig time. Walter's house is the last one on the Gaffney road, just take it out of the shed, it's not locked.'

This time Jenny got a reaction. My face fell with disappointment, and then clambered into a false expression of gratitude. I was going to have to be more direct.

'I was wondering if you knew whether Mr Robertson, Jackie that is, the gardener, was awful busy at the moment?'

This was transparent but I was beyond caring.

'Och you don't need him. Go up and get that Flymo and do your own garden. You'll get a lot of pleasure from it. The mower's there if you want it, Walter will be pleased someone's getting the use of it.'

I supposed I should be grateful, after all I had told Jenny my problem and she'd provided me with a solution. At last I was seeing a bit of the famous Highland hospitality. I could mow the grass myself, I wasn't doing anything else. Jackie wasn't coming back to finish it and the sooner I got over this garden phobia the better. I'd make a good job of it and whenever he cycled past he'd see that Jenny was right, I didn't need him.

The Flymo was great. After all the time I'd spent worrying about it, I mowed the whole garden in an hour. I was annoyed when I ran out of grass. The rest of the garden still terrified me though but, I thought, one step at a time. Along the edge of the grass were big clumps of weeds. I tried to go over them but the hover wasn't happy, it squealed like a pig and I was scared I'd broken it. I left the weeds alone after that, one step at a time.

I desperately wanted to leave the other weeds alone and so I crumpled the cardboard packet and threw my Last Ever Packet of Fags in the kitchen bin. Maybe not my first Last Ever, but it was going to be my last, definitely. I didn't even count how many there were in the packet, what did it matter?

The next day, a long silent day, I estimated that there were a minimum of four fags in the packet. They sang to me, a siren's song from the bin, 'We're here!' They were in bits when I rescued them, not a whole one left. But desperation is the mother-in-law of invention. I rolled a filtered butt between my fingers, hollowing it out enough to be able to graft another longer stump on. So long as I held it vertically it was smokable. As I limbo-danced beneath the fag and carefully sooked at it, I couldn't work out what was more satisfying: creating the Frankenstein fag or smoking it.

My next attempt to give up was, like every other, useless. This time I'd doused the packet of Silk Cut in the sink, soaking the tobacco and then throwing the packet in the outside bin. Inevitably I went to the bin in my nightie, in the dark and freezing cold, and dug out the sodden fag packet.

I separated and removed the wet paper and laid out

157

the tobacco in the grill pan. I turned on the oven but I had to turn the heat down to a peep. It was burning the tobacco before I was getting a chance to smoke it. As I wafted the smoke from the grill pan towards my open mouth I was fully aware that I was a pathetic addict, a sad case, and hated myself.

The weather was beginning to pick up and Rebecca and I were walking further and further each day with Bouncer. We ambled along but Bouncer was always keen to go further, wanting to see what was around the bend.

Rebecca was a chatterbox and, through her, I quickly became acquainted with the pupils and staff of Inverfaughie Primary School. I discovered that, although she had *absolutely nothing up top*, Sheila McGhee's mum had bought her a trainer bra. I knew too that Rory Anderson smelled, Helen McCardle never had lunch money and Miss McGivern wore the most gorgeous green eyeshadow. When Rebecca became involved in an ongoing feud with Ailsa Robertson, previously her best pal, I waited every day for the next instalment.

'Do you miss your old school friends, Rebecca?'

'Yes, but we're better here. As a family.'

That sounded like it was straight out of Roger's mouth.

'Your mummy seems awful homesick, is she all right?'

'Mummy's not homesick, she's got stress. She caught it in London, that's why we moved here. She has medimacation to make her better, and Old Nurse Time, that's what Dad says. Anyway, lots of kids at this school have mums with medimacation.'

As a rep I'd sold an antidepressant for a while. I knew the market, depression was endemic, the company was cock-a-hoop as sales figures went through the roof. But living in the Highlands, living at a slower pace, could that be a cure? As far as I could see it just created a different kind of stress.

As with Steven, I'd managed to avoid smoking around Rebecca. She seemed to look up to me and I didn't want her getting the idea that it was cool or trendy. Her dad hated me enough as it was. I had no idea that she knew until one day when we were going up a steep hill and I was talking, she asked me to stop and get my breath back.

'Auntie Trixie, I don't want you to smoke. I don't want you to die from smoking.'

There were tears in the wee soul's eyes. It was now or never, I had to beat this bastard smoking. I cuddled her and promised.

We took the packet of fags down to the sea. It was Rebecca's idea.

Bouncer kept trying to get in on the act, as we built the tiny raft.

'See, Auntie Trixie? Bouncer's trying to help, he doesn't want you to smoke.'

'Actually when I think about it pet, he always leaves the room when I light up.'

'Well he won't have to any more.'

Rebecca wanted to light it and she was just about to when she suddenly decided that I should do it. With shaking hands I lit the fire. It was nearly extinguished by the sizzling froth at the water's edge, but Rebecca pushed our little Silk Cut longboat out to sea. It rocked a bit on the surf before a wave carried it further out. Darkness was falling as Rebecca and I watched the brief flames die and the pyre sink into the water. I knew then that I'd never smoke again.

Steven, worried that I wasn't settling, asked me repeatedly about my friends in Inverfaughie. I reassured

159

him by telling him I had friends from six to sixty. Technically this was true if I included Michaela the six-year-old snitch and Jenny the sixty-year-old swinger, but I made out I had a vast array of mates. Steven asked about Jackie and I told him I hadn't seen much of him recently. Except for once when I'd spotted him in the distance on his bike, I hadn't seen him at all.

I wanted Jackie to see the garden. When I'd replaced Walter's Flymo Jenny said I could use anything else in the shed so long as I looked after it. A day hardly went by when I didn't spend an hour or so farting about in the garden. I tidied and trimmed, looking the part in my borrowed gardening gloves. I knew that proper gardeners planted things in spring but I didn't have a clue where to start. The garden was doing it for me, anyway. The sludge greys and browns became greens and then yellows and blues. What I had mistaken for weeds were coming through as daffodils and bluebells. I could hardly believe how cheerful it looked compared to a few weeks ago. Even before I'd come to Harrosie, when the ground was ice hard, the flowers and leaves were here. They'd been here all the time, hiding under the ground, biding their time.

Now that they had put in an appearance I wanted Jackie to cycle past, but he never did. For such a small community it was remarkable that I never bumped into him. Maybe he saw me coming. Jenny never mentioned his name. It was as if my short but intense friendship with him had never happened.

I was making do with my small social circle until disaster struck when I had an unpleasant, and ultimately very revealing, altercation with Jenny.

Chapter 15

Jenny was nearly wetting herself with excitement when I went into the shop. She stood on the top step of her wee ladder stacking shelves and shouted, 'HOLD THE LINE!' in a strange accent.

'Sorry?'

Then down the ladder she comes, right up to my face, and says, 'When I give the command unleash hell.'

I would have laughed but her expression was grim.

'D'you think Russell Crowe is a bent shot? A lot of these Hollywood actors are, you know.'

Then the penny dropped. *Gladiator*. It had finally arrived. Jenny had been going on about it for weeks. She hadn't gone off her head, she was quoting lines from the movie. Jenny had the serious hots for Russell Crowe, she couldn't stop talking about him, on and on she went: was he gay? Had I heard if he was married or not?

'It doesn't make much difference, he's not likely to be up in this neck of the woods now is he, Jenny?' I said.

I managed to stop myself from saying *and if he ever was, he's hardly going to fancy an old dear like yourself.*

Then, as usual, she starts to tell me the plot.

'He's a general who's tired of fighting and all he

161

wants is to go home to his wife and get the crops in, but the emperor . . .'

Jenny had ruined every movie I'd seen in Inverfaughie. My hand went up as if I was stopping traffic and before I knew what I was saying, the words were out.

'Wait a minute Jenny, don't tell me any more. I want to see it for myself, I want to enjoy this one.'

That clamped her. It was the first time I'd stood up to Jenny like that and I don't think she was expecting it, but it didn't take her long to come back.

'Well, you'll have to take your place in the queue, other I.R.V.C. members have priority, there's plenty in the village who have put in advance orders for it.'

'Fair enough, I'll wait my turn. I'm not bothered, I've managed fine without Russell Crowe up to now, I'll just have to manage a wee while longer.'

There was a right frosty atmosphere after that. I'd actually gone in for a bottle of wine, among other things. She never said anything, but sometimes when I bought drink, or more drink than Jenny considered reasonable, she tilted her head to one side as she served me. I noticed, although I pretended not to, that her accent was always more sing-song on those occasions. I resolved the problem: I just bought less drink more frequently. It meant more trips to the shop but we both enjoyed that. Or we had, up until now. I couldn't buy wine now, I was bloody sure I wasn't going to let her look down her nose at me.

'Just a loaf today thank you Jenny,' I said.

I held out two days but the freezer was getting empty and I realized that if I wanted to eat I was going to have to face her. She had the *Gladiator* poster up now. It was huge, taking up most of one wall, but I kidded on I didn't see it. The look on her face when I bought a few bottles of wine! Her head inclined so much it was resting on her shoulder. I'd hoped she might behave a bit more professionally, what with her twelve years' experience in middle management at Woolworth's and all. If this atmosphere kept up it was going to make things a bit tickly.

Jenny's was the only shop for miles and she knew it. Thank God I had stopped smoking but unless I was prepared to pay off-sales prices from the Calley hotel, I'd have to go to her for drink. My face burned when I thought of her mock sympathy for my drinking. If she wanted her head permanently at that angle I could oblige her with a swift karate chop. Then she'd have difficulty in indulging what was no doubt her other great hobby: slobbering all over her stinking *Gladiator* poster when she shut up shop for the night.

I considered doing a big shop in Inverness. I looked up in the phone book and there was a shop where you could buy kits for making your own beer. It would be quite expensive initially with the plastic barrel and all the tubes and everything, but in the long run it worked out at five pence a pint. On the phone the man said he sold wine-making kits as well, but wine took a few weeks longer to mature. I asked him what was the quickest beer and he said I could be self-sufficient in three weeks. I decided to go down to Jenny's and give her one last chance before I took my business elsewhere. If she wouldn't straighten her face it would be the home brew for me.

When I went into the shop it was empty and Jenny was nowhere to be seen. This was good. This put me in a position of strength. When she came back she'd have to apologize for keeping the customer waiting. She'd be raging that, on this occasion, the customer was me. I'd give her a warm forgiving smile thereby letting bygones be bygones, and we could take it from there.

Actually it wasn't that unusual for Jenny to be absent when the shop was quiet. Locals knew that they just had to shout 'Shop!' and eventually Jenny would stop what she was doing, stocktaking or whatever she did in there, and come through. Her multicoloured plastic fringe curtain was the dividing line betwen home and work and she popped between them all day long. Although we were friends, it was strictly front shop. I had no idea what her living quarters were like, seeing as she'd never asked me in.

I'd never passed through the curtain, and I often thought that it could be another world in there. Sometimes at night, when time hung heavy, I entertained myself imagining what lay beyond the fringe. I pictured it like Narnia or the Land of Oz or London of the Swinging Sixties. How my long dark evenings would fly in as I fancied Jenny's decor in swirling psychedelic purples and greens. This would be broken up by posters of topless black girls with outsize Afros smoking outsize spliffs. Curled inside one of those white plastic egg-shaped suspended chairs, Jenny maybe smoked a few spliffs herself.

Jenny footered about in the back shop even when she knew she had customers, she could hear the bell on the door. At first it annoyed me but later, as I adjusted to the pace of village life, it didn't. I wasn't one who shouted 'Shop!' If Jenny wasn't there I'd take the opportunity of getting a free read at her magazines.

A precedent had been set a few weeks ago, in those happy days before our *Gladiator* tiff. Jenny was leaning across the counter, mug of tea in hand, reading the *Press and Journal*. This reminded me that I wanted one and I asked her for a copy. Cool as a cucumber she finishes what she is reading, folds it up and hands it to me. I had to laugh.

'I'm not having that, it's second-hand. You've just read it.'

Jenny was laughing as well but it didn't stop her making an excellent retort.

'Och no dear, you're mistaken, I wasn't reading it, I don't have time to read while I'm at my work. I was checking it for mistakes, typing errors and the like, smudged photos. I wouldn't want you getting a defective newspaper. It's not second-hand, it's quality-assured. We aim to please.'

So it was a two-way street: if she could read my newspaper, I could read her magazines. She didn't mind. She'd come in from Narnia and catch me reading *Chat* or *Take a Break* and ask me if I'd read the one about the woman who killed her kids. If I hadn't she'd open it for me and make me read it while she packed my bag. Then we could have a good old gab about it. We'd always have a laugh at the headlines: *My Lover Ran off with My Son! I Lived on a Jaffa Cake a Day for Nine Years! Arthur Sawed My Leg off And I Took Him back!*

As I looked for something juicy to read I noticed that most of the mags were already a bit dog-eared, but then again most of them had photos of Russell Crowe on the front. I made a point of not looking at those.

Two women visitors came in while I was reading. They were Dutch by the sound of them, one a teenager and the other ages with myself, probably mother and daughter. I explained that the shop assistant would be through in a moment, and went back to my magazine. They seemed to understand and we nodded and smiled at each other. It was important to be polite to visitors, the village depended upon them. I might have broken my rule and given Jenny a shout but I wanted her to come in and find me here, and anyway, I hadn't finished reading *I Stabbed My Husband and Walked*

Free! I could have gone behind the counter and served them, I supposed, but I thought, no. In the current political atmosphere I would be overstepping the mark and I'd get no thanks for helping out.

I was aware of music from behind the curtain when I'd first come in. Jenny was a great fan of Andy Robertson on Inverfaughie fm, but the same music had been playing too long for it to be the radio. It was kind of ethnic music, Indian maybe. Now that my attention was caught I moved over towards the curtain, getting as close to it as I could from this side of the counter. I couldn't see a thing through the fringes but at least I could make out the music better from here. It was New Age. Aha! So I was right all along, Jenny was an old hippy after all! I sniffed the air trying to smell incense, sandalwood or, even better, hashish. After the superior looks she bestowed on me for a couple of bottles of wine!

But something wasn't right. I couldn't believe it of her, and even if she had ever smoked the weed, which I doubted, Jenny was too business-minded to skin up during shop hours.

The Dutch women were getting restless. When they first came in they'd chatted away to each other but after a while they fell silent. Their eyes darted to the window when any traffic passed on the road, and then back to the plastic curtain. I guessed their coach had stopped for a comfort break and they had taken the chance to nip into the shop. They seemed nervous that the bus would leave without them. When I moved across the shop towards the curtain the women took this as a signal that something was about to happen. They followed me, forming an orderly queue behind me. And, in fact, something did happen.

I could still hear the strange music but over the top of that, I could hear a new sound.

'Ohhh, uhhhh, nuhh, mmhh.'

The women heard it too. They looked to me for explanation but I could only shrug. Then I recognized the music. The *Gladiator* theme, I was sure of it, I'd seen the trailer at the cinema and heard it on the radio.

'Mmmhhh, uhhh, nuhh.'

Mother and Daughter burst into Dutch again. I couldn't understand the words but their tone was urgent. What the bloody hell was that noise? It almost sounded like someone having sex. Of course, I realized, someone was. Jenny was having sex. With herself. She must have been so carried away she didn't hear us come in. Through the curtain, only a few yards away from us, Jenny was entertaining herself. Now there was a steady rhythm to the noises she was making but her pitch was getting higher.

'Oh, ooh, ooh, ooh.'

She was approaching the tickly bit. The women exchanged more rapid-fire Dutch and then, on the command of Mother, Daughter jumped onto the counter.

I only had a few seconds to think. Obviously there was a misunderstanding here. One of us was getting it wrong. They seemed to be interpreting the noises Jenny was making as distress rather than passion. Mother was sending Daughter in to investigate.

I supposed there was a chance that Jenny actually was in distress, she might have fallen off her wee three-step ladder. At her age there was always a danger that she'd fall and break a hip. She could be lying horribly twisted with her feet pointing up and her chest on the floor. Maybe I was the one making the mistake; maybe it wasn't ecstasy I was hearing but delirious moans of agony. If Jenny was in pain we needed to get to her fast. Daughter had swung her legs up and over, her feet were about to reach the floor. On the other hand, if she wasn't . . .

I could see that Jenny might not appreciate someone bursting in on her at any time, never mind at such a private moment. I would though, I'd appreciate someone bursting in on her. For one thing I'd finally get to see what her house was like. For another I'd get to see her covered in embarrassment. There'd be no more head-tilting at my alcohol consumption after that.

I had to make a decision, Daughter had reached the curtain now. She pulled aside the fronds and took a step inside the back shop.

'Shop!' I shouted at the top of my voice. 'Jenny, quick, you've got customers!'

Amazed at me suddenly finding my voice, the girl stopped in her tracks.

'Shop!'

As if by magic, Jenny appeared. Daughter got the fright of her life and swiftly retreated to the customer side of the counter. Jenny, unruffled by this intrusion, took the time to smooth her overall until the women were organized on their own proper side of the counter.

'Yes, what can I get you, ladies?'

They wanted sanitary towels. Jenny directed them to the darkest corner of the shop where such things were hidden away. In any other shop the signage would read 'Feminine Hygiene', in Jenny's it read 'Lady's Emergencies'.

Up until now Jenny's phrase had struck me as a quaint euphemism but now I could see the truth of it. The women had hung around for ages and risked their coach leaving without them. They had been prepared to storm the private quarters of the proprietor. It really was a Lady's Emergency.

As they scuttled out the shop I took a good look at Jenny. She was perfectly composed, her cheeks were rosier than usual and her eyes were brighter but she wasn't flustered in any way. And why should she be? I had to admire her nerve. Who would have thought it of her? Jenny was sixty, a Highlander and the post-mistress to boot. Forbye all that she was an unashamed gusset typist.

I wouldn't say she was sugary sweet because she wasn't. Obviously she was grateful that I'd saved her neck, but never in a million years would she say so. She didn't try to sook in with me, she never even mentioned her special offers. She was all chit-chat about how Walter was doing in hospital and was Bouncer keeping all right, all the while with the gigantic *Gladiator* poster looming over us. I took the opportunity to stock up, I'd run out of nearly everything.

She helped me pack my bag but she didn't overdo it and she never batted an eye, nor did she even lift her head, never mind tilt it, when I bought two dozen bottles of Grolsch. I thought I'd better get bottles with replaceable tops just in case I ended up having to do the Inverness home-brew run. I was about to leave the shop when she called me back.

'Trixie.'

She said my name in a kind of no-nonsense way. I could tell she was embarrassed, I was a bit embarrassed myself.

'*Gladiator* is available for hire tonight if you want it.'

I didn't know what to say. Jenny was bumping me up the waiting list. This was an illegal manoeuvre and flew in the face of everything the I.R.V.C. stood for.

'Thank you Jenny,' I said.

I tried to be as gracious as I could.

'Now, put your purse away,' Jenny said, putting her hand up to stop me the way I'd stopped her the other day, 'this one's on the house.'

Chapter 16

What a movie! Even Bouncer enjoyed it and he could never sit at peace when a good film was on. He would be either up and down like a yo-yo at the window every time a car went by, or whining to get out, or crashed out in front of the fire leaving me to watch it on my own. As a special dispensation, because the film was so good, I let him sit up on the couch with me. We watched it three times, the first two times back to back. The third time, to make it more like the pictures, I made microwave popcorn and turned off the lights and shut the curtains. There was none of the jiggery-pokery that Jenny had got up to, not with an impressionable young dog in the house, but oh it was brilliant! I was nearly greeting when I had to hand it back.

I took it back to Jenny in the plain brown envelope in which she had given it to me, and slipped it to her when the shop was quiet. We were back to being friends again, thank God, I was dying to talk about the film and I knew she was. As soon as the lunchtime rush died down Jenny disappeared into the back shop. Not to interfere with herself but to make us a mug of tea. I left the exact money on the counter and cracked open a packet of Tunnock's caramel logs. When Jenny came back I had already made myself comfortable in the care-with-a-chair. At first we discussed the artistic merits of the film and argued the case for its Oscar awards.

'As the slaves were brought through the city and into the Coliseum, I thought the director's vision of ancient Rome was perfectly rendered,' I said.

I was quite impressed by how highbrow this sounded. I'd read it in a review but if Jenny had read it she never let on.

'Oh yes!'

Jenny agreed with everything I said, she was enthusiastic about all of it, especially the men.

'And the bad guy, the emperor's son, he was quite tasty as well, wasn't he?'

I had to agree, he was quite tasty.

At last Steven came. I cleaned the house from top to bottom and stocked up on crisps and juice. The cupboard was groaning with ingredients for my curry recipes. I had already baked and stockpiled batches of snowballs, brownies and a traybake of almond slices. I was getting quite good at the traybakes.

I picked up the boys from the train at Inverness. Steven shied away from any kind of emotional reunion, probably because he had Gerry with him. I was a bit disappointed not to get a hug at least. Steven and Gerry instantly took to Bouncer, clapping and petting him as he bounced around the platform. A smiling nod and 'All right Mum?' was as much as I got.

Gerry was very well mannered. We weren't out of the station and he was thanking me profusely for the invite. I'd harboured uncharitable thoughts about Gerry intruding on our holiday, so now his gratitude annoyed me and made me feel guilty. It was so over the top that he could have been taking the piss.

On the way home they both sat in the back. I tried to

keep up a conversation with Steven, asking him about school and Nettie's, but it was difficult. I felt like a taxi driver. Steven asked if they could play a CD. What could I say? They were on holiday.

I'd tried to have this debate with Steven when he was first getting into this kind of music. When I was growing up the most uncool music in the world was metal. It was so old, so American, even when it wasn't. I'd chucked a boy because he played his big brother's Quo record. Steven would argue that this was death metal, thrash metal, nu metal, but it was basically the same shite, different decade. And it still wasn't cool. No right-thinking person could do other than despise it. Even with the windows up, Cradle of Filth could be heard screaming as we came through the village, with the two boys headbanging along.

Within days a routine was established. Steven and Gerry would lie in their beds till lunchtime, then get up and slob around watching TV and raiding the cake tins. Every day I asked them what they wanted for tea and every day they would say chicken curry. At first I was flattered but after a week I was sick of it. I called it quits when one night, getting undressed for bed, I sniffed my oxters and discovered I was exuding vindaloo. They took the dog out in the afternoon, point-blank refusing to put his tartan coat on him, and after tea, they'd go down to the Calley.

The first night they arrived they walked down into the village and straight into the Calley bar. They were chancing their arm but were delighted to discover that Ali did not require ID. The boys behaved calmly, resisting the urge to try the more exotic drinks. (Steven had once been thrown out of a pub for attempting to order two Beziques.) With quiet satisfaction Steven and Gerry would while away their evenings in the Calley bar, supping their pints manfully. I asked them what the place was like, never having been in it myself. Steven said it was quiet, depressing really, with a few old men and losers propping up the bar. I suspected he was just saying that to prevent me from ever popping in.

I offered to pick them up but Steven went mental, accusing me of deliberately trying to ruin the one good part of his holiday. The *one* good part? On my insistence Gerry got his mother on the phone and asked if he could go to the pub. She spoke to me saying indulgently, as if she was doing me a huge favour, that Gerald could go to the pub *within reason*.

It was the same every night. After dinner Steven would push his plate away and casually say to Gerry, 'Fancy a pint?'

Gerry always yawned and stretched and pretended to think about it.

'Aye, if you like.'

Then began the grooming rituals. Steven and Gerry would spend an hour apiece in the bathroom. I didn't want to go near it for a few hours until the steamy sickly intermingled smell of aftershave and jobby subsided. There had to be women in the Calley bar. The lads washed and dried their hair, flicking it around like girls. They ironed their jeans and stood in front of the mirror adjusting their hair partings and fine-tuning the casual arrangement of their clothes. Never once did they invite me.

I didn't mind, I liked having the house to myself for a few hours. I was used to living on my own now. I'd been looking forward to the company but the boys were useless. Most of the time they deliberately excluded me by talking in a made-up code they called 'egg language'.

At first I was baffled. I considered phoning Bletchley Park for a loan of their Enigma machine, but the name 'egg language' turned out to be a dead giveaway. They

173

were simply putting 'egg' in front of the first vowel sound. Right in front of me they would discuss such delicate subjects as neggookie beggadges and bleggow jeggobs. They were good at it, their young minds racing ahead, simultaneously translating as they spoke. I was usually a few sentences behind but I could catch the sense of it. They may have been suspicious, I heard Steven say, 'Legget's meggurder Meggum,' but it was just a test. I had to be careful to remain impassive. I didn't want to spoil their top-secret schoolboy fun and anyway, this way I got to hear everything.

While they were out I got the chance to catch up with the housework. Steven, never the tidiest person, showed off in front of Gerry by draping his cast-off clothes over furniture from one end of the house to the other. Gerry, obviously comfortable with this, followed suit. With Gerry in the house I didn't have the freedom to bawl at Steven the way I usually did. It was easier just to accept the fact that I'd have to be a full-time skivvy for the duration.

Neither Steven nor Gerry had worked out the difficult technical task of putting a new toilet roll in the holder. One of my daily janitorial duties was to replenish the loo paper. We were going through it like nobody's business and I cursed myself for not buying more of Jenny's special offer.

Since chucking the fags I'd rediscovered my sense of smell. This had been, until now, a blessing. Every night a delicious pot-pourri of Steven and Gerry's socks, dog farts and curried armpits would put me off my dinner. But it wasn't all bad. At least now I had someone to blame whenever I couldn't find things.

And the boys were popular with the wee girls next door. Steven thought it was hilarious hearing them call me 'Trixie'. Rebecca, who became a constant visitor during those two weeks, was in love with Steven and

174

followed him around the house, giggling at everything he said. Rebecca and Michaela would come in some mornings even though they knew the boys wouldn't be up for hours. It was the only time they volunteered to help me in the garden. Once when the girls were round Steven got out of his scratcher unaccountably early. He stumbled into the kitchen, still sleepy and tousle-haired. The girls had brought Smidgy in to show him. Steven sat stroking the rabbit on his knee before taking him out the room. Used like a ventriloquist's dummy, poor trembling Smidgy's head poked round the door. All we could see was an apparently four-foot-tall rabbit.

'Can you see me?' Steven said in a Smidgy Rabbit voice. 'Can you see me now? What about now?'

With every question Smidgy got taller and the more the girls giggled, the taller he got. Then he disappeared and who should bound into the kitchen but Skippy the Bush Kangaroo.

'Look, I'm Skippy! And here's me little joey!' Steven said in an Australian accent. Steven had turned his hooded sweatshirt back to front. Now Smidgy's head was peeking out of Steven's pouched belly. He, or I should say Skippy, was hopping around the kitchen tutting, terrifying poor Smidgy. Bouncer and the girls wanted in on the act and the kitchen floor vibrated with the bouncing of two wee girls, a dog, a big daft boy and a frightened rabbit.

'What's that you say Skip?' My Australian accent veered more towards Irish but the kids got the idea. 'Gerry's hung-over and you caaan't wake him up?'

Skippy tutted and nodded furiously.

'Quick kids, that Gerry feller needs help, this could be serious!'

They all bounced up the stairs to Gerry's room, Bouncer doing his best to get a sniff of the rabbit. Not in a predatory way, more a nosey youthful exuberant kind of way. Steven was tutting and laughing and bouncing while protecting Smidgy from the dog. This was a glimpse of the real Steven. When he was like this, free, uninhibited, he reminded me of his dad, the best of Bob, the side of Bob I hadn't seen for a long time.

I could hear them all squealing and jumping on Gerry's bed. Gerry was drinking more than was *within reason*, despite what his gushy mother said. Either that or he didn't have the same tolerance for alcohol as Steven. It was genetic and slightly worrying, another family trait, one that Steven got from me.

Gerry was not amused, making it plain that playing children's games was uncool, and the hilarity quickly died down. Thanks to Gerry, once the girls had gone home, Steven retreated back inside his cocoon, a pupa of insecurity and teenage huffiness.

That was one of the few laughs we'd had since they'd arrived. I was getting cabin fever spending so much time in the house. Now that the boys were taking Bouncer out I was missing my daily walk. One morning I played Inverfaughie fm at full volume in a bid to drive the boys from their stiff-sheeted beds. This was in revenge for all the Slipknot and Cradle of Filth I'd had to listen to. An hour or so of accordion music would get them on their feet, I reckoned, and I was right. Two hung-over disgruntled teenagers clogged up the kitchen. Over coffee and almond slices I tried to talk them into a day out with me.

'D'you fancy a wee run in the car today? You've not seen much of the countryside, it's lovely.'

'We saw it on the way up, Mum.'

'Yes but that was from the train, you've not seen the real Highlands yet.'

'I'm a bit tired Mum, could we leave it and maybe do it tomorrow?'

I didn't let him see how pissed-off I was. I considered my position and a possible strategy: the presence of Gerry meant that insisting was going to be out of the question, and I'd already tried cajoling without success. I was going to have to use the most powerful tool in the box.

With my head bowed in disappointment, I nodded my silent acquiescence. As I stood quietly washing the dishes I didn't reproach my son with how I'd hardly seen him; I never mentioned the cakes and curries, the tidying, the toilet rolls. But he knew.

'I suppose we could go today Mum, I don't mind either way.'

'Och no, not if you're too tired. I'll need to get this place cleaned up anyway.'

'No, I'm not, I'm fine. That'll be good to get out and see a bit of the place, won't it Gerry?'

'Eh, yeah.'

'Och, we can maybe do it some other time. You lads need your sleep, and I've a big traybake to do.'

'Can we go out Mum, please? Can we?'

'Well . . . och, OK then.'

Chapter 17

The boys weren't keen to leave Bouncer in the house on his own.

'He's fine,' I told them, 'I leave him all the time when I pop down to Jenny's.'

Nevertheless, Steven insisted that we leave him fresh water, a bowl of Chappie and his plastic snowman to play with. I put on Inverfaughie fm so's he wouldn't get lonely, he always seemed comforted by the local voices.

Steven, unbidden, sat in the front with me as I drove the coast road.

'Where are the Highlands? All I can see is mist,' said Gerry.

It was true, it wasn't very scenic. Due to the heavy mist we could only see about two feet beyond the grass verge on the road. Steven drew Gerry a look of absolute disgust.

'What d'you want man, a free holiday *and* a view?'

That clamped old Geraldo. As Steven turned round again his hand grazed mine on the gearstick and when he winked as well, I knew it hadn't been accidental. To wind Gerry up I gave a running commentary describing the islands and lochs as we passed along the grey tunnel of mist.

The mist lifted long enough for us to see a group of old people at the side of the road. There were four of them, two women, two men. The men were sitting on a bench facing out to sea. The women were behind the bench, squatting. At first I thought the ladies were having a naughty outdoor pee. I wasn't going to draw the boys' attention but then I noticed their trowels. They weren't peeing, the women were digging up the wild irises that grew by the side of the road, not just cutting the flowers but scooping the bulbs out of the ground and putting them in a poly bag. I did an emergency stop and rolled down my window. Steven and Gerry were dumbfounded by what happened next.

'What the bloody hell do you think you're playing at?' I said to the oldsters.

They tried to ignore me. The men stared beyond me and the mist, straight out to sea. The women squatted lower and dug faster.

'Hey! Stop that right now. If you want flowers go and buy them, you mean old gits! You might just be passing through but this is where we live. We don't come to your place and dig up your flowers, do we?'

Although they still ignored me, the men at least seemed to see the force of my argument. They turned towards the women. The women slowed but didn't completely stop.

'Right that's it. It is my duty to inform you that we are off-duty volunteer conservation officers and are making a citizen's arrest. Out of the car lads.'

Steven was giggling until I nipped his arm. Gerry got out without question.

'You have the right to remain silent,' I said, 'but anything you do say . . .'

Luckily the old folk got off their mark, dropping their poly bag to give them more speed as they hobbled towards their car.

179

'That's it, run you buggers! Hirple for it, it's the conservation volunteers!'

Steven and I laughed and laughed so much we induced hysteria. The fact that Gerry didn't laugh seemed to make it even funnier.

'We could be the ones who get arrested. Those people could report us,' Gerry said.

'What for?' said Steven.

'For impersonating an officer, that's what!'

Gerry was gritting his teeth and getting quite steamed up. I dug the irises back into the ground but, as the flowers listed like drunks, I didn't hold out much hope for them. The old women had left their wee trowels in the bag. Oh well, I thought, I'm sure I can find a good use for them, that's what conservation was all about.

'Yes, but I said we were *volunteer* conservation officers and technically we are. Anyone can make a citizen's arrest.'

'Intimidating pensioners, how sad is that?' Gerry sneered.

This was too much for Steven.

'Shut it Gerry, it's a long walk back to Glasgow. Just chill out man.'

Steven walked off into the mist. Gerry had nothing to say after that. I felt a bit sorry for him. After all he was just a fifteen-year-old boy, but he'd started it and anyway, he'd had Steven to himself since they'd arrived. Nevertheless, I was the adult and should apologize, and I was about to when Gerry muttered, 'Sheggite deggay eggout.'

Oh very brave, I thought, not only is he too scared to say it loud enough or in proper English, he's too scared to say it in front of Steven.

'Fegguck eggoff!' was, I felt, the most appropriate reply.

180

Gerry's eyes nearly popped out of his head. I would deny it if Steven asked.

I was still up a few nights later when they came back from the pub.

'Guess who we met tonight, Mum?'

I knew. The only person in Inverfaughie that we both knew.

'You met Jackie in the pub? What was he saying?'

'No, he wasn't in the pub, he just came past, on his bike. It was him that recognized me.'

'Did he ask after me?'

'Yeah, he said how's your mum.'

'And what did you say?'

'I said she's fine. He's going to take us out fishing tomorrow.'

'All of us?'

'Eh, no. I think it's just me and Gerry. I didn't think you'd want to come.'

'Well, no. I don't.'

'So. Just as well then.'

'What time is he coming for you?'

'I said we'd see him at the pier for half eight.'

'Half eight! You'll never make it out your beds for half eight.'

'Yeah we will. Jackie's got a boat and rods and stuff, he's going to take us out. We've to bring a packed lunch.'

I didn't know Jackie had a boat. He'd never offered to take me out in it.

I got the boys up at half seven and gave them a cooked breakfast. I made up a tin with loads of sandwiches and cakes, plenty for them and Jackie as well.

'What time will you be back, Steven?'

'I'm not sure Mum. Shouldn't be too late.'

As I waved them off down the hill I shouted after them.

'Tell Jackie he's welcome to join us for dinner if he wants, nothing special.'

'Nothing special? It'll be a full-on fish tea, fresh from the sea, and I'll be providing it.'

I ran around cleaning up. I didn't want Jackie to see the house a mess but I didn't do the make-up thing. Jackie had made it plain he wasn't interested. Hopefully he'd get the message that he was quite safe with the boys here and realize that I only wanted to be friends.

The boys were back at four, with three fish each, but no Jackie.

'What do you make of these beauties then, eh? I told you I was bringing home dinner, didn't I?'

The boys were so chuffed with themselves they rattled on for ten minutes, boasting about how they caught them.

'Oh, and Jackie says thanks very much Mum, but he can't make dinner. He's got a booking for the boat later on.'

So that was why I hadn't seen much of him, he wasn't a gardener, he was a sailor. He probably had a girl in every Highland port.

'He gave me this to give you.'

Steven produced from his rucksack the bottle of malt whisky I'd left in Jackie's coal bunker.

'He says thanks very much but he doesn't drink. It would be wasted lying in his house, he said. It won't be wasted here though, eh Mum? This'll come in handy for celebrating the catch.'

'So Jackie rents out his boat to fishing parties, is that it? How much did he charge you?'

'Nothing, it was free. He's a brilliant guy. He said seeing as we're local we can come any time, but it only runs from Easter to September. You want to see some of the fish he's caught, big conger eels and everything man, he's got photos of them.'

I sighed as I got out the whisky shot glasses and the frying pan. I'd learned more about Jackie second-hand from Steven than I probably ever would from the man himself.

Steven and Gerry went fishing another twice with Jackie before they went home, but I never saw hide nor hair of him. I comforted myself with the thought that at least he was being kind to my son, which meant he couldn't completely hate me.

I was all jolly when I took them to the station, I waved and laughed as the train pulled out. On the way back I was so blinded by tears I had to stop the car. When I was helping him pack I'd asked Steven what he thought of Inverfaughie. It took him a while to answer.

'It's OK,' he said.

'OK to live here, or OK but not special?'

'Dunno.'

I took to my bed and thought of Polly through the wall. Rebecca came in for me after school but I told her I'd walked Bouncer already. She came the next day as well.

'Sorry pet, I'm not really up to it today, I think I've got a bug. I took him round the garden for ten minutes at lunchtime.'

'Oh please Trixie, just down the hill and back, please. I've been looking forward to it all day.'

I pulled my jeans on over my jammies and marched down the hill and back up again.

'I'll ask Mummy if you can join her group if you want, Trixie.'

It suddenly dawned on me how rude I was being. I

hadn't spoken a word since we left the house and we were nearly home.

'Och I'm awful sorry pet, I didn't mean to ignore you, I'm just a bit fed up since Steven went away.'

'You could join Mummy's Imhag group. It's for ladies who are fed up. Mummy's having them over next week, it's her turn and me and Michaela have to play quietly upstairs.'

'Imhag? What does it mean?'

'I don't know, Mummy says it's for people who have problems but I think it's something to do with health. Daddy said that you must have piss-poor mental health to bring a bunch of loonies into your home.'

Mental health, Inverfaughie Mental Health Association Group? No, not association, awareness, that was it. That was all I needed, to sit around with a bunch of saddos moaning about how miserable life in the Highlands was. They were probably English anyway. Well I was made of sterner stuff, OK I was a bit down because Steven had gone, but I wasn't mentally ill.

'No, I don't think so Rebecca. But I think it's great that your mummy is doing something about getting better.'

At Rebecca's age everything showed on her face and she couldn't hide her disappointment.

'Anyway, now that we're out, why don't we continue on down to the village and get sweets at Jenny's?'

That cheered her up and her concern for my mental health was a wake-up call to me. I'd need to keep a check on my moods. I must remain cheerful, keep my head down, get on with it.

Chapter 18

It was getting into the summer season and still I couldn't decide about running the B. and B. I was too busy with the garden. I found a garden centre out by Thessie and I pestered the man for ages with questions about what I should plant. I ran around filling my trolley until I realized how much it was all going to cost. The poor wee guy was crestfallen when I went to the cash desk with a few packets of seeds.

The weather was warmer, warm enough now to spend as long as I liked outside without getting frostbite. Jenny told me to take Walter's old garden furniture and give it a lick of paint. There was still no word on when he was getting out of hospital, but Jenny was always thinking about him. I brought four picnic chairs and a table from Walter's and, with Rebecca and Michaela's help, painted them bright yellow. It was lovely sitting there, with no mist and hardly any cloud, the views were spectacular.

Now that I had the furniture, and the weather was nice, I decided to have my dinner alfresco. The girls had gone home for the night to follow their usual routine: homework, telly, then bed. I fancied something special for a change so I defrosted a steak. Fried mushrooms and onions gave it a proper steakhouse feel and I thought to hell with poverty, and opened a bottle of wine. It took ages to prepare and when everything was ready I took it out to my lovely rustic garden.

I hadn't even sat down to eat when the midgies started. They hadn't bothered me much until now but I wasn't usually in the garden this late in the day. This was the midging hour. I was walking to and fro with the cutlery and the HP, but the minute I stopped I could feel them on my forehead. I rubbed my head and flicked the tiny black specks away. It wasn't often that I took the trouble to cook a proper dinner so I wasn't going to be put off by some tiddly wee flies. I went back inside and got my secret weapon.

The citronella candle described itself as 'insect repellent' and cost seven quid. Except for a three-inch exclusion zone around the candle itself, it didn't work. The midgies kept on coming. I tucked my trousers into my socks and pulled my sleeves down. The smell from the candle made my eyes water.

While I was moving the midgies couldn't get me, it was staying still that was the problem. I got up and walked around the table, popping mushrooms or a tottie into my mouth every time I passed my plate. After a few circuits they fell away. Midgies were so small that a few times round a four-foot table must have been equivalent to a thousand-mile trip for them, ha! Chuffed with the successful ruse, I sat down to enjoy my meal.

But I had mistaken retreat for reconnaissance. They had only been marshalling their forces; now, team-handed, they redoubled their efforts to bite me. This was a full-scale attack.

I'd fooled them once, I'd do it again. I'd just keep circling the table. You had to be hardy in the Highlands and I rose to the challenge, pitting my wits against nature. If I kept moving I'd still get the views and the great outdoors as well as my dinner, and I'd burn calories into the bargain. Stopping to cut my steak might have proved problematic, but on the spur of the moment I invented an anti-midge manoeuvre. While I cut with one hand, I whirled the other arm like a windmill. That worked reasonably well but I could feel them again at my ankles, I had to stay mobile. By now I was moving at quite a pace around the table. The arm-whirling alone didn't offer full body protection. I was getting breathless and my dinner was getting cold. I needed a seat and something to keep the midgies away from my legs. I brought the candle back into use, putting it on the ground between my legs. Immediately I felt an uncomfortable heat in my groin. To avoid singeing I was obliged to flap my thighs.

Almost by accident I had hit on a workable solution. Simultaneous thigh-flapping and arm-whirling was the answer. This permitted sitting down and left one hand free to cut up food. I'm not saying it was relaxing, but the Highland midge had not got the better of me.

Unfortunately, that night, sated with steak and the full bottle of wine by way of a victory celebration, I forgot to close my bedroom window. Next morning I'd been eaten alive. I looked as if I'd been carpet-bombed, my face, neck and wrists scattered with pustulating sores. If I'd known the midgies were so determined I would have opened a vein and left out a saucer for them. They could have queued up in an orderly fashion and drunk their fill of my blood. At least that way I wouldn't have had such an allergic reaction. The bites made me bloated and scabby. Over the next few days I coped as best I could with antihistamines and calamine lotion, but one particularly nasty bite over my eye became swollen.

Jenny said I should see Dr Robertson. Maybe she was right, but my previous career made me reluctant to go anywhere near doctors. I was pleased to have someone, even Jenny, so concerned for my health. I was feeling pretty sorry for myself, it was good to have company.

'Och no, honestly Jenny I'm fine,' I said, although I was nearly blinded by the bite over my eye.

'But it looks awful sore. Och you're a brave soldier Trixie, so you are! And do you know who you put me in mind of?'

I shook my scabby misshapen head.

'That, what do you call him,' she waved her hands in front of her face, 'him in the church, och what's his name?'

I would have liked to be able to help her out but I didn't know which particular cleric she meant. There was that guy who'd been the bishop's envoy and ended up in captivity for years, he was pretty brave, but as far as I knew he wasn't actually in the church himself. She might mean Nelson Mandela but he wasn't a church-man either. It could be Joan of Arc but she was a woman. I tried to think of a famously stoic member of the clergy.

'Och,' Jenny clicked her fingers and smiled, 'I know it now. Quasimodo!'

The midgie bites had a bad effect on me. I didn't want to go over the door. It would be just like the thing for me to bump into Jackie when I had a face like a pizza. Apart from brief sorties down to Jenny's when I knew the shop would be quiet, the plukes made me a virtual prisoner. Even mad Polly was getting out more than me. The last few mornings she'd taken the girls out to meet the school bus.

Rebecca was beside herself with excitement. Mummy was having an Imhag meeting, and everyone would bring biscuits. It was a rule. She and Michaela would feast on KitKats for a week. But even better than that, the two girls were being shipped off to Ailsa's for a sleepover now that they were friends again. Everyone had a social life, except me.

Rebecca was on at me to go to her mum's meeting but I demurred. Just my luck, I thought, the one time anything happens around here and I'm not fit to be seen in public. I watched the Imhaggers arrive. Three cars drew up: a Volvo, a Lexus and a wee Audi sports car. Was it just posh women who went mad? Only posh women joined awareness groups, visiting each other's houses, being *aware*. When it had all gone quiet I took Bouncer out for his evening wee.

I supposed I could have gone in but I had three good reasons: one, I wasn't looking my best and I was a firm believer in first impressions. Two, the only biscuits I had were half a packet of soggy ginger snaps left over from when the boys were here, and three, what was I going to say? 'Hello, my name's Trixie and I'm aff ma heid.' It wasn't even true. I was a fraud. From outside I could only hear the faint sound of murmuring with the occasional short blast of one person's manic laugh. That was reason number four.

I remembered from drug training that it was in-advisable to take drink with antihistamines. It could potentiate the effects of the alcohol. One glass of wine and I'd be fleeing. The way things were going, that would be a result.

I awoke the next morning to a snuffling sound at the end of the bed. Through an antihistamine haze I was aware that Bouncer was holding a dirty white fluffy thing in his mouth. He was bringing me a gift. The full horror of the situation became apparent when I realized that it was the body of Smidgy Rabbit.

The rabbit's legs were sticking up in the air and his mud-spattered fur was dirtying the duvet. Fucking hell,

189

what was I going to do? How the hell did Bouncer get into Smidgy's cage? Bouncer could be very expressive when he wanted to be. He managed to look surprised and deeply wounded when I screamed at him. He took the huff, slinking out of the room, leaving me holding the rabbit.

After I chained Bouncer in the kitchen I made every effort to revive Smidgy. I shook him, I poured whisky down his throat, I blew into his slack mouth. I pulled the wires out the toaster and tried defibrillating him. Nothing worked. After my big slip-up with Bouncer I had to be sure that Smidgy was definitely one hundred per cent dead. No pulse, no breathing, no condensation on the mirror. Nothing.

In case he really was alive but just shy – I knew rabbits were shy, I'd seen *Watership Down* – I put him in front of the fire and waited in the kitchen while Bouncer farted and whined. Three quarters of an hour later Smidgy's body had grown a lot bigger. The heat was causing some kind of chemical reaction, and still he hadn't moved. I had to face the facts, Smidgy wasn't coming back.

Next door's car was gone and the house was quiet so they must have gone to pick up the girls from the sleepover. I could just stick him back in the hutch, make it look like he'd died of natural causes. Roger would be suspicious but he couldn't prove anything. I examined Smidgy for bites but although he was filthy, there wasn't a mark on him. That idiot Bouncer must have dragged him through the dirt. To stand any chance of getting away with it I had to clean him up.

Most of the dirt I managed to brush off with my fingers but his fur was grubby so I gave him a quick shampoo. I set the hairdryer to cold, I didn't want Smidgy's body getting any bigger, there was always the danger that he might explode. Laying him across my knee I gently fluffed up his fur. He scrubbed up lovely. On the pretext of hanging out a washing, I sneaked Smidgy back into the hutch. Apart from being a bit swollen, he just looked as if he was sleeping.

It would look more suspicious if I wasn't at home when they found him, so I stayed where I was. It wasn't long before I heard the kids wailing and howling in the garden. I had to have a wee steadier before I could face them, particularly Rebecca, but I stuck to vodka so they wouldn't smell it. Pretending to bring in the washing, I popped my head over the fence.

'Morning! Everything all right?'

'No. Actually it isn't,' said Roger, his face tripping him.

'Oh no, it's not the rabbit, is it?'

I had to mention it because Roger was squatting at the hutch with his head in his hands.

'Yes, it is actually, Trixie. Smidgy died yesterday. We buried him yesterday afternoon. The kids were just getting over it and some sick bastard has dug him up and put him back in the hutch.'

Kids recover quickly. A few days later Rebecca was as right as rain. My spots were beginning to clear up so our long walks were back on. I asked her if she was OK about Smidgy.

'Och aye,' she said.

It was funny to hear these words through her English accent.

'Daddy asked if we wanted another rabbit but I said no. I think it's cruel to keep animals locked up. And anyway, I always have to clean the hutch.'

Oh well, I thought, things had turned out not so bad after all.

'Daddy's a bastard.'

'Oh Rebecca, don't swear, it's not nice. Why is he a bastard?'

'He says we're not to have any more sleepovers at Ailsa's.'

'Why not?'

'And Mummy's not to go to the Imhag meetings but she says he can't stop her. He says he's not having any more lunatics in his house, one is enough to cope with. Daddy says a person who would put a dead rabbit in the hutch needs locking up.'

I patted her wee thin shoulder and resolved to buy her and Michaela a present the next time I went to Inverness.

'But the worst thing is, he won't drive me to my guitar lesson. He says he can't trust Mummy alone in the house and he won't leave Michaela.'

'Oh but Rebecca, you can't miss your lesson. Tell Daddy I'll look after Michaela.'

'I already asked him but he said no. I don't think Daddy likes you, Trixie. He doesn't like anybody. He's a bastard. He makes Mummy cry.'

'OK, OK. Look, why don't I take you to the guitar lesson? Would he be all right with that?'

'Could we go in your car? Can Bouncer come too?'

Roger might have been a bastard and he definitely didn't like me, but even he didn't want Rebecca to miss her guitar lesson. He agreed that I would take her. Guitar lessons were with a man who lived about four miles the other side of the village. When I dropped her off Rebecca insisted that I bring Bouncer in to meet everybody. Her pal Ailsa was there along with some other kids from school. Jan, the guitar teacher, was very friendly. He didn't seem to mind that the lesson was being disrupted by a dog bouncing all over the giggling kids and their oversized guitars.

Jan, pronounced *Yan* apparently, wasn't a local. He

had a strange accent that might have been Dutch or South African. When I managed to get Bouncer under control Jan said I could wait for Rebecca if I wanted, but I felt daft hanging around. When I came back for her all the other kids had gone.

'Rebecca told me you volunteered to bring her to the lesson.'

Jan was smiling at me.

'I'm glad. She is very talented you know, Trixie, a natural musician.'

I was smiling too. Jan was like me, an incomer. When he said the word *glad* his accent made it sound like *gled*, like a Glaswegian. I was gled too.

The exams were upon us and Steven was on the phone every night. I was forced to admit that staying with Nettie had been great for his studying. If he wasn't studying he had to sit and listen to her boff on about the damp running down the walls or her sore ears, so swotting was infinitely preferable. Despite it, Steven was suffering a crisis of confidence.

'Mum, I'm not going in, I'm only making a fool of myself in there. I won't be able to write anything but my name.'

'Steven. You'll be fine. What is the worst that can happen, eh? It's not the end of the world if you fail an exam. You'll still have your pals and your dad and me. And Auntie Nettie.'

'And that's supposed to motivate me?'

'You know what I mean. You won't have lost any-thing. If you fail you can appeal or resit or leave it alone. You have choices. You've done the work son, I know you can do it. This is only exam nerves. Go in Steven, eh? Go in and give it your best shot, nobody can ask any more of you than that. We love you no matter what.'

All day my arse was knitting socks, I couldn't sit down, couldn't go out in case something happened and he phoned. Eventually the phone rang.

'A total scoosh case. I checked my answers with everybody when we came out and I reckon I've done OK.'

'Oh that's great Steven, well done son, I was sure you'd do well.'

'Yeah, so was I.'

This was pretty much the pattern, or the pattren, for the rest of the exams: a tense insecure run-up followed by Steven bumming about how well he thought he'd done. The boy was becoming a man.

Chapter 19

I had a bit of bad news. Walter was getting better, they were letting him out of hospital. I supposed this was good, Walter was on the mend, but also bad, I'd have to give back the gardening tools and furniture. And Bouncer.

I had a phone call from Jenny. This was surprising, she'd never called before; I had no idea she had my number. Would I come with her to the hospital to pick up Walter? I readily agreed, it would be a wee day out of the village for a change. She had keys for Walter's house, she was going to get the place cleaned up and ready for him. I said I'd help. I'd only ever peeked in the back windows of Walter's house, this way I'd be able to get a good nosey inside.

Jenny was a wee dynamo, she had twenty years on me but she put me to shame the way she got stuck into Walter's housework. I hardly had a chance to look around. Move along there, I thought, nothing to see here, no trophies from exotic places or priceless antiques, no evidence of Walter's scandalous dissolute life. Just an old man's house with worn-out carpets and chairs. Was my life so empty these days that I had to get vicarious thrills from snooping in an old man's house? Instead of this respectable shabbiness, would I have been tickled to find something seedy? I was ashamed of myself and, alongside Jenny, scrubbed Walter's house from top to bottom.

Walter looked half dead when we picked him up at the hospital. He was quiet and humble but, despite his long stay in hospital, he seemed uncomfortable accepting help. Bouncer, recognizing him right away, tried to jump on him and had to be restrained. He was far too eager for my liking, with a lot of indecorous panting and whining. Walter tried to match the dog's enthusiasm but he looked scared.

Not usually one to cast things up, I couldn't help but think about everything I'd done for that dog. All the walks and the biscuits and the letting him up on the couch, even covering for him when he exhumed Smidgy. Maybe this was the real Bouncer I was seeing. Maybe he'd always felt this way about me, desperate to get away but humouring me for fear I'd try to bash his brains out again. It was just as well he couldn't talk. As Bouncer lunged forward again attempting to lick Walter's face, I gave his lead a good tug. Trying to dub me in, his yelp was a wild exaggeration. A drama queen *and* a grass.

Matron Jenny took charge right away. She made Walter comfortable in the back seat and got in beside him. As unpaid taxi driver, I was stuck with Bouncer in the front with me.

'Now Trixie, we're in no hurry home. Walter hasn't been out for a while so let's just enjoy the countryside. None of your Grand Pricks stunts on the way back now.'

It was true I'd driven fast on the way there, but it was Jenny who'd nagged me to step on it.

She treated Walter like a china doll. They muttered away in their sing-song Highland accent and I could hardly make out a word. Jenny had draped a white hospital blanket around Walter's shoulders. The old guy was away with it, maybe doped with painkillers or just resigned to the ignominy. He had the sort of beneficent expression I'd seen on pictures of the Pope. From my rear-view mirror, with his white hair and almost transparent skin, Walter looked like an angel. I saw Jenny lift his hand and kiss it. She kissed his palm. Not in a kiss-it-better type of way. In a slow sad way. And then she laid her head down, her face cradled in the palm of his hand. As if she was a wee girl. It was nearly an hour before she spoke to me again.

'Trixie, would you mind making a wee detour on our way home?'

'Not at all, just let me know where you want to go. You've picked a fantastic day to get out of hospital, Walter.'

Walter gave me a papal nod and smiled, keeping his energy and conversation for Jenny.

Unlike my last excursion, the sky was clear and the views were amazing. Jenny directed me to take a wee side road that didn't seem to lead anywhere. There was nothing signposted, it was a road to nowhere. The single track wound up and over a few hills before petering out at the edge of a wee lochan. I thought we must have come the wrong way but Jenny was pleased when we stopped.

'Oh look, there's the boathouse! See? I told you!'

'Many nights I dreamed of here,' said Walter.

It was a simple thing to say. He said the words quietly, privately, like a prayer. This place which, to me, was a miserable boggy midge-ridden lochside, was dreamed of. *Many nights I dreamed of here*. I don't know if it was his accent or the sadness in his voice but it sounded like poetry. We all sat in silence, even Bouncer, for what seemed like a long time.

When we arrived at his house and brought in his

stuff, Walter tottered from room to room. Jenny wanted to go with him but he refused. As he passed through the rooms picking up ornaments, he smiled. Each time he returned to the kitchen where Jenny and I were sorting out the lunch, Walter looked better. With every room he got taller, straighter, had more colour in his cheeks. This was a different man from the one who was led out of hospital with a blanket round his shoulders.

Not until Walter had concluded his tour of inspection did I let Bouncer off the lead. He bounced and romped from room to room like he owned the place, sniffing everything. As we ate lunch at the kitchen table Bouncer, the traitor, sat at Walter's feet. I was amazed at the healthy appetite Walter displayed. Back in his own environment, his recovery appeared remarkable. After a hearty lunch of mince and doughballs he cheerfully excused himself and went to the toilet.

'That mince was lovely but if you'll excuse me, ladies, nature calls.'

He was gone a long time.

'D'you think he's OK in there? He's been away a helluva long time.'

'It's his condition,' Jenny whispered, 'for God's sake don't mention it when he comes back.'

What did she take me for? As if I would say *just been for a shite then have you Walter? And how are your diseased old innards?* While he was away Jenny brought up the subject I had been dreading, that of Bouncer.

'Walter looks grand but that will wear off, he'll tire quickly. He's to take it easy. You didn't know him then but at one time Walter was a big strong man. You can see for yourself how weak he is, Bouncer will knock him down like a skittle if he jumps on him. And as for walking the dog, he's not fit.'

I carried on cutting my doughballs, saying nothing.

'Oh go on now Trixie. It'll only be for another few weeks until Walter gets back on his feet. You can keep the gardening stuff for now if you want. He'll not be doing much in the way of gardening for the next wee while. I'll get Jackie to come up and keep the place in trim.'

Mid doughball chew, I drew her a dirty look. She knew what it was about. She'd ask Jackie for Walter but she wouldn't ask him for me.

'Och come on Trixie, you're a fit and healthy young woman. It's done you the world of good doing your own garden and you know it. And having the dog. I didn't like to say, but what a difference it's made to your figure.'

'What do you mean?'

'Toned your muscles, lifted your bum, that's what I mean. Look at you! It's halfway up your back!'

If she'd left it at that I would have been quite chuffed, but, typical Jenny, she didn't.

'Not that I was looking, I'm not that way inclined, but when you first came to Inverfaughie your arse was sweeping the ground. Sorry, och, I never say the right thing but Trixie, please. Please please please will you take the dog?'

'I will, for Walter's sake.'

'Och Trixie you're good-hearted, I don't care what anybody says.'

'How's Trix?'

'Hey, don't get cheeky, it's Mum to you, pal. So, tell me about the job. CEO is it?'

'JWO actually, Junior Warehouse Operative, and don't knock it, it's five quid an hour.'

'That's brilliant, Steven. Good on you.'

'And I can work all the hours I want. They can't get enough of me. Gerry works there as well.'

199

'Suits me, that means you'll have your own cash when you come up. I won't have to provide the refreshment allowance for your nightly trips down the Calley like last time.'

'Well, actually Mum, you won't have to anyway.'

I knew it, I knew it. I'd tried to keep it light but I knew the minute he said he'd got a job.

'Don't tell me, are *you* maybe going to give *me* an allowance?'

I was making it harder for him but I couldn't help myself.

'Mum, what happened was, when I went for the interview Gary, the supervisor, said he needed somebody for six weeks. I had to promise or else he wouldn't give me the job.'

'Och well, just don't let them work you too hard. You can still come up for the weekend, can't you? You can bring Gerry, anyone you like. Come any time.'

'I'm awful sorry Mum.'

'It's OK. Honest.'

I felt numb when I put the phone down, an absence of any emotion. He had been such a clingy baby. He bawled if I left the room. If I went to the toilet he stood outside, anxious in case I should climb out the window and down the drainpipe.

Steven phoned every night for a week after that. Guilt made him very attentive. We spent hours chatting and making each other laugh. I told him about Smidgy and he did a brilliant impersonation of Nettie in full flow. But although he joked about her, Steven seemed genuinely fond of the old dear.

'God love her, she could do with a holiday you know, Mum.'

'Not with me she couldn't.'

'I'd feel bad coming up to Inverfaughie again without

her. She moaned for weeks about it the last time. I felt really guilty.'

'Just tell her there's no room.'

'She's not daft. She knows it's a B. and B., you told her yourself when you were bumming about it. She's not likely to forget.'

'But Steven, she does my head in!'

'Could she not come up with me? One weekend wouldn't kill you, Trix. I feel bad, man.'

'Oh for God's sake! What's this? You can't come unless Nettie comes, is that the deal? Right, OK, she can come, but she's your responsibility. And don't bloody well call me Trix again! You're not too old for a skelp, you know, boy!'

Steven laughed.

'Mum, I'm sixteen and you're still coming away with this patter, *you're not too old*. When will I be too old for a skelp?'

Automatically I gave him the stock reply I had used since he was wee, my euphemism for never.

'When you grow a beard.'

Steven found this even more hilarious.

When they got off the train the first thing I noticed was their luggage. Steven and Gerry had a sports bag each, Nettie had a suitcase on wheels. The next thing I noticed was the bum fluff on Steven's chin. A beard. I had to laugh. This time I got a hug before Bouncer, which was an improvement.

'Oh there you are Trisha love,' Nettie babbled. 'Thanks very much for inviting me, I won't be any trouble. You look terrific! Country life certainly suits you.'

I hoped the look I drew her would convey my distaste for such transparent flattery. She was here for the weekend, then she was out on her ear.

I had a funny feeling that when we got to the car Nettie would be in the front with me while the boys took the back seat. That would set the tone for the weekend, the lads *larging it* down the Calley and the old woman lumbered with the even older old woman. I wasn't wrong.

Chapter 20

It was all go back at Harrosie. I had new neighbours on the other side. Three women were unloading their car into the house next door that had so far lain empty. I had a good idea it wasn't the owners, Clive and Helen from Sussex. These women must be renting the house for a holiday. They seemed friendly enough, waving and smiling as we passed them. I didn't get time to investigate further, I had to get Nettie and the boys settled in the house.

'Oh you've got the place lovely!' said Nettie.

'Well I haven't really done anything, it was like this when I moved in.'

'Och no but you've got all your own wee bits and bobs about the place, that's what makes it home. Look! I remember when that picture was taken!' Nettie had picked up the old photograph of the wee girl from the mantelpiece.

'I don't think so Nettie. I found that photo here. I just stuck it up there because I felt sorry for the wee soul.'

'Och your bum! I went with Elsie to the studio. The photographer had to work for his money that day, I'll tell you. He was running about with a big golliwog doll, wagging it on his head, trying to make you laugh, but you wouldn't smile for him. It was strange because you were always a smiley baby. He kept shouting *look at the golly dolly!* He was very arty. *Look at the golly dolly!'*

The old dear had finally lost it. At that moment, when I should feel sorry for her, I hated her. Steven had chosen this senile old woman over me.

Rebecca and Michaela were in like a shot as soon as they saw my car was back. Rebecca's face was red when she told Steven she liked his beard. Michaela related the strange mystery of the resurrected rabbit and although the boys sniggered, they didn't spill the beans.

'Rebecca, I saw people going into the house next door when we came in. Have you seen them? Are they here on holiday d'you know?'

'Aye,' said Rebecca, 'Daddy says we've not to bother them.'

All day I was dying to get a chance to go next door but my guests had no sooner had their lunch than they wanted taken out.

'Come on Mum, we're only here for the weekend and it's a cracking day, let's not waste it. We want to see the sights don't we, Nettie my old love?'

Nettie giggled like a schoolgirl. *My old love.* She didn't know when she was being had. Steven was only entertaining his sniggering pal Gerry.

'Why don't we take the boat ride round the islands? You would enjoy that, wouldn't you Sweetcakes?'

There was no end to Steven's inventiveness when it came to affectionate names for Nettie. Throughout the weekend there was Dollface, Sweetheart, Candypants, Tiger, Gorgeous and Sweet Pea. He even called her Hun. As in Honey I presumed, and not as in the football refrain *Go home ya Hun*. It was easier to keep my mouth shut and do as I was told. Despite the fact that I had new neighbours I hadn't even met yet, we went on the boat trip.

It was a beautiful bright day. I hadn't brought sunglasses and had to constantly shield my eyes from the sun glinting off the water like thousands of mirror pieces. At the kiosk Steven wanted to buy tickets for me and Nettie, even though they were twelve quid a head. Automatically I pulled out my purse, it was a nice gesture but it was too much for Steven to shell out. While Steven was speaking to the ticket man Nettie put her hand on my arm.

'He's working, let the boy get it,' she whispered.

Making sure Gerry was watching, Steven handed me my ticket as casually as he could.

'There you go Mum, my treat.'

'Thanks son.'

Steven crooked both arms, one for Nettie and one for me, and affected an old-fashioned manner.

'Shall we go in?'

Once aboard, the boys went up on deck while Hun and I were parked inside out of the wind. Nettie did everything she could to please me. She went and got us coffees and bars of chocolate from the buffet bar.

'That's a wee special coffee. Just to say thanks again for inviting me, hen.'

The coffee had whisky in it, loads of it.

'Cheers Nettie. It's me who should be thanking you, for taking Steven in.'

'Not at all Trisha, it is a pleasure to have him. Can I just tell you that he's a credit to you. Never done talking about you, he told me how you stood up to those people stealing the plants. Steven thinks the world of you. You've done a smashing job bringing up that boy.'

That warmed me as much as the whisky.

'I hear the kids calling you Trixie, I like it. Can I call you Trixie too?'

'Only if I can call you Sweetcakes.'

'Oh that boy of yours! He's full of carry-on. I know he's at it but it's a good laugh isn't it?'

She wasn't such a bad old stick really. Sometimes she could be so like Mum.

Steven rushed down the stairs towards us.

'Hurry up or you'll miss them. Dolphins!'

He bolted for the deck but then remembered and rushed back to help Nettie on the stairs. Nettie was right, he was a lovely boy, a credit to me. Steven's face was flushed with excitement as he hustled us upstairs towards the dolphins. He might have a beard but he was still a wee boy, my wee boy.

On the way home, Steven informed us that we were going on a distillery visit tomorrow.

'And if you're good, I'll take you out to lunch.'

None of us had ever been to a distillery but Steven was confident that we'd enjoy it.

'They take you round and show you how they make the whisky, and Nettie Hun, you'll like this bit, they give you a wee half.'

'Oh, that sounds smashing,' said Nettie. 'Can we go, Trixie?'

'I don't see why not.'

We were all knackered by the time we got back, but as I got the dinner on, the boys hit the bathroom. Nettie pottered round the kitchen helping me.

'I hope they photaes turn out, it'll be just like the thing if they don't,' said Nettie. 'Oh that was a dream come true, so it was! I've seen dolphins on the telly obviously, but to see them right up beside us like that!'

'Och you see all kinds of wildlife up here, every day. See that road outside the house, Nettie? Two nights ago there was a big stag, with antlers out to here, standing on the road, just standing there for ages. I sat on the couch and watched him, it was fantastic. Better than any wildlife programme.'

206

'But what was he doing out there?'

'D'you know, I've no idea. Maybe he was waiting for a bus!'

At that moment Steven walked in wearing ironed jeans and howfing of Paco Rabanne.

'Och that's just stupid!' he said. 'Everybody knows the bus doesn't stop here!'

It was quite nice, us all sitting down to eat together, and we were ready for our dinner. The lads were going off down the Calley as usual but for once I didn't mind being left. Nettie and I would just settle down and watch telly, there was a good film on at half eight. As I was clearing the plates Rebecca came in the back door.

'Trixie, the ladies next door want you to go in and see them.'

'They want *me* to go in? What for?'

'I don't know.'

I sorted Nettie out with a cup of tea and a plate of home baking on her lap and she was quite happy.

'Nettie, I'm just popping next door a minute with Rebecca, I'll not be long.'

I wondered what they wanted me for, surely if they had a problem with the boiler or anything they would have asked Roger. But this was a good chance to meet them and get a nosey at the house.

They were dead nice. Nurses they were, Julie, Eileen and Sarah, Glaswegians, working out in Saudi. Rebecca had insisted that we take Bouncer with us, and when they saw him they made a big fuss. They had obviously taken a shine to Rebecca as well. It was great to be back in Scotland they said, see a bit of greenery. They were here for a week and were going to make the most of it. I told them about the dolphins and they said they'd take the trip the next day.

They were going that night to a ceilidh, they'd seen a

poster in the tourist office for one in the hotel at Cullsnoddy, about twenty-five miles north.

'Is it any good?' the small one, Julie, asked.

'I'm sorry, I couldn't tell you, I've never been.'

'Och let's go anyway,' said Eileen, 'there's a spare seat in the car if you want to come with us, Trixie.'

Typical, I thought. I've been in Inverfaughie for months and the first time I get an invite, I can't go.

'I really would love to come, I haven't been out for months, but I've got my family up this weekend.'

They were fine about it and said another time then. As I was leaving I remembered what I'd come in for.

'Rebecca said you wanted to see me about something?'

The girls looked at each other and then back at me.

'No,' said Sarah, 'Rebecca said you wanted to see *us*.'

I looked at Rebecca and she stared at the floor, her face turning crimson. God love the wee soul, she was networking on my behalf.

Nettie was sitting where I'd left her, quite the thing. The lads were upstairs getting ready, they had a CD on, up full blast. I had been knackered earlier but now, now I was full of beans. I couldn't sit down. I tidied round Nettie and then moved to the kitchen, banging the dishes about as I cleaned. The music the boys were playing was pumping me up. Rebecca must have sensed my mood because she stayed in the living room with Nettie. Bouncer gave me a wide berth too.

'You've become a dab hand at the home baking,' said Nettie as she tottered into the kitchen, 'Rebecca and me have eaten the whole lot. Where do you want me to put my plate?'

'Just leave it on the table thanks Nettie.'

I had my arms up to my elbows in the washing bowl and my back to her.

'Och I'm fair wabbit with all that fresh air today, so I

208

am. I cannae concentrate on the telly with all that's going on in this house. Those boys playing their records and you banging about in here.'

Outraged, I spun round. Nettie, standing at the table, had her back to me. I gritted my teeth so hard it hurt. I considered stoving the selfish old cow's head in with the pot I was scrubbing.

'I'd be happier on my own in here tonight. I cannae hear the telly right if somebody else is with me, it's my ears you know. It'd be nice to get a bit of peace and quiet, get the place to myself for a wee while.'

My mouth fell open in amazement with an involuntary squawk. Rebecca. She had nobbled her. I was astonished by the implausible story about her ears, but what was remarkable was that Rebecca, at age eight and a half, had trained Nettie, a woman nearly ten times her age, to circumvent the whole guilt trip, giving me the opportunity to go out with a clear conscience. After talking Nettie through the TV remote control and where the tea bags were kept, I ran upstairs and got my kit on.

I couldn't remember the last time I'd had my good clothes on. I howked everything out the wardrobe and threw it on the bed. There was a bit of colour in my arms and legs from all the gardening I'd been doing. This would be a perfect opportunity to show off my tan in a strappy wee dress. Maybe I was getting old or had lived in the Highlands too long, but everything I tried on, everything I would have once considered *pulling apparel*, felt indecently scanty. I decided to play safe with a pair of smart trousers and a wee top. It was a ceilidh I was going to, not a lap-dancing club. I hardly thought then that it was going to be such a night of revels and revelations.

Washed, dressed, perfumed, made-up and bejewelled, I stood at the nurses' front door.

'Room inside for a wee one?'

Chapter 21

The nurses were ages with myself, maybe a bit younger. The big four oh being such a sensitive number, it wasn't the sort of thing I could ask directly. Without giving them the full inquisition I was able to find out that they were single and had no kids. I got the idea that they were career girls, and party girls. Big drinkers anyway. Before we left, except for Julie who was driving, we all sank two large voddies.

Clotheswise, they were covering all eventualities. They wore hip-skimming jeans and skirts with back-less tops under fleeces and cagoules. They even had balaclavas. Haven't adjusted yet to the climate, they said, as they drank long vodkas in their woolly hoods.

'I hope Culsnoddy hotel is warmer than this house,' Julie said.

I doubted it. The house was bloody roasting, they had the central heating on full blast.

I tuned the radio to Inverfaughie fm in the car and we caught the mood, heuching and cheuching on the way there. It was disappointing when we arrived at the hotel. After we'd paid our five pounds each, we discovered that we were the only people who weren't with a coach party. There was a coach tour from England, one from Holland and one from Germany.

Most of them were a good bit older, pensioners really. They sat at big circular tables waiting for the band.

It didn't seem to put the girls off. We hardly had our coats off and Sarah was up at the bar getting the first round in. I told them that I admired their spirit, on holiday to the Highlands and making the best of it. I felt as if I had said the wrong thing because they were very quick to assure me how much they loved it.

'When we're in Saudi all we think about is Scotland: Glasgow and the Highlands,' Eileen said, and the others agreed. 'You get sick of the sunshine, you know, there's more to life. There's home.'

I thought they were about to burst out greeting so I proposed a toast. 'To home,' I said, raising my glass.

'To home.'

I took to calling them the Three Nurseteers and subsequent toasts were based around the *one for all and all for one* theme. Julie only had one drink seeing as she was driving, but the rest of us were quite well on when I noticed a man setting up a microphone.

The guy looked amazing, he had grey-white hair, loads of it, pulled into a tight ponytail on top of his head with curls reaching down to his shoulder. Although he must have been fifty-fiveish, he had incredibly bright eyes, like a baby. Not exactly a handsome man, but very striking. In full Highland dress, he could have just stepped out of a Scotch House catalogue, he was that clean-looking. He introduced himself, said his name was Spider, and welcomed everyone.

Then he said that due to circumstances beyond anyone's control the band were unavoidably detained on Lewis and were unable to be with us this evening. I don't think the tour-party people really got this, because they didn't seem to mind or want their fivers back.

'Not to worry, friends,' said Spider through the mic,

'in true Highland fashion we'll make our own entertainment.'

He pulled out a boran, the only musical instrument in the whole place, and banged away at it while he sang a song in Gaelic.

'This is ridiculous,' I whispered to the girls, 'there's not a man under sixty here and now the band aren't coming. There's literally no talent.'

We were giggling and whispering between ourselves that we should go back to Inverfaughie, there at least we wouldn't have to sit in polite silence. The song ended and Spider sang another, the whole time with his bright eyes boring into us, disapproving our whispering. He finished and, as we were trying to sneak our fleeces off the backs of our chairs, Spider came over to our table and grabbed Eileen.

'Now ladies and gentlemen, we may not have a band but it won't stop us dancing!'

He took her by the arm and pulled her to the stage.

'With the help of this lovely young lady we're going to demonstrate for you the Gay Gordons.'

Eileen was embarrassed and unsure of the steps but she let him walk her through it slowly. When Spider stopped to explain the moves he held her, his arm around her waist. Of the three of them, Eileen looked most like a Highlander. She was a curvy freckled girl with lovely red hair. Sarah and Julie had tans and bleached hair but Eileen's skin was classic Scottish peely-wally, except for her face, which was beetroot red with the attention she was getting. With Spider hanging round her like a tramp round a bowl of soup, Eileen was mortified. We thought it was hilarious. Spider was now asking couples onto the floor and, I'll say this for him, just by humming 'Mairi's Wedding' through the microphone, he had a hundred and fifty pensioners birling across the dance floor. Sarah and I got up too, it was too good a laugh to miss. Only when we'd all danced twice would Spider let Eileen go back to her seat.

The oldsters, the coffin-dodgers from the coach tours, they knew how to party. They were on the floor for every dance, and each time Spider picked a different old lady as a demonstration partner. He was an unbelievable flirt and he soon had them giggling like teenagers. You would have thought he was Elvis. My first impression of Spider had not been good. Anyone who called strangers 'friends' was, in my book, an automatic creep. But I had to admit he was doing a tremendous job keeping the party going. He was on the go the whole time, demonstrating, calling the dance, humming the tune and bashing the boran. After about an hour of everyone birling themselves silly, Spider announced a short break. He looked knackered.

He came and joined us at our table. We hadn't asked him to, but we were pleased to have him. With his celebrity status well established, we basked in Spider's reflected glory. He brought a woman with him and introduced her as Kathy, his wife. Poor Kathy, what a sight she was. Although she was a good ten years younger than Spider, beside him, she looked a frump. Kathy had on a suit she must have had since the Eighties, either that or from a charity shop. It looked like something out of *Dallas*. When she found out I was living in Inverfaughie she homed in on me.

It turned out Kathy was a Glaswegian too, originally from Govan. I got the whole story. She'd married Spider and moved to the Highlands sixteen years ago. Sixteen years she'd lived here and still she was treated as an incomer. Up until now I had been enjoying myself, I didn't really want to hear this. She would never be accepted. Even the kids, Jill and Kay, every year they entered the Mod, the Gaelic cultural competition, and every year they came away with nothing. The vodka had obviously kicked in because I giggled, picturing Anne Robinson in a kilt, sneering at two wee girls: *Jill and Kay you leave WITH NOTHING!*

'Whereabouts in the city are you from?' Kathy asked us.

The Nurseteers were southsiders like her, but from the wealthier suburbs of Giffnock and Pollockshields. I was from the West End, I told her.

'Partick, is that?'

'Near Partick,' I said.

Did I know Jimmy McLean from Partick? No, sorry, I didn't. Or Anne and Shona McLeod? No, sorry. They lived above the fruit shop in Dumbarton Road, very involved with the Scouts they'd been, everyone knew them, big tall women, I'd know them if I saw them, twins they were, with long dark hair down to their bums, ring any bells? No. Well what about George Bell?

To get away I asked if she wanted a drink, it was my round anyway. Thankfully when I came back Kathy had gone to the loo. Just as well because Spider only had eyes for Eileen, he kept directing his chat and his charm towards her. Eileen did her best to deflect it. The old ladies were starting to approach the table. Spider spun out the break for as long as he could but eventually he had to go back to his fans.

I think he had run out of puff for the dancing and, starting with a self-penned ditty, he enthusiastically initiated some community singing. Was there no end to the man's talent? He went round the tables singing and we sang the last line.

Spider sang:

> '*Spider don't you make those eyes at me,*
> *Spider don't you make those eyes at me,*
> *Spider don't you make those eyes at me,*'

214

And we had to sing:

> '*Aye but I will says Spider!*'

Even the men joined in. As he moved around the room Spider teased the ladies: holding hands, making eyes, pulling legs. They seemed to think this was the raunchiest thing out. He was a pensioner heart-throb. I was waiting for someone to throw their knickers. The verses became increasingly racy:

> '*Spider don't you hold the hand of me,*
> *Spider don't you put your arms round me,*
> *Spider don't you tickle the thighs of me,*
>
> *Aye but I will says Spider!*'

On the thigh-tickling verse he arrived at our table but only one of us saw any action: Eileen, predictably enough.

The next thing was, he called for people to come up and do a turn, explaining that the true essence of a ceilidh is to have everyone take part. Such was his charisma that Spider managed to get two Dutch sisters, who were sixty if they were a day, to do the cancan while the rest of us sang dah dah dahdahdahdah and clapped out the beat. The old guys wolf-whistled. There were no more volunteers so Spider persuaded each tour party to sing one of their national songs.

The Dutch were really sweet, they sang a sad song and all of them joined in. The Germans were great too and to be fair, the English sang 'Roll out the Barrel' with brio. But Spider was keeping the best to last. With national pride at stake, he insisted that our table sing 'Flower of Scotland'.

This wasn't fair, we protested, there were only four of us, but Spider paid us no heed. We endured an excruciating minute and a half of shoe-gazing and

215

embarrassed giggling. This being our country, the tour parties were expecting great things of us. We tried to reason with him but Spider would have none of it. When we made no moves to start he introduced us, giving us a big show-biz build-up, getting them all to applaud.

'Ladies and gentlemen, all the way from bonnie Scotland at no expense whatsoever, I give you the Scots Blue Belles!'

Spider encouraged loud cheering, raising the level of expectation to fever pitch, whipping them into a ceilidh frenzy. We had to do it. Although we didn't discuss it, we knew we couldn't take the piss but the situation was so ridiculous it was difficult not to laugh.

We stood up and I was surprised when Eileen, the shyest of the girls, with her hands behind her back, started to sing. She had a lovely voice and we followed her. I was scared to look at anybody in case I burst out laughing so I stared straight ahead, stony-faced. People on telly at New Year singing heuchter-cheuchter songs are always stony-faced, I thought. Maybe they're trying not to laugh.

Kathy approached and added her voice to our four shaky ones. She had hidden talents too, by the second verse she'd introduced a harmony. This could have been disastrous, I for one was always hopeless at anything fancier than the basic tune, but we pulled together, concentrating, trying to sing louder, to not let the harmony throw us.

Our volume increased again when Spider himself joined in. A spontaneous burst of applause broke when the audience heard his bass voice. Spider struck a dramatic pose with one kilted leg cocked on the chair and one hand on his knee. Smoothly, as if he had done this before, he stepped onto the table, a cross between

Harry Lauder and Ricky Martin. Out of nowhere Kathy produced the boran and handed it to him.

With the gravitas brought by the lonely elemental drum, suddenly it wasn't funny any more. We were no longer at a tourist do in the function suite of a hotel. Suddenly it was 1297 and we were standing shoulder to shoulder with Wallace at Stirling Bridge on a cold September morning, ready to fight and die for Scotland's freedom.

Spider's eyes were glassy as, at the final chorus, we gave everything we had to the last few lines:

> and sent him homeward
> to think again.

The tour parties loved it, we had done Scotland proud.

The ceilidh seemed to end abruptly after that. With bus engines turning outside, the function suite emptied in minutes. We were sad to see our English, Dutch and German pals go. The next morning I had a hazy recollection of hugging people. After our triumph we were still high as kites as bar staff cleared the tables. We didn't want to go home. Spider invited us back to his place *by way of a nightcap* and Kathy didn't seem to mind. At the time it didn't bother me that it was a further twenty-seven miles in the opposite direction from Inverfaughie.

Chapter 22

There were two young guys at Spider's house. Spider and Kathy went in ahead of us and as we followed we could hear frantic tidying up. The lads looked as if they'd been snoozing by the fire. We caught them mid tidy and there was a smell of farts in the air that everybody pretended not to notice.

The two guys were brothers, Spider introduced them as the Bell Boy and Keek. They could have been quite handsome but for the fact that the Bell Boy had several top teeth missing and Keek had a terrible squint.

'The lads work for me at the double glazing,' Spider told us.

Keek and the Bell Boy had been babysitting. As soon as we heard this we began speaking in hushed voices but Spider flapped his arm dismissively.

'Don't be daft, those kids will sleep through anything.'

The brothers were still in their working clothes by the look of things, they wore muddy denims and holey knitted jumpers.

'Boys, this is Sarah, Trixie, Julie and Eileen.'

'Also known as the Scots Blue Belles!' said Sarah.

The lads hung back and Spider tried to bring them out of their shell. 'The girls are from Glasgow,' he told them, although they must have been able to tell from our accents. Kathy offered us tea from mugs that were stained brown on the inside while Spider poured us large whiskies from a two-litre plastic Coke bottle. I expected it to be rough but it was excellent.

'That's a lovely Speyside, Spider, it's not Glenfarclas is it?' I asked him.

He looked impressed and then a wee bit alarmed but he just laughed. 'Och, now, ask no questions . . .'

Kathy collared me again, moaning about how isolated she was up here, miles from anywhere and Spider out all day double-glazing and all night hosting ceilidhs. I was rescued by Spider giving us a guided tour of the house. It was a big old farmhouse which looked as if it could do with a good clean. The furniture was quality even if it was old, but the place needed freshening up and a lick of paint wouldn't have gone wrong. He took us into the conservatory which he'd built himself. I expected something like you see advertised on the back page of the Sunday papers, but this was very much a home-made job, with windows of different shapes and sizes. The views were fantastic though, a river ran straight past the house and away in the distance you could still make out the tops of the mountains against the sky.

'Och it's a shame you've missed the sunset, girls, I sit out here in the evening and a lovelier view you'll not see,' Spider said. 'And do you see the river down there? It has all the salmon you could ever want, and the biggest. You'll have to see the size of the salmon I have out in the freezer!'

Without knowing where we were going, we trooped outside and followed Spider into a big byre.

'Now, there's no electric out here ladies, so just be careful.'

It was pitch black inside. The byre was more like a

warehouse with rows and rows of shelves set out in aisles. Spider led us up one aisle and down another, all of us tripping and giggling in the dark. He stopped and our faces were suddenly lit from underneath by the light from a big chest freezer. He hadn't been kidding about the size of the salmon, it was about a yard long.

We started sniggering – the salmon was comical, its mouth open as if it was surprised to find itself in this situation. As Spider was showing us it, accidentally on purpose I was convinced, the salmon's bottom lip caught the hem of Eileen's skirt. She ran away down an aisle screaming in the darkness as we stood holding onto each other, howling with laughter.

'Spider don't you poke that fish at me!' Eileen shouted, but she was laughing too.

'Aye but I will says Spider!' he sang back, and then ran down the aisle after her. We were killing ourselves. Eileen dodged him and then Spider was running back towards us. We raced away but he caught up and was thrusting his salmon at us as we ran and screamed and laughed. At the top of the aisle we split up and ran down different aisles. For a few minutes he couldn't find anyone, but that was no fun so Julie gave him a clue. 'Oh, Spi . . . der!' she called.

'Over here Spider!' Sarah joined in.

Spider rushed up and down the aisles towards the voices, a couple of times nearly catching us. I heard the door open and wondered who had come in or gone out. My eyes were getting used to the dark by now and I saw Spider run past me. He saw me too, but he wasn't interested in me. This made me realize how silly I felt, running around a barn in the dark. I made my way to the door and slipped out.

It was a gorgeous starry night and I decided I'd wait here until the girls had finished their game and go into the house with them. I didn't want Kathy cornering me again and telling me all her troubles. After about fifteen minutes or so, it could have been more, I was cold and I decided I'd have to take my chances with Kathy. I went into the living room but the lights were turned out. As soon as I came in they all froze. There was enough light from the fire to see that Julie was on the couch with the Bell Boy and Sarah was sharing a chair with Keek. There was no sign of anyone else. In my embarrassment I walked out of the room but I quickly recovered and went back to rescue the whisky. All activity once again ceased while I rummaged around on the floor to find it. I went out to the conservatory. I wondered what had happened, Kathy must have gone to bed and Eileen must still be out in the byre with Spider. Everyone had copped off, except me.

Oh well, I thought, always the bridesmaid. I'd just have to make the best of it. The girls would come and get me when they were ready. Fifty miles from Inverfaughie, how else was I going to get home? I sat in a big leather armchair that had a patchwork quilt thrown over it. I pulled the quilt round me and snuggled down with my lumber for the evening, the plastic bottle of whisky, and watched the moon and the stars move across the sky.

I must have dozed off. The next thing I knew Spider had his arm round me and was fondling me. But that was just sleep confusion. He was actually trying to get the Coke bottle away from me. I'd wedged it down the side of the chair before I'd fallen asleep.

'God Spider, I'm sorry, I didn't realize I'd drank so much.'

'Och not to worry, there's plenty left.'

The darkness had faded to a thin grey light. I watched him pour substantial measures for us both. My head was thumping. Curled up in the chair my legs were stiff and I was cold to my bones.

'Not for me thanks.'

'C'mon now Trixie, keep me company, everyone else is asleep.'

I was dying to know where Eileen was but I was scared to ask. Spider seemed to have a whisky-drinking ritual. He threw it into his mouth, swished it around, chucked it down his neck, showed his teeth and then sighed a long slow sigh. My sipping technique was tame by comparison but then, I thought, mine wasn't a satisfying after-sex slug, unfortunately. I lifted my drink and knocked it back. It did warm me up. Spider took the other armchair and we sat in silence looking down at the river. At this time of the morning Spider had lost all vestiges of his stage persona. I tried to think of something to say, something to cheer him up, to make him think I was good company.

'D'you ever do any ceilidhs out Inverfaughie way, Spider?'

'Aye, the odd time. I'm booked to do the gala day ceilidh at the Calley in a couple of weeks. Is that where you're staying, Inverfaughie?'

'Aye. Harrosie, d'you know it?'

'Och aye, of course I do. I grew up in Inverfaughie. It's a grand place for a holiday, are you girls having a nice time?'

'I'm not on holiday. I live there. The girls have hired the house next door and they invited me out. I've only just met them.'

'You live at Harrosie did you say?'

'Yes. I inherited it.'

For some reason Spider seemed to find this hilariously funny.

'Oho, the rightful heir! That'll put Jock's nose out of joint, so it will.'

'Jock?'

'Aye Jock Robertson, it's his house, or at least it was

his father's. Harry swore Jock would never see a penny but I never thought he'd do that! The old fella held a terrible grudge.'

'Did he? Why?'

'Och him and Jock never got on, not even when he was a boy, but when Rosie died Harry said it was his fault.'

'Whose?'

'Jock's.'

'Does Jock still live in the village?'

'Oh aye.'

'Oh Christ, that's all I need, another claimant. I've got enough trouble with my Auntie Nettie wanting in on it.'

'Och I'm sure you're quite safe. If I know Harry he'll have done everything by the book, all legal and correct. It's your birthright, no-one can take that away from you.'

Bells were ringing all over the place. Harry? Rosie? Jock? Birthright? Harry and Rosie, that's where Harrosie came from. Harry, short for Henry. Harry, the name of the wee man at Mum's funeral who fixed the karaoke machine. Why had I not made this link before now?

'Spider, what was Harry like? I mean, what did he look like?'

'He was smart enough. Small, thin, snappy dresser.'

'Oh my God! I think I've met him. He came to my house, he gatecrashed my mother's funeral!'

'Oh now don't be so hard on the old fella, he only wanted to do right by you.'

Bells were ringing all over the place. I felt as if I had the 1812 Overture going off in my head.

'Spider, what is Jock short for?'

'It's John.'

'But can't John be Jack as well?'

'Aye, that's what he's calling himself these days,

223

Jackie, but I'm not calling him that. He was Jock when we were at school and Jock when he went into the army. It was the English wife that christened him Jackie.'

'You were at school together?'

How old was Jackie then? But that was hardly important. I was coming on to the question of birthright when the conservatory door burst open.

'You, ya dirty hoormaister!'

Kathy flew at Spider and dug her nails into the top of his head. He had a job getting her off. They were both making grunting noises but with his ponytail swinging, Spider finally shoved her away. She bounced into the front window wall, making the whole structure of the conservatory sway. Next she went for me.

'And you ya fucking dirty weegie bastard! Can you not get a man of your own?'

She made a breenge for me but she had further to come and by the time she reached me I was on my feet with Spider standing between us. She screamed at me over his shoulder.

'Get out of my house you dirty fucking cow! And leave my man alone!'

'Get a hold of yourself woman! Trixie is a guest in my house. There's no occasion for insults.'

I noticed he didn't deny being a dirty hoormaister but neither did he defend my honour.

'Ya manky auld slapper! Get to fuck away from my man!'

I heard a child crying somewhere in a room above us. As the slurs rained down Keek came out in his Y-fronts to see what was going on and soon the house was a hive of post-coital activity. Over Spider's shoulder, beyond Kathy's foaming lips, there was enough light now to see the river and the mountains, all of nature, and it was so peaceful.

Chapter 23

On the way home I tried to make sense of it. No doubt there would be an element of truth in what Spider had said, the names all rang true, but I didn't get the birthright thing.

I tried to sneak in the back door but Nettie shouted.

'Is that you Trisha?'

'Yes.'

The fact that Nettie was awake alarmed me. It was six in the morning.

'Where are the boys? Are they in?'

Nettie came into the kitchen in her nightie and my dressing gown.

'Aye the boys are fine. They keep better hours than some I could mention.'

She said it ratty but she was smiling.

'Sorry. We went back to someone's house for coffee and, och, you know what it's like.'

'D'you want a cuppa?'

Seeing as she wasn't going to give me a hard time, I agreed. I was knackered and it was nice just to be back sitting in my own kitchen.

'Sorry Trisha, I mean Trixie, I borrowed your goonie, I hope you don't mind, I was freezing.'

'No, help yourself.'

'That's a smashing view you get from your bedroom window. It wasn't till I saw it that I remembered. Elsie was right, it's a fabulous view.'

'What do you mean?'

'This is the place!'

'Sorry?'

'Where she worked, it must be.'

This was too spooky. Nettie was about to finish what Spider had started. Please God, let her keep it simple, I thought, don't let her start on about the golly dolly again.

'Nettie I'm interested, honestly I am, but I'm tired. Tell me again, slowly, and try to just stick to the story.'

She took that quite well for Nettie, rather than waste time taking the huff she launched in.

'Well, you know Elsie: headstrong. But folk didnae get divorced in they days, hen. I could sympathize, if my Tommy had been away all the time like that I would have had something to say about it.'

'Mum wanted a divorce?'

'Naw, no really, but she was fed up with Hughie being away all the time.'

'You mean when he was in the Merchant Navy?'

'Aye, och you'll no remember it, it was before you were even born, but Hughie was all over the place, Hong Kong, Taiwan, you name it. Mind you, he always remembered us. Every time he came home on leave he brought back fantastic gadgets: battery-operated toys, painted coconuts, lovely silk scarves for your mammy. In they days you couldn't get a lot of things, no like it is now.'

She was off on one, I had to get her back on track.

'But Nettie, what has that got to do with Inverfaughie?'

'Oh excuse me! You're the one that wants to know.'

It was at times like this, when Nettie reminded me so much of Mum, that I most wanted to strangle her.

'Sorry Nettie. In your own time.'

That was sarcastic. Nettie said nothing.

'Sorry Nettie. Please go on.'

That was apologetic.

'OK, well, I think they were going through a bad patch. Elsie wanted a family you see. I mean, it's not as if she hadn't given it a fair chance, twelve years they'd been married and she was nae spring chicken. I don't know what was wrong, they'd been for tests and everything but I never heard any more about it. Our Elsie never told me nothing. But Ma told us that when Hughie was home on leave Elsie gave him an ultimatum: leave the Navy or she was leaving him.'

While she'd been telling me this, Nettie struggled with the cake box and finally got it open. She paused momentarily to stuff her face with an almond slice before continuing, spitting cake crumbs on the table.

'But it wisnae just as easy as that, Hughie was under contract. So next thing was, she turns up at Ma's with her bags packed and says she's got a job in a hotel. If he can go to Honolulu then I can go to the Highlands, she says, and off she goes. Oh she loved it, she wrote home how much she loved it. Mind you, she told us it was a hotel. By no stretch of the imagination is this place a hotel. But she described the view all right, the islands and the loch and the wee town and that, I remember it clear as day.'

'She worked here? In this house?'

'That's what I'm telling you. Mind you it didnae last. It was only a matter of months before Hughie brought her back down the road. He left the Merchant Navy and got a job in the shipyards along with my Tommy. Next thing we know, hey presto! Your mother's pregnant.'

Steven brought me in a cup of tea. I'd woken from a dream about Dad. I felt my eyes, they were dry, but I knew I had been crying.

'Can you get your own breakfast this morning son? I got in quite late last night.'

'Breakfast? Try lunch, it's half twelve. Good night was it?'

'Aye, no bad thanks son, and yourself?'

'Aye no bad.'

I never drank tea on top of a hangover. It only made me worse. Irn Bru was my cure or, if I was really bad, a few spoonfuls of honey. Since I'd moved here I never went to sleep without filling my bottle and putting it at the side of my bed.

When I first saw the sports water bottles I could hardly believe it. So simple yet effective, like all the best ideas. Some genius had the vision to create these bottles so that cyclists or runners could, any time anywhere, pull up the nipple and drink. Whenever I was unable to raise my head off the pillow, struck down and hung-over, my sports bottle was a comforting, non-spill, Irn Bru dispenser. Sometimes I just lay and sucked. But not in front of Steven.

He sat on the edge of the bed.

'So what time are we going then?'

'Going where?'

'To the distillery.'

'Oh God Steven, do we have to go? Can we not leave it till tomorrow? I'm not feeling too braw.'

'We're going home tomorrow.'

I kept my mouth shut and sipped my tea. Steven sat in silence. By not whining or casting up that I'd promised, or mentioning my hangover, he took the moral high ground.

I caved. I had to, they were leaving tomorrow. I wasn't emotionally strong enough to spend the day with the three of them hanging about making me feel guilty. It was easier just to drive.

I was OK once I was on the road so long as I drove

slowly, no sudden movements. Steven had them well warned and Nettie thankfully stayed quiet. Gerry brought his CD Walkman. The boys took an earpiece each, headbanging noiselessly in the back. Applying the rule of one hour per unit of alcohol, I worked out that I'd be safe to drive sometime next Monday. But now that I was no longer a rep I didn't have to worry constantly about losing my licence. You never saw the police up here anyway, and when you did they were all smiles.

I must have known it all along, I thought. Mum's deathbed scene. *'Young women can be daft sometimes.'* That wasn't advice, it was a confession. And the man turning up at the funeral. When I thought back, he'd had a Highland accent. I didn't recognize it at the time but that's what it was. I'd just thought he had asthma. What was it he said? I couldn't remember, but it was along the lines of it being a pleasure to meet me. I bet it was. I bet it was a pleasure fathering me as well, taking advantage of an innocent young girl. OK not that young, she must have been twenty-seven or twenty-eight by that time, and married, and separated, but still. Why didn't Harry tell me? I would have taken it all right, for God's sake, it was forty years ago, a lot of water under the bridge. I could have met him, properly, got to know him. Instead I ignored him while he fixed our karaoke machine. What a bloody waste!

They must have stayed in touch. Nettie said the hotel sent lovely presents when I was born. That's why he had my photo. A wee memento. That's why it was down the back of the cupboard shelves, hidden from his wife, his dirty wee secret, the cheating bastard.

The Auchensadie distillery was a beautiful building and so were all the wee houses around it. The place was so well kept that my eyes were hurting with the light bouncing off the concentrated whitewash.

Auchensadie had done its marketing. It knew how to give the tourists exactly what they wanted: clean, cute, oldey worldey, a whisky theme park. Any other day I'd have been up for it.

'Right, I've got the tickets, they weren't dear. Mum, put your purse away, this is on me. We're lucky, the last tour starts in five minutes. Over there, in the malting shed.'

'And we get to drink as much whisky as we want?' asked Gerry.

Now I understood why the boys had been so gagging to come.

'Do not fear my friend, we'll drink the barrels dry. OK, let's go to work.'

A big fat posh woman in a kilt and full-length tartan cape introduced herself as our guide. Then she played a video which informed us, by way of old photographs and an English actor's voice-over, of the glorious history of Auchensadie. From humble beginnings as an illegal still in the woods to lucrative respectability, and back to a humble existence as an outpost of a multinational.

As it was the last tour of the day there were only ourselves and two carloads of French people. We'd missed the tour buses, thank God, I didn't want to run into anyone from the ceilidh. I had a vague memory of us driving alongside the German bus, me with my head out of the window singing 'Will Ye No Come back Again'.

The fat woman was rushing through her spiel, anxious to get finished up for the day. Using her cape to catch stragglers, she herded us together and moved us from shed to shed explaining the distillation process.

Halfway round we stood beside enormous circular vats. The guide opened the wooden lid and invited everyone to take a sniff. The French people, probably scared of her, did as they were told. When the French all started laughing Steven and Gerry tried it too.

'Oh man, see that?' said Gerry. 'You get so far down and then it's like a punch in the mouth.'

'Try it Nettie, it's a great buzz.'

Nettie tried it and agreed.

'Oh so it is, I wasnae expecting that!'

'C'mon Mum, we've all done it, you have to do it too.'

'Nah, you're all right son.'

Steven pulled me over to where the lid had been lifted.

'Just stick your head down there, it's good fun, honest.'

As if lending moral support, he put an arm around my shoulder. Steven just wasn't getting the message. He was really pissing me off but he knew I wouldn't argue in front of all those people. I forced a smile and gingerly lowered my head under the lid. The mixture, or *mash* as the guide had called it, didn't smell that bad, a faint sickly sweet smell but that was all. What was turning my stomach was the sight of the stuff. It looked like a giant pile of sick.

'D'you smell it?' Steven laughed.

Still with his arm around me, he pressed my head a further inch down into the vat. It was an inch too far. Suddenly I was caught in a searing atomic nose explosion. Trapped and under attack, my body reacted. Before I could stop it, half a mouthful of boak escaped and plopped into the vat. Steven let go of my head immediately.

If anyone saw me, they pretended they hadn't. When the tour moved to the hospitality suite I disappeared and sat in the car.

I was a bit emotibubble when I put them on the train. Steven's wee face crumpled, he even forgot about my

231

front bits and gave me a proper cuddle. He kept saying, 'I'll come again soon Mum, I promise.'

But it wasn't that. The truth be told I was glad to see the back of them. Between them, Nettie and Spider had delivered such a bombshell that I needed a bit of time to myself. I was still absorbing the aftershocks.

I drove home and sat drinking tea for hours. I hated everybody. For forty years they had been saying behind my back, *oh god love her, the wee soul, she doesn't know her real father*. Most of all I hated Nettie and Spider for telling me the truth.

Bouncer was upset that I was upset, and was about as hangdog as a dog could be. He snuffled into me as I sat on the couch in a state of catatonia. His affection gave me a sudden surge of emotional energy. I threw my arms round his neck and burst out crying.

'You're the only one I can trust, boy. My only real friend. It's only me and you now, Bouncer!'

I hadn't a hanky and Bouncer let me wipe my tears and snotters on his fur. Later, I heard him give himself a good hard shake in the kitchen. He came back with his lead between his teeth. There was none of his usual excited begging, he was doing it for me.

The dog was right. Moping in the house wasn't going to change the fact that I was a bastard. Born out of wedlock, well, actually in wedlock but not to my mother's husband. Did that still make me a bastard? The world had been knocked off kilter. Uncle Henry. There was no Uncle Henry, it was Harry and he was now Dad. Dad was now just Hughie, my mother's husband, no relation. Strangers were my closest relatives. Including Jackie.

Chapter 24

I felt bad sneaking past Rebecca's house but I needed time to work out my complicated life. I marched down the hill and right through the other side of the village. I'd never walked as fast or as far before. Bouncer was struggling to keep up with me for a change. I kept thinking about everything that had happened with Jackie. As cars passed me, all they saw was a purple-faced woman out walking her dog; a weather-beaten country lady. But my cheeks were burning for the cheesy moves I'd made on my own brother.

He must have known. Why hadn't he told me? I should have realized something was amiss when he worked so hard and then refused payment for the gardening. And who drove to Glasgow and back in the middle of the night just to be neighbourly? How stupid was I? I'd thought he fancied me, and I'd thrown myself at him. It was disgusting. I was disgusting. He was disgusting.

I was halfway to Gaffney before I tired, several miles from home. Walking wasn't doing it for me. I was still a bastard, only now I was a tired, blistered, limping bastard. Even the dog was footsore, but poor old Bouncer's legs would be bloodied stumps before my rage would recede.

Walter lived about quarter of a mile further along the road, he'd let me phone a taxi from his house. Maybe he'd give me a cup of tea and a foot massage. Or at least let me use his basin. I could pretend I'd brought Bouncer out to visit him.

Thank God, Walter was as pleased to see me as I was him. He was looking well, a bit too well. Walter and Bouncer spent at least five minutes kissing and cuddling on the doorstep and I began to worry that he'd want me to leave Bouncer there. Maybe coming here had been a mistake. Walter put the kettle on. I was hanging around chatting to him when the back door opened and my long-lost brother walked in.

Jackie's face went white. He mumbled something to Walter and ducked straight out again. I wasn't having that. He wasn't going to get away from me this time. Ignoring Walter, I flew out the door after him. I'd expected him to jump on his bike and hightail it back to Inverfaughie, his long legs a blur on the pedals, but no, he was in the greenhouse. Good, I had him cornered.

'Jackie?'

'Oh hello there Trixie, how are you, not seen you for a while.'

His voice was jolly. He fiddled about with something in a pot and, although I pushed my face at him, he couldn't look at me.

'Oh Jackie don't waste your breath. I know. I know why you've been avoiding me.'

He stopped fiddling. And then started again.

'You don't know anything.'

'Look, do I have to spell it out? D'you want Walter to hear? I. Fucking. Know. OK?'

'So?'

'So? That's all you can say? Why didn't you tell me? You could have saved me making an arse of myself, it was in your power. And then you wouldn't even speak to me for Christ's sake! Oh aye, you're all avuncular with Steven but you won't even answer the door to me. Look, I know now and I'm OK about it, thanks for asking. I mean I'm not OK about it yet, but I will be when I get used to the idea. Just don't . . . don't freeze me out like this. Can we not turn the clocks back, start again? We were all set to be good mates, weren't we? Jackie, I could do with a friend, and since Mum died I need all the family I can get. I'm sorry I embarrassed you but in all fairness, I wasn't to know. You can relax, I'm not going to jump on your bones, I'd just like a big brother.'

'Is that how you want to see me, as a big brother?'

'I don't spend my evenings lusting after you, if that's what you mean. You're quite safe. And anyway, you're a bit old for me.'

That was meant as a joke but Jackie was awful sad-looking.

'I've never been a brother before.'

'Neither have I, but you don't need a City and Guilds certificate! D'you want the job or not?'

'I'll take it.'

Rather than spoil the moment I left it at that and went back into Walter, acting as if nothing had happened.

And in a way, nothing *had* happened. Everything went on as before, walking Bouncer, driving Rebecca to her lessons, gabbing with Jenny, phoning Steven, that was it. Jackie didn't take up his post as my new brother, he didn't visit or phone. I wasn't surprised. The girls next door went back to Saudi and I was sorry to see them go. I got stuck into the garden. I would dig and hoe and clip and rake and weed and mow and mulch all the livelong day.

As time went by I realized my mistake of not questioning Jackie when I had the chance. I was kicking myself that I'd flounced off, I had so many questions. Did he feel I had stolen his inheritance? Did he want Harrosie? Had the gardening just been a pretext to check me out? I thought we were getting on great, didn't he like me? Or was it the snogging incident that had put him off? Had Harry ever mentioned me? What was Harry like? Even stupid little things niggled me: why did Jackie return the whisky and not the sweeties?

I wanted to talk about it. Bouncer knew as much as I did but he had nothing to say on the matter. I couldn't tell Steven, not when he was waiting for his exam results, and Rebecca was too young. I tried to raise the subject with Jenny.

It was no accident that the shop was empty when I went in. I always timed my visit for when it was quiet, lurking outside until I had her to myself. If Jenny had customers she would look through me and say, 'Yes dear? What can I get you?'

She was stacking shelves, up and down her wee three-step ladder as if she was at the gym. I casually mentioned that I bumped into Jackie up at Walter's.

'I've been rushed off my feet all morning. I've hardly had a chance to get this stock out.'

'Want me to hand the tins up to you?'

'Och no, it's the only exercise I get, sitting in this foosty old shop all day.'

I lifted three tins and passed them up to her anyway. She took them, filed them into their space, and turned to me expectantly. I bent down and got three more.

'Jackie and I had a good talk.'

She made a sympathetic face and nodded. This confirmed what I suspected, that she knew already. I continued to pass her up the tins.

'Peas now Trixie please, that box.'

236

'We managed to sort things out.'

'Oh well that's grand.'

'I mean we talked a bit, but there are still loads of things I don't know.'

'I'm wondering if I should bother with the butter beans, nobody buys them this time of year, they're just taking up space.'

'I meant to ask Jackie about Harry.'

Jenny turned with a tin of butter beans in her hand.

'Harry?'

'Yeah, what he was like, if he ever talked about me. You knew him didn't you Jenny, what was he like?'

'Well Jackie is the man to ask about all that kind of thing.'

'Aw c'mon Jenny, don't you do it too. It's all out in the open now, I'm fine with it.'

Jenny came down off the ladder and put her hand on my arm and looked into my face.

'I am, honest. I'm entitled to know about my father.'

'Yes, Trixie, you're right, and Jackie has a duty to tell you.'

She might have said more but customers came in. Our chat was over.

It was four young men, backpackers, all speaking at the same time, one of them waving a poly bag.

'Nih parley pah Fransay,' said Jenny with a friendly smile.

'I think they're Spanish, Jenny,' I said.

I had spent enough holidays on the Costa del Sol to know that much.

Jenny held up her hand to halt their chatter.

'Righty-ho.'

She slid her hand under the counter and unfastened the bolt. Lifting the hinged flap she displayed an A4 sheet of paper with one sentence translated into various languages written on it. She picked one out and demonstrated, with her finger going along the line as she read the words.

'*No hablamos español.*'

Again she smiled. But the lads didn't, they started speaking again, this time louder and faster. The one with the poly bag shoved it at Jenny and pointed towards the till. I was suddenly very conscious of our situation. This was the first time anything like this had ever happened to me. I grabbed for Jenny's hand and moved closer to her.

'Jenny, don't be alarmed,' I whispered, 'but we're being held up. He's telling you to put the money in the bag. Just do what he says.'

To my astonishment Jenny laughed as she took the bag from the boy.

'*No es catolica!*'

He seemed to be saying something about Catholics. Maybe it was a political protest. Jenny opened the bag and looked inside. Now she threw her head back and really laughed. Jenny held her left hand flat and waved her right hand around in front of it, making a rude gesture towards the Spaniards. She nodded her head and the boy nodded back.

'*Es* rotting! *No es catolica!*' the lad said.

'For God's sake Jenny, don't provoke them, they're Catholic!'

'*Si, es catolica, pero no es mantequilla!*' Jenny said as she pulled a plastic knife, six rolls and a half-pound of lard from the bag.

I was confused. Maybe they weren't trying to rob us.

'You've bought lard, you bunch of diddies! You don't put that on a roll! Here,' she reached into the fridge and handed the boy a packet of McSpor's Scottish butter, 'this is what you're after.'

'*Es mantequilla?*'

'*Si* BUT, TER. Ask for it properly the next time,' she

wagged her finger at the lot of them, 'it's not my fault if you buy the wrong thing.'

'BUT, TER. *Gracias, señora.*'

'*Señorita, actualmente,*' Jenny said in a flirtatious tone.

Everyone laughed except me, I didn't know what the hell was going on.

'*Gracias, señorita.*'

'*De nada. Adios, guapos.*'

I waited till they were out of the shop before I got the story. It turned out it wasn't a rude gesture at all, she had mimed spreading butter on a piece. We laughed at that one. When we sobered up a bit I complimented her on her grasp of Spanish.

'Och well, I wouldn't go that far. I had a friend in London, I picked up a wee bit from him.'

'More than a wee bit Jenny, you're too modest, you sorted those boys out. I was amazed.'

'Och well Trixie, we Highlanders can turn our hand to anything. You can't tell just by looking at people. Sometimes you have to look further than your nose.'

Steven thought it was hilarious as well when I phoned him that night. It was the first time we'd laughed since he'd gone back to Glasgow.

'It's good to hear you laugh Mum.'

'Aye well, you've just got to get on with it haven't you?'

'You know what you are Mum, you're *indefatigable*.'

'Thanks. We Highlanders can turn our hand to anything. Is indefatigable one of your new words? What does it mean exactly?'

'Dunno. I think it means cheery.'

'Oh well, I'm certainly that.'

I could manage about twenty minutes of cheery before I had to get off the phone.

*　　　*　　　*

Two days later Jackie showed up. He cycled up, casual as you please, parked his bike and took a walk round the garden. I gave him twenty minutes to settle, then I came out to meet him.

'All right Jackie?'

'Nae bad, thanks, and yourself?'

'Aye, couldn't be better, thanks.'

The conversation continued in this laconic style for a wee while. I went in and brought out the cake tin and mugs of tea for us. I felt a bit awkward standing about with the cake tin under my arm but I wanted to take things at Jackie's pace. Eventually he sat down. It was a lovely day and the midgies weren't too bad, a perfect Highland day in fact. He was full of compliments about the home baking and the garden.

'You have the place looking lovely, the roses are coming up grand. They're the nicest I've seen in the village, those would easily take a prize at the gala day flower show. You've worked wonders, I think you have a wee hidden talent there, Trixie.'

'Aye well, it runs in the family.'

Jackie's face flushed. Oops, wrong thing to say.

A decent interval after he'd finished his tea, Jackie got up to leave. I made no effort to keep him. I thought of the last time he left, limping bootless across the gravel. It was only when he was astride his bike, ready for a fast getaway, that he seemed to relax.

'Are you busy on Thursday Trixie?'

'Now, Thursday, let me think. No, I don't think I am.'

'I'm taking the boat out, I have a booking in the morning. I'll bring them back about one. We could go out to the waterfall after that.'

I'd never heard of the waterfall but it sounded good.

'Yeah OK, if you like.'

'OK.'

He pushed off and wheeched down the hill.

'Can I bring the dog?' I shouted after him.

Without looking back he held up his hand, which I took to be a yes.

'Bring cakes!' he shouted back.

Jackie's boat, *La Belle Dame Marie*, was nothing like I expected. For one thing it was much bigger than I'd thought it would be and painted a jaunty blue and yellow. It was comfortable inside too, it even had a wee bar. Bouncer was in an excitable mood. As soon as we got on board he did his usual, sniffing everything. The dog was reckless, I had to keep pulling him back from the edge. I was scared he was going to fall in.

'The last time Steven visited we went out on a boat past the islands and saw dolphins, it was brilliant, I got loads of photos.'

'We can go and look for them if you want.'

'Och no, I'd rather see the waterfall.'

I was impressed by how confidently he manoeuvred the boat around the wee harbour. As we negotiated our way past the other boats Jackie told me he'd had her for years now, did all the maintenance himself, made just about enough money in the summer to keep her in the water. He took us out of the loch, past the first island along a narrow channel with steep cliffs on either side. Stone-coloured seals lolled about on sharp rocks, only sliding into the water when Bouncer barked hello. Jackie took us in so close to the edge I could touch the cliff walls and see wee crabs scuttling in the clear water. Now entering another sea loch, Jackie cut the engine and pointed into the sky. Away in the distance there was a dot circling in the hills.

'Eagle,' he said.

'I'm amazed you spotted it. It's only a tiddly wee thing in the sky.'

'I'm used to it, it's my job. And I wouldn't let him

241

hear you calling him tiddly. If that fella was standing here now he'd be up to your middle.'

It was another quarter of an hour of slowly phut-phutting up the loch before Jackie stopped.

'There's the waterfall over there.'

He pointed inland to a dribble of water falling off a hilltop ledge.

'It's great,' I said. I laughed when I said it, it was difficult to sound convincing.

'The weather's not been great for it.'

'What d'you mean Jackie? The weather's been lovely.'

'Exactly, no good for a waterfall.'

He was right. I'd seen burst drainpipes that were more spectacular but I didn't like to say.

'We could still go and look for the dolphins if you like, Trixie.'

'Not at all. Don't be daft, it's nice to be out. We couldn't ask for a better day, there's not a cloud nor a midgie for miles. And I've brought the cake tin.'

'I'll get the kettle on.'

I waited on deck, taking the rays, until Jackie handed me my tea.

'*La Belle Dame Marie*, is that after your restaurant?'

'Well, after my wife really.'

'Och that's nice.'

Things went quiet again after that. Jackie seemed to find the view up the loch fascinating, squinting into the sun, away from me, until I played my trump card.

'I met him, you know.'

'Who?'

'Harry.'

Jackie turned and looked at me.

'He came to Mum's funeral. I mean, I didn't know who he was, but he spoke to me, introduced himself. What was he like?'

'You're asking the wrong person.'

'You're the only person I can ask. If you won't tell me I'll have to ask Spider.'

'Spider? How do you know Spider?'

'I met him at a ceilidh. He said he knew you at school, is that right? He looks older than you.'

'I'm fifty-six.'

'You don't look it.'

He was squinting again, embarrassed.

'Oh for God's sake Jackie, I wasn't meaning anything. I'm not trying to flatter you, I was just being honest, you don't look fifty-six. I would have taken you for about . . . fifty-four. Fifty-four and a half.'

I was watching his face so I could see he was suppressing a smile.

'Tell me about him. I want to know about Harry.'

The smile faded.

'Look Trixie, it won't do any good. Let it go.'

I let it go, not because he told me to, but to re-consider my strategy. I wasn't going to let him off the hook, not when I had him captive, he couldn't hop onto his bike this time. The direct appeal had met a brick wall, as had the jokey approach. My whole family, Mum, Harry and now Jackie, had kept the truth from me. It wasn't fair, I had a right. The water in my eyes wasn't entirely tactical but nevertheless, I sniffed loudly. This served the dual purpose of alerting Jackie whilst at the same time preventing spillage. Spillage would be overplaying it.

'There isn't much I can tell, and none of it is good,' he said.

I was dangerously close to spillage, time to close him down.

'I don't care. Just tell me, please?'

'OK.'

Bingo.

243

It was a long and sad story and told me as much about Jackie as it did Harry. Every time Jackie curled his lip and said 'my father' I wanted to correct him and say 'our father', but he was on a roll and I didn't want to interrupt the flow. The way Jackie told it, Harry was the bad guy. Our father had thrown Jackie out of the house when he was only sixteen. Jackie didn't set eyes on him for more than ten years, and then he brought Marie back to Inverfaughie to set up the restaurant.

'My mother welcomed Marie with open arms, but not him. He was jealous, jealous of how beautiful and clever she was, of our success. Within months *La Belle Dame* had four times the turnover of Harrosie. I could have bought and sold him.'

Jackie skimmed over the car crash that wrecked his marriage and subsequent divorce. It was obviously painful to him, his voice dropping to a whisper when he mentioned Marie. His jaw tightened when he told me that Harry never visited Marie when she lay in hospital with two broken legs.

'He drove my mother to the door and waited in the car. There were always his fag ends lying on the road where he'd parked.'

After Marie left him and went back south to her family, Harry forbade Rosie, Jackie's mother, to visit him at all.

'But Ma told him she'd leave. She wasn't keeping well by this time, but she would have done it. We saw each other whether he liked it or not. We'd sit in the kitchen blethering over a dram, it was always my favourite room in the house. He'd make himself scarce when I came.'

I didn't want to hear pessimistic stories like these, we were having too nice a time. I wanted to hear about the lovely presents Harry sent when I was born. I wanted to hear if he ever took out the photo of the wee girl and gazed at it, but I let him go on. Talk about opening the floodgates. What with the broken legs and the divorce and all the bad blood, I didn't think it could get any more depressing, but it could.

'He said it was me, but he killed her.'

'What?'

'He started it. It was his fault.'

'Started what, Jackie?'

'The argument. The night she died. Ma wasn't very well, she looked terrible, her skin was an awful yellowy colour. I'd brought a bottle to cheer her up. As soon as I came in he marched through to the kitchen and lifted the whisky off the table. He was away to pour it down the sink. Ma tried to stop him but she couldn't, she had terrible swollen ankles and a big tummy, her legs had ballooned as well, she could hardly move. He was upsetting her. What was I supposed to do? I told him to leave the whisky alone, I gave him fair warning. Then I had to struggle to take it off him. Ma was screaming. The old man ran out of the room with tears in his eyes, I didn't like doing it but I had to, for her.

'She calmed down eventually but a wee while later Mum started being sick, really sick, it was horrible. Not just sick, blood. I had to get him to help me. He tried to put me out the house but I refused to leave her. By the time the ambulance arrived she was unconscious. The paramedics took the old man's side, they wouldn't let me in the ambulance. By the time I got to the hospital my mother was gone, she never woke up.

'He blamed me. He told everyone I'd attacked him and the shock had killed her. I had caused her heart attack. He wouldn't let me come to the funeral, my own mother's funeral. I went anyway, he wasn't going to keep me away. The whole village was there but that didn't stop him shouting. Telling them that I'd killed her. I didn't stand up to him. I should have, I know that, but things were bad enough.

'I'd taken a drink that day, probably too much. It was raining hard when I walked up from the village behind the cars. I got soaked and my trousers were muddy. I knew how much I'd already let her down. I didn't want to draw attention to the state of my trousers. So, as they lowered her coffin I stood and let him shout at me.'

Jackie looked ready for a bit of spillage himself. Anything I thought of to say just seemed facetious. The best policy was to keep my mouth shut. With anyone else I would have automatically put my arm around them. Jackie turned away and looked back down to the loch.

There was something not ringing true here.

Chapter 25

At six o'clock in the morning it dawned on me. I had been lying awake for about an hour, turning over in my mind everything Jackie had said. It didn't fit; his mother Rosie's symptoms were too weird. Yeah, the swollen ankles were obviously oedema, but vomiting blood? That was no heart attack. Swollen abdomen and yellow skin? Sounded more hepatic to me. But a little knowledge was a dangerous thing, especially in medical matters. I should ask an expert. Archie Marshall would tell me. It was too early for Archie to be in his surgery but my mind was buzzing so I got up, made a big pot of tea, and waited.

'Dr Marshall? Hi, it's Trisha McNicol.'

'Hello Trisha, how are you?'

'Aye I'm grand thanks Archie, and yourself?'

'Och, same old shite. Patient topped himself yesterday, depression, age twenty-four.'

I'd forgotten how often Archy was distressed, just in the normal course of his job. We spent a few minutes on the pleasantries before I got down to it.

'I'm actually phoning to pick your brains. Is this a good time?'

'Good a time as any.'

'Can I run a scenario past you?'

247

'Fire away.'

'Imagine if you will a patient, female, drinker, early fifties, with jaundice, swollen abdomen and ankle oedema. Poor mobility, obviously.'

'Obviously. Tell her to seek medical help immediately.'

'Too late. She haemorrhages, vomiting vast quantity of blood, loses consciousness and dies soon after. This was a while ago, no records are available.'

'Uh huh. Is this a quiz?'

'What do you think is the cause of death?'

'Christ's sake Trisha, how the hell am I supposed to know? Without seeing the patient . . .'

'Could it be myocardial?'

'You're not suing one of my overworked colleagues, are you?'

'No Archie. I'm not trying to get anyone in trouble and this is strictly off the record, between you and me. To tell you the truth, a friend of mine believes this woman, this patient, had a heart attack and that he was responsible. I'm just trying to help.'

'You said she was a drinker, a heavy drinker?'

'I'm not sure, possibly.'

'What do *you* think was the cause of death Trisha?'

'Oh come on Archie, you're the doctor, give me a diagnosis, I won't hold you to it, I promise.'

'Could be a few things. The haemorrhaging could be from oesophageal varices, the ascites and the jaundice make it sound most like liver failure, but without examining . . .'

'Not M.I.?'

'I think your friend is off the hook. Anyway, I'm supposed to be ministering to the sick. I better get on. Will that satisfy you?'

'Yeah thanks Archie, that's brilliant.'

*   *   *

I decided to have another go at Jenny before tackling Jackie. I needed verification of the facts before I did anything. I wasn't confident; she'd been as tight as a drum when I'd asked her the last time. For someone who loved to gossip, Jenny could be very discreet when she wanted to be. I'd have to take a different tack.

I caught her on her own in the shop the next afternoon. I'd gone down on the pretext of handing in my application forms for the gala day competitions.

'Jackie told me about his mother's drink problem,' I casually mentioned.

Jenny didn't fall for it. She coolly looked me up and down and went back to reading *Hello!*

'I'm glad I never knew him, Harry must have been a right bastard.'

I was trying to be controversial, to spark debate, but she wasn't taking the bait.

'It wasn't Jackie's fault that his mother was an alcoholic. It sounds like living with Harry would drive anyone to drink. Poor Rosie. But I suppose if she didn't get it here she would have got it somewhere.'

This notion had only just popped into my head but as soon as I said it I realized I had hit a nerve. Jenny started to bustle, moving things around on the counter without any apparent purpose. I had accused her of supplying Rosie with drink. It had to be true: she wasn't denying it.

'Bad enough that he let Jackie think he was responsible, but to tell the whole village . . .' I sighed.

'What Jackie thinks is *his* business,' said Jenny.

At last, a response.

'Yeah, but everyone thinks he caused Rosie to have a heart attack.'

'Trixie, everyone knows that Rosie was a sick woman who died and didn't suffer any more, and that's all anyone needs to know.'

'Jackie says that at the funeral Harry . . .'

'Jackie would be lucky to remember anything that went on at the funeral, so stinking he was with the drink. He nearly fell in the grave alongside her. Harry had to catch him by the seat of his trews. It was a right wet miserable day. Jackie sat down there in the mud and cried like a baby. Harry was no better, shouting like that at the graveside. He should have let the boy come in the car, show his respects like everyone else. It was the worst funeral this town's ever seen, a disgrace. Rosie didn't deserve that. Aye, she took a drink, she was no different from yourself, but she was never a bother to anyone.'

Ouch, Jenny was comparing me to someone who died vomiting blood when her liver packed in. But Rosie was Harry's wife, she had no genetic link to me, thank God.

'Rosie was good at keeping it quiet. You wouldn't know she'd had a drink. Even when she fell ill she didn't stop, she didn't want to stop. She wouldn't have Dr Robertson in the house. Harry begged me not to serve her. It was a sore thing to refuse her, she needed it, but I couldn't give her it. Rosie was always a determined person, she would have went to the ends of the earth for a drink. She went out and hitched a lift off tourists, and got as far as Inverness. She spent all the money she had on drink and then phoned Harry to come and bring her back. Nobody in the village ever knew about that, not even Jackie. After that Harry said I was to give her what she wanted, no more than half a bottle a day. God love her, she would have wept to see the state of Jackie at her funeral. He's never touched a drop since. That's why I told you not to take whisky to him, I didn't want him tempted.'

'He gave me it back, Jenny. He didn't want it. I didn't know why at the time.'

'He's a good lad. Och, he's done a lot of stupid things, but haven't we all? The car crash, that was when it all started to go wrong for him.'

'In what way?'

Jenny had forgotten her earlier reticence. She was bursting like an overripe grapefruit now.

'He won't tell you this and I'm trusting you never to mention it, but Jackie was drunk that night. Rosie told me.'

'I'd assumed Marie was driving!'

'No, it was him. His wife was left a cripple. Her family hated him after that, who could blame them? They took her back to England. It was her father who had set them up and it was him that forced Jackie to close the restaurant. He was in no fit state to run it anyway. You'd think that crippling your wife would sober you up, but it had the opposite effect on Jackie. Things went from bad to worse, first he lost his wife, then his business, then his mother. And Harry blamed him for all of it.'

'Poor Jackie.'

At least I'd be able to set the record straight and let Jackie know he hadn't killed his mother. It was the least I could do for him.

I was tempted to go round to his house immediately and tell him, *hey Jackie, good news, your mother was an alcoholic! It wasn't you, it was the drink that killed her!* Maybe it wasn't such a good idea after all, maybe Jenny was right, it was Jackie's business what he believed. But still and all, he should know the truth. I'd have to judge when the time was right and break it to him gently.

Meanwhile, Steven was waiting for his results. The morning they were due to arrive, I called him.

'Right. The envelope feels quite heavy.'

'Steven, that isn't an indicator. It'll be the same weight whether you've passed or failed. Just open it.'

'No. I need to be mentally attuned before I can open it.'

'OK.'

We observed about a minute's silence.

'Ready?'

'Shhh!'

We observed a further minute's silence. I didn't mention that at peak time long distance, Steven's mental attuning was costing me an arm and a leg.

'Right I'm ready.'

'Thank God. No, Steven, wait!'

'What?'

'Don't open it yet.'

'I'm going to, it's OK, I'm attuned.'

'Yeah but hang on. I just want to tell you that no matter what is in that envelope, we, your dad and I, will think no better or worse of you.'

'Yeah yeah, I know.'

'And if it's not good news I don't want you to take it hard. You've done your best and we're proud of you.'

'Yeah yeah. I've opened it.'

Another big long silence, which this time felt more like an hour, while Steven read his certificates.

'And?'

'And I've passed! Everything, even maths! I've got six ones and two twos.'

'Steven that's brilliant! Fantastic, son! What a guy!'

I was shouting down the phone but he couldn't hear me. I could hear him whooping and laughing, running, crashing into things.

'Yes! He shoots, he scores, goal!'

I pictured him dancing around Nettie's living room, taking applause from his imaginary stadium crowd.

'Steven,' I said, when he finally came back to the

phone. 'That's it, there'll be a big fat cheque in the post to you this week as promised and when you come up next weekend we'll celebrate properly. It's the village fête and gala day, I'm entering some of my roses and I've put Bouncer's name down for the dog show, it should be a laugh. After it we can go to that hotel you fancied at Bengustie. I'll book a table. Let's get lobster and wine and everything, the full bhoona. I've been dying to try that place ever since you mentioned it.'

'Oh, I can't do next weekend Mum. Sorry, I meant to tell you, I've made arrangements.'

'Well just bring Gerry with you, you know I don't mind. I'm getting to quite like the wee twerp.'

'Aye, but, it isn't Gerry.'

'Well whoever it is, it's OK.'

'It's actually a crowd of us Mum, girls and that. We're going out, it's been planned for a while.'

'Och that's OK, no bother. Come up when you can, there's no rush. You have a good time son, well done, I'm proud of you.'

'I'm sorry I'm going to miss the gala day. Inverfaughie's always so quiet, just my luck to miss the one day in the year something actually happens. I hope you win something.'

'Oh aye, Bouncer and I'll knock 'em dead.'

Rebecca was as gutted as I was that Steven wasn't coming for the gala day.

'But I'm playing my guitar and Jan says I'm going to win the eight-to-twelve-year-old category. Steven has to see me pick up my trophy!'

'I know pet, but he can't make it. He has to work.'

I didn't have the heart to tell her that we were no longer the only women in Steven's life.

'Never mind, we'll still have a good time. You can

253

help me with my traybakes. Jan's asked me to help raise funds for the guitar club's trip to Glasgow.'

'What trip to Glasgow?'

'Has he not told you? Jan's hiring a minibus so you can see some amazing Spanish guitarist at the Royal Concert Hall. But it wasn't me that told you, for God's sake don't dub me in, OK?'

'Cool! I've never been to Glasgow.'

'You'll love it, it's a great place. But we'll have to shift a lot of cakes to pay for the bus. Jan wants us to run a stall.'

'Jan fancies you.'

'Away you go, he does not! He's just trying to raise funds.'

'He does so! He told Ailsa that you were a nice lady.'

'I thought you weren't speaking to Ailsa?'

'Aye, I fell out with her but then we fell back in.'

'Good, that's nice.'

'You're nice, that's what Jan said.'

'Well that was nice, it's nice to be nice. But it doesn't mean he fancies me.'

'And he wears aftershave, he never used to, he pongs now.'

Rebecca giggled and held her fingers to her nose while she started a nasal sing-song.

'Pongy Jan fancies Trixie! Pongy Jan fancies Trixie!'

'Get a grip Rebecca, he's only after my French fancies.'

Of course I behaved grown-up and redirected her attention, but Rebecca's childish chant sang in my head all day.

Chapter 26

Jenny was almost as gutted as I was that Steven wasn't coming for the gala day. Although she'd never actually met him, she knew as much about him as I did, as much as I could tell her, and she was always hungry for more information. I spent all my time bumming him up. It was strange and somehow sweet that this childless elderly woman took such an interest.

'Och that's a shame Trixie! And me with a wee present for him for doing so well in his exams!'

'I'm sorry Jenny.'

'Och it'll keep until the next time. No, it's you I'm disappointed for. You were looking forward to trying out the Bengustie hotel. Here, what about this for an idea? Me and you could go anyway! I could close up early on Sunday, make a wee day of it. We could book a nice Sunday lunch at the Bengustie, celebrate on Steven's behalf.'

'Oh Jenny that sounds great. I've been a bit fed up since he said he wasn't coming. I could do with a wee treat.'

'I think we both could. So, it's a date then? Get your glad rags on Trixie, we're going posh.'

*   *   *

The Bengustie was better than I could have expected. Everything was fresh and prepared on the premises, none of your frozen fish from London or your microwaved individual portions, everything was homemade: bread, fish soup, venison stew, raspberry flan, it was fabulous. Except that we had to share a table.

Annacryne, a town just north of Bengustie, was in the midst of its Highland Games, and the hotel was booked full of American caber-tossers. Jenny knew the manager and he managed to squeeze us in, but we had to share with two women tourists from Yorkshire. Jesus, these women could moan: they didn't like the weather, they didn't like the hotel, they even moaned about the food. These old bags could have put a right dampener on our day out but Jenny saw the potential for a bit of sport.

She pretended to sympathize, clucking and tutting at everything they said. She was way over the top but they didn't catch the sarcasm. Putting different inflections on it, sometimes sounding scandalized, sometimes empathizing, Jenny said 'Oh, I know!' twelve times in a row. I sat quiet, marvelling at her talent for taking the piss. Encouraged by Jenny's under-standing, the women told us how disappointed they were that there was no Marks and Spencer up here. They had brought their charge cards especially, *it makes the holiday, having a bit of a shop, and let's face it, if you're going to shop, Marks is the place to do it. Oh I know!* They couldn't believe that there wasn't a Marks and Sparks for a hundred miles, they had never been so far away from one in their lives.

Jenny leaned across the table conspiratorially and whispered, 'Oh, but there is.'

The women gasped. 'Where?'

Jenny tapped her nose. She leaned back in her seat,

took a sip of coffee and licked her lips. She was stalling, trying to think up a plausible story.

'You know how when you go into Marks and you see a nice cardi but it's forty-five pounds and you think you'll wait for the sale and see if they reduce it and anyway, you've seen one similar in Littlewoods for twenty?'

The women nodded, they knew exactly.

'But when you look at the Littlewoods one again it's not really the same and you prefer the Marks one?'

Vigorous nods from both of them.

'And when you go back to Marks the cardi is gone and they're not getting them in again?'

Nods all round, I was even nodding.

'Well, they're here.'

'Where?'

'Market forces. That cardi is taking up valuable space. If everyone waited for the sale Marks wouldn't make any money. So they sell them off cheap, but far enough away that it's not going to affect their trade. Next time you'll pay top dollar for the cardi because you know it'll be gone otherwise. Unless you know where to find it.'

The women were hanging off the edge of their chairs.

It was plain that Jenny didn't get out much. She was being very naughty: tourists provided a living for nearly everyone in the Highlands, it was an unwritten rule never to be rude to them.

'About five miles along the coast road, ten minutes after the turn-off to Dressar, there's a road on the left marked Quarry. Up that road about three miles you'll find an unmarked shop. From the outside it just looks like a hut but from the inside, oh, from the inside there are all the wonders of Marks at a fraction of the price. You just have to be in the know. Ask for Big Wullie, it's code, show them your card, tell them you're Fanny and that you're looking for Big Wullie.'

Jenny turned to me. 'Daphne, get our coats please, we must get home, Mother will be worried.'

We had a run of glorious sunsets every night for a week. An old couple in a green Audi with a German registration plate began parking outside Harrosie every night as the sun went down. The first time I spotted them I got comfy so's I could watch the fun. It was going to be a laugh watching these pensioners running around, slapping and scratching, trying to beat off the midgies. But this was obviously not their first visit to Scotland.

The Germans were fly for it, they didn't get out of the car. Every night they sat with the electric windows locked, cocooned in their luxury vehicle. Every night they sat entwined, not speaking or even looking at each other, just gazing out to sea, watching the big red ball slide down behind the island, not kissing or any funny business, just her nuzzling his neck and him stroking her hair, both of them watching my sunset.

That was something I'd noticed since the tourists started arriving, the amount of hugging that went on. It seemed that as soon as they unpacked and pulled on their holiday leisurewear, they started pawing one another. You could hardly go anywhere but there were couples clasping and squeezing each other, and not just the young ones, the Old Marrieds were just as bad. Long-term spouses embracing openly on the street, it was hideous.

Three nights of the green Audi lieblings was enough for me. I considered painting a No Parking sign but Roger next door would probably go mad. I wasn't brave enough or daft enough to go out and confront them. I got the idea from a *Roadrunner* cartoon.

The annoying thing was that I never found out whether it worked or not. I expected to hear at least one loud bang as their tyres burst on the nails I'd dropped in the parking bay. But to my great disappointment, the Audi pulled away smoothly. They never came back but maybe that was the end of their holiday anyway.

I went down to the shop to get the stuff for the traybakes.

'Och now, I didn't tell you did I?' said Jenny, 'Ali and his wife are having a . . . och now what do you call it again?'

'A baby?' I said, trying to be helpful.

'Don't be ridiculous! She's over forty, she hasn't the eggs!'

I didn't think that was very nice but that was Jenny for you.

'Och, what's wrong with me, I can't remember the word.'

I could see she was struggling but I kept my mouth shut.

'I'm having one of my senior moments again,' she said, annoyed with herself. 'I think I'm coming down with that CRAFT disease.'

She said this as she wandered into the back shop. I could hear her ripping up boxes and muttering to herself.

'What's CRAFT disease?' I shouted through, I thought I'd better ask.

She poked her head through the plastic fringe curtain and said, 'Can't Remember A Fucking Thing.'

Always the joker. Jenny was a cheeky swine but she could always make me laugh.

The bell rang on the shop door and it was Ali himself.

'I was going to make the posters for the ceilidh,' he said.

'Och yes yes, the ceilidh, I was just telling Trixie all about it. Ali's going to run a ceilidh for the gala day, just to round it off.'

'But I don't know how to spell it!'

Poor Ali had to stand there like a schoolboy while Jenny gave him a row about his inability to spell in Gaelic. I knew all about Ali from Jenny. She had filled me in on almost everyone in the village. Calley Ali, as everyone called him, bought the hotel three years ago. Jenny said that at the time there were a few in the village that weren't pleased.

The previous owners, the Dougal family, had owned the Caledonia hotel for generations but they couldn't make a living from it. It was too big and they didn't have the capital to maintain it. The place was falling apart when Ali bought it. He put money in, renovated the bedrooms, modernized the restaurant and brought in the Folk Club. He got a deal with the Continental tour companies. Even if they didn't stay at the Calley, the tour buses stopped there for lunch and spent money in the village. Ali could have halved the staff, cut his costs, maximized his profits, but he kept everybody on. Some people in the village owed their living to the Calley hotel and everyone else benefited from it.

Jenny wasn't long in taking over the poster production. She shooed Ali out the shop, telling him she would sort it out. The minute he was out the door she was scribbling on the side of her paper bags. I gathered up all my flour and glacé cherries and the like and attempted to pay her.

'How much is that I owe you Jenny?'

'It's for funds for the wee ones' trip, isn't it?'

'Yes, Jan's taking them to Glasgow for a concert.'

'He's a nice man, for a foreigner. He thinks you're a nice lady.'

'And so I am! What's the story with Jan, has he not got a wife? Is he gay?'

'No he's not gay, there's no poofs in the Highlands. That'll be seven pounds please.'

'Seven quid for all this stuff? That's not right Jenny, you're doing yourself.'

'I'm not charging for the baking stuff, that's for the children. Seven pounds for your box of wine, please.'

'Och, thanks very much Jenny, that's awful good of you. I'll be sure to tell Jan about your donation.'

'Don't you dare tell a soul, they'll all be round here looking for handouts.'

All the while she spoke to me, Jenny was still scribbling on the paper bags. She had her hand cupped round what she was writing but when I went up on my tiptoes I could make out cheildi, cielihd, cielidh.

'It's c.e.i.l.i.d.h.,' I said.

'I know it fine!' she said, 'I was only practising for writing on the posters.'

Chapter 27

Rebecca and I worked like demons, baking till we dropped, for the gala day cake stall. We made apple, coconut and cherry flapjacks. We made tablet, coconut ice, brownies, almond slices, snowballs, and millionaire's shortbread. By way of an experiment I baked two massive slabs of sponge.

It was a qualified success, the one in the top shelf of the oven was fine but the lower-shelf sponge sagged like a hammock in the middle. Not to worry I thought, as I set about performing a bit of cake first aid, I'll just layer it. I spread raspberry jam on the saggy one, filling the crater with extra jam, and then I spooned thick white icing sugar on top of the nice flat one.

We made so much stuff that Rebecca was actually fed up licking the bowls. I went for a pee and came back to find her letting Bouncer have a lick. He thought he'd died and gone to heaven.

Even although she'd stuffed her face all day with cake mixture, Roger insisted that Rebecca go next door for her dinner. The man had no sense of fun. When she came back her face was tripping her.

'Trixie, will you give me a lift to the gala day?'

'Of course I will pet, but are your mummy and daddy not coming?'

'Our car is broken. Daddy got nails in two of his tyres last night. He says we have to wait till he gets paid before he can get new ones. But he says that about everything. He hasn't been paid for ages.'

'Go and tell your dad that I'll take you all to the gala day, it's no bother. Rebecca, hold on a minute.'

I quickly filled a tin with a selection of cakes and gave her them to take next door. It was the least I could do.

'Mum and Dad say thank you very much for the cakes,' said Rebecca when she came back.

'Are they coming to the gala day?'

'Yes, Mum and Dad are very much hobliged and I've to ask you what time you're going.'

'Well I'll have to get down there early before it officially starts, so will you if you're going to help me with the stall, but if your dad comes with us he can bring the car back here, it's insured for any driver. That way they can come whenever they want.'

'Oh it's going to be brilliant!'

'Hey, hey! Calm down!'

Rebecca was jumping around the kitchen, Bouncer was starting to get excited too. I was nervous that the cakes, which filled every available space on the work-tops, still cooling or in various stages of preparation, would get damaged.

'Trixie, can I use that ball of tartan string you have?'

'If you like, what d'you want it for?'

'We can tie the cakes with it and sell them to tourists for double the price.'

I had to admire the eight-year-old's business acumen.

'D'you think it will work if we tie some around Bouncer? I think he's going to win Best in Show.'

'He's definitely going to win Smelliest in Show unless we get him in the bath.'

Getting him in the bath was trickier than I had

anticipated. Although Bouncer was always keen to explore the muddiest bogs he could find, he refused point-blank to sit in the bath. He started his bouncing malarkey, nearly throttling himself with every upward bound as I held him rigidly by the collar.

'For God's sake Rebecca, scoosh him now!'

She did her best but it's a difficult thing to scoosh a moving target, never mind a leaping one. Much easier to scoosh the person holding the target.

'Get him!'

Bouncer's rhythmic yelps were punctuated by our random squeals whenever we caught a ricochet. After five minutes I gave up and let him go. I was soaked from head to foot, the bathroom mat was saturated and Rebecca was dripping. Bouncer was barely moist.

'Don't let him in the kitchen!' I screamed, but it was too late.

Stuck for space, I'd moved the iced sponge slab down from the table onto a chair while I cut and cling-filmed the coconut ice. By the time I got to him Bouncer had the iced sponge pinned down with a soggy paw, ready to devour. His feet were wet, not from Rebecca and my efforts, but from contact with the wet bathroom floor. When he realized that jumping wasn't going to deter me from throwing him out, he dragged his arse along the ground until we reached the garden.

'Oh no Trixie, it's ruined! He's slebbered all over it and there's a big dirty paw mark on it! Bad, bad dog!'

It was true. First aid wouldn't do it this time; the cake was too far gone. Damn my foolish generosity I thought, I should never have given Roger and Polly all those cakes. I had expected to get at least sixteen slices out of the sponge. Now it was contaminated with dog germs, unfit for human consumption. I was going to be short of stock for the stall. And yet . . .

I asked Rebecca to stay in the garden and give

Bouncer a good scrub with his brush. While she was gone I rubbed a wee drop of McSpor's kitchen scouring cream onto a J-cloth and scoured the brown paw stain off the white icing on the sponge.

Roger was genuinely grateful for the loan of the car.

'This really is very kind of you,' he said, as we drove down to the gala.

'Not at all, any time Roger. The car's insured for any driver, I hardly use it, except to nip down to the village for my messages or when my son's visiting. Please, use it any time you need it. Here, that's the spare key, why don't you keep a hold of that for the moment? Then you can take the car when you need it.'

'I must say, I'm rather overwhelmed by your generous offer Trixie, you've already been so good to us. We do appreciate you taking Rebecca to guitar class, she thinks the world of you, don't you darling? I'm afraid I misjudged you Trixie, and for that I apologize. We got off to a bad start and I dare say Polly and I haven't been the best of neighbours.'

'Och, you're not the worst.'

I hardly knew where to put myself. If Roger knew the half of it.

'The fact is, Polly's not very well. We need our car just to escape occasionally. The children love Inverfaughie but we find the Highlands . . .'

We were just coming down the hill into the village. Laid out before us in vibrant blues, purples and greens was the magnificent vista of loch, sea, mountains and hills.

'We find it quite oppressive sometimes.'

That was the first time I felt truly sorry for them.

In the fields on the lochside which had been set aside for the gala, white marquees dwarfed the red and white striped tents dotted around them. The brightly painted kiddie rides and bouncy castle were set up opposite the areas that had been squared off with rope for the races and dog shows. The unmistakable smell of smoked mackerel wafted across the fields from a roughly improvised barbecue pit. This is going to be brilliant, I thought.

Jan spotted us driving in the gates and directed us to our stall. We had a good pitch right next to the entrance to the main marquee. Rebecca went with her dad into the marquee for a look round, this was where the guitar competition would be judged. When they came back Roger kissed her and left, saying he'd bring her mum and Michaela down in plenty of time to see her play.

'Trixie, you have baked many cakes, this is wonderful!' said Jan.

'Well, I couldn't have done it without my lovely assistant Rebecca.'

This was the first time that I'd properly looked at Jan, or looked at him in a certain light. In a certain light he was actually quite ugly: big jaw, big nose, scowly face, but he was ugly in a manly kind of way, it suited him. But maybe I just thought that because I knew he liked me. Maybe I was so lacking in attention from the opposite sex that I was automatically warmly disposed to any man who might fancy me. Living in the Highlands was making me less picky.

Jan was well organized, he had prepared a cash float for us and bought a programme so we all knew when our own events were scheduled. He'd worked out a rota so that all the kids in the guitar group got a turn of serving at the stall. Even with the help of Jan and Rebecca's friend Ailsa who turned up, it took us three quarters of an hour to lay out the stuff and write the price tags. Considering all the excitement, Bouncer was very well behaved. After he had a good sniff, he was happy just to lie down under the table and enjoy the sunshine.

We had only just finished getting ready when we heard the pipe band come along the road from the town. Villagers and visitors walked behind and when the band came through the gates, the gala officially started. The locals, aware of the bargain they were getting, flocked to our stall. We sold half our stock in the first fifteen minutes. After that, trade slowed dramatically.

'Trixie, you will need time to get your dog ready for the competition, it will begin soon. Ailsa and Rebecca and I can manage here.'

'No, I've done everything I can with that dog, which isn't much, he's as ready as he'll ever be but I wouldn't mind nipping over to the flower-show tent, I want to enter my roses.'

I carefully removed the flame orange stems from the tinfoil and showed them to him.

'Oh they are beautiful! Beautiful roses, wonderful cakes, you are a woman of many talents, Trixie.'

He was a silver-tongued devil, that Jan.

I was the last entrant and so I didn't get a very good display spot, but the other entries didn't unduly worry me. It wasn't until I looked at them that I realized just how lucky I had been with my roses. My leaves, stems and petals were in peak condition.

Having never entered a flower show before, I didn't really know what they were looking for, but I assumed leaves, stems and petals were important, along with size and colour of the blooms. As I wandered along the aisle checking them out, I began to feel a bit sorry for the other entrants. Although they had been expertly trimmed to hide the worst, most stems showed some evidence of bug blight. Some colours were dreich, more like a boilwash accident than nature's paintbox. One or two just looked knackered.

'Harold, look at these,' I heard an American woman say to her husband, 'aren't they just the prettiest, I love that orange colour!'

I smiled at her in what I hoped she would recognize as bashful pride but she looked right through me.

'Thank you. I wasn't sure whether to enter them or not,' I said, directly to her.

'Oh, are these flowers yours? They're gorgeous, I just love that shade, it's so exotic!'

I nodded shyly. 'Well, the Highlands are not generally known for exotica but we do our best.'

The American couple, hand in hand, apparently superglued to one another, moved off.

'Aye, I would be proud of them myself,' a voice behind me said.

My face flared as I realized that the voice was Jackie's. He had caught me showing off, bumming my load, talking cheesy nonsense to tourists and taking the credit for his ancestral roses.

'Hi Jackie,' I said with a high-pitched laugh, 'have you entered any flowers yourself?'

'Och no, the competition is too fierce,' he said, but his smile was kind.

He was a bit embarrassed as well, I think. He hadn't contacted me since we'd been out in his boat.

'Are you enjoying our wee gala day?'

'Aye, it's great.'

'I suppose it's not what you're used to in Glasgow.'

'How d'you mean?'

'Och well, it's not very exotic.'

'Oh you must have missed the exotica tent on the way in. It's just next to the Boys' Brigade tombola.'

The banter broke the ice and we both relaxed.

'Jackie, I'll need to head back, I've left Bouncer and he's entered for the dog show which is about to start but can I catch you later, maybe in the beer tent?'

'Sorry Trixie, I'm . . .'

Roger and Polly appeared at our side.

'Well done Trixie, your roses look terrific!'

'Thanks Roger.'

There was a moment's silence while Roger and Polly eyed Jackie. Where were my manners?

'Polly, Roger, can I introduce you to my . . .'

I instantaneously grasped the reason for the terror that passed across Jackie's face. He didn't want me to tell them he was my brother. But he *was* my brother. I wanted Roger and Polly to know that I had family. Most of all I wanted Jackie to, if not be proud, then at least acknowledge me.

'. . . gardener,' I said.

'Oh, so *you're* the chap responsible for these lovely flowers then?' Roger joked.

'No, it was all Trixie's work,' said Jackie.

He looked relieved and grateful and sorry and embarrassed, all at the same time. Roger looked confused. Polly, dishevelled and with a faraway look in her eyes, looked like she couldn't care less.

'Sorry, I've got to get back, the dog show's about to start,' I said.

'Yes,' said Roger with a forced jollity, 'we'll come and watch you putting Bouncer through his paces, that should be fun.'

'Nice to see you Trixie,' said Jackie.

I shot him a filthy look and walked away, leaving Roger trying to hurry along the listless Polly.

I got back to the stall to discover Jan missing, Ailsa in floods of tears and Rebecca with her arm around her.

'What is it? What's wrong? Where's Jan?'

For one horrible moment I thought she'd been poisoned by my iced McSpor scouring cream. I saw myself before the Procurator Fiscal with the half-chewed cake, recovered at autopsy from Ailsa's stomach, as exhibit number one.

'He's gone to get her mum. Ailsa's upset. She made a mistake playing her guitar piece.'

Rebecca stage-whispered this to me, which was totally pointless as Ailsa could hear every word she said.

'I got mixed up,' Ailsa said between heaving sobs, 'I stopped and I couldn't start again, I was looking at the music but I couldn't read it. I was rubbish!'

She started to wail again. Bouncer came and sat at her side. He didn't like it when anyone cried but he never knew what to do.

'You were not rubbish! You were good,' said Rebecca.

'I'm sure you were fine, Ailsa.'

Rebecca was such a nice wee girl, sometimes she put me to shame. Just then Jan returned with Ailsa's mum. As she was being led away Rebecca called after her.

'Ailsa! You've forgotten your guitar!'

Not only had Ailsa forgotten her guitar, she'd forgotten how old she was as she threw a tantrum worthy of a two-year-old.

'I don't want it. I hate that stinking guitar!'

Once she was out of sight Rebecca shrugged.

'She was rubbish, actually.'

'But that was very kind of you not to tell her, you're a good girl Rebecca. Michaela and your mum and dad are here. They're coming to watch Bouncer in the dog show.'

'Oh, Trixie, we better hurry! It's five past, it's already started. Jan, can we go now? The dog show's started.'

'Yes of course, go on girls. Good luck Trixie, and good luck to you too Bouncer.'

'Jan, I wouldn't put any money on Bouncer winning.'

Chapter 28

Andy Robertson, the deejay from Inverfaughie fm, was commenting on the action through a scratchy-sounding megaphone speaker system. Andy was a local celebrity and he drew a big crowd. To start with, he announced the rules. Then as each dog appeared, he introduced them by name with a brief description and CV. As they progressed through the contest he provided a running commentary.

There was an assault course, problem-solving and an obedience test. It was the *Krypton Factor* for dogs. They came from everywhere, from the islands and from John o'Groats to Inverness. Dogs of every shape, size and breed had gathered. Every competitor had to slalom across the field, jump a fence, walk along a wall and crawl under a net. They had to manoeuvre a route through a purpose-built chicken-wire maze. Each was required to execute commands without question, to sit and stay and walk; to resist temptations such as sausages placed as booby traps for the ingenuous or poorly trained. Bouncer was of course rubbish.

Not entirely rubbish, he was not bad at the physical stuff.

'Bouncer is a two-year-old of unspecified breed whose hobbies include long walks, personal grooming and bouncing up and down, it says here,' Andy Robertson announced. Bouncer was making a good round until I spotted Jenny and Walter in the crowd and made the mistake of waving to them. It may have been my fault. Bouncer might have thought I was telling him to go to Walter. He dashed through the throng, knocking over two wee boys who were sitting at the front on the grass. That raised a laugh from the crowd, at least, and might have got him marks for charm. But when I tried to get him to complete the circuit he was all over the place. He wouldn't sit, then he wouldn't stay. He lifted the sausage in his mouth and then put it down again.

'Ah yes, as you see, ladies and gentlemen, Bouncer picked it up but he didn't inhale,' said the radio wag.

Despite his shambolic performance Bouncer got a good round of applause when he finished. Walter was delighted anyway.

'He's a good boy!' Walter said triumphantly.

As usual Bouncer was all over Walter like a rash. Jenny had to keep the dog at bay for fear that he would knock Walter off his feet.

'I've shut up shop for a couple of hours, the village is deserted anyway and Walter hasn't been out for ages. It's doing him the world of good to get out and see people,' Jenny said while Walter was busy canoodling with Bouncer.

'Now Trixie,' said Walter. He beckoned me closer to him. 'I want to suggest something and I hope you'll be agreeable.'

'It depends what it is, Walter,' I said with a cheeky grin but my stomach was churning. This was it, I was going to have to give Bouncer back.

'Jenny tells me that you and Bouncer get on well enough. Is that right?'

'Och he's all right.'

'You've been good to him and I'm very grateful. Och it's a sore thing to give up an animal, so it is. But if you want to keep Bouncer I'll put up no objections. Anyone can see the dog loves you.'

'Oh Walter, are you sure about this?'

'Yes he's sure,' Jenny interjected.

Suddenly I wasn't sure if I wanted the dog. He walked the feet off me every day and cost me plenty in dog food. It would be nice not to have to take him out morning noon and night, not to sit and smell his poisonous farts of an evening.

'Now, if you don't want him I understand,' said Walter.

Bouncer was sitting at our feet, looking up at us, too daft to understand what was going on.

'No, I do. I do want him, Walter. Thanks very much, it's very generous of you.'

Rebecca wasn't due in the guitar competition for ages yet, so she and Michaela and their schoolfriends took Bouncer for a walk. Jan had arranged for two mums to take their turn on the stall although business was pretty slow by now, all the good stuff had gone. Jan invited me to take a wander round the stalls with him.

As we moved around the craft stalls we passed Roger and Polly a few times in the crowd. Polly looked terrible. She had lost a lot of weight and it didn't suit her. The flesh drooped from her perfect bones, the English rose complexion had become a prison pallor.

I was fascinated by the long-jump event. There was no shortage of entrants, it seemed that all the men from the village were taking part, some of them the worse for drink. Most of them did quite short long jumps, landing arse first on the sand amidst loud cheering and great hilarity.

Jan and I stopped and bought smoked mackerel in

burger buns and sat on the grass and ate them. They were absolutely wonderful. I fancied a pint from the beer tent just to wash it down but I was too shy to suggest it.

'The cakes have been a great success. We have enough money for the minibus and tickets for the show. Now we can tell the children, they will be so excited.'

I just hoped Rebecca could keep her mouth shut.

'Thank you for all your help Trixie, you have been wonderful but I wonder if I can ask you something again?'

I was obviously getting too good at this baking carry-on.

'Well, you can ask,' I said. I was thinking, *but you'll be wasting your time*.

'Calley Ali has asked me, I mean the guitar group, to perform at the ceilidh tonight. I must tune guitars and sort sheet music. I will need someone to supervise seating and music stands. It is their first professional engagement, the kids will be so excited. But perhaps you are tired from making all these cakes.'

'Oh no, not at all, I'd love to help. I hadn't planned coming to the ceilidh but I'm happy to. D'you know Jan, in all the time I've lived here I've never set foot in the Calley.'

'Yes, I know what you mean. I have lived in Inverfaughie for four years but I have only been to the pub a few times.'

'What brought you here, Jan?'

'You do not want to hear my very long, very sad story.'

'I do.'

He stared at me and I met his gaze. I wasn't just being polite, I did want to hear it.

'I was ill when I came here. I was looking for

274

someone but I was crazy. My girlfriend went to work one morning on the tram in Amsterdam where we lived. She died there on the tram, her heart stopped. She was healthy, just one of those things. They showed me her body but I refused to believe it. I was crazy, a nuisance, I looked for her everywhere. Every day I saw her in the street and ran after her, but it wasn't her.'

Oh dear, I thought, he *was* a bit fruit loops. Typical, the only man for a hundred miles who fancied me was off his head.

'She didn't like Scotland, we visited once. She didn't like the midges. She swore she would never go back, we used to laugh about it. When they told me she was dead I thought it was a lie. I thought she was hiding in Scotland, knowing it would be the last place I would look for her. I was crazy.'

'It isn't crazy to grieve, Jan.'

'Rebecca told me that your mother died. Maybe you felt something the same?'

'Yes, something the same.'

'I am better now. I have accepted things, I don't see her any more.'

I giggled nervously, nerves made me do that, and always at the wrong time. I fought the impulse to go, *oh look Jan, there she is over there!* I pulled myself together and changed the subject.

'I'll have to go and buy my ticket for the ceilidh before they sell out.'

'No! Of course you will not pay for a ticket. After the show when the children go home I hope you will stay and allow me to buy you drinks.'

Superb, I thought, a night out, not any old night out but Inverfaughie's hottest ticket of the year, and better than that, on the drinks front Jan was talking plural.

'Performers do not pay for tickets. With the guitar group you are on duty, you are with the band.'

'Oh I like the sound of that. That makes me sound like I'm in show business. And tell me this Jan, do I get a backstage pass?'

How desperate was I? Not only was I flirting with a crazy man with a dead girlfriend but I was doing it while mackerel grease ran down my chin.

'For you Trixie, access to all areas.'

And he, it seemed, was flirting back.

A wee boy came round selling raffle tickets in aid of the Mountain Rescue Volunteers.

'Yes, I'll take some, give me ten.'

'They're a pound each,' said the wee boy as he tore off a strip and offered them to me.

Instinctively I shrank back. But I was having such a brilliant day, the best day I'd ever had in Inverfaughie. My cakes had been a sell-out success, Bouncer was now officially my dog and I had a date for the ceilidh.

'Och to hell with poverty, give me them! I'm feeling lucky today.'

As we walked back to our stall Bouncer barked hello. He was with Rebecca and Michaela who were now with their mum and dad. Roger and Polly were just ahead of us. I didn't need to hear what they were saying to know that they were bickering. Roger glanced behind and as soon as he spotted us he rushed over.

'When on earth is Rebecca going to get her turn? We've had to wait around all day!' he almost shouted at Jan.

Jan was a bit taken aback but he answered politely.

'I'm sorry Mr Atkins. The judges have many children to test, they go as fast as they can.'

'Yes but it says in the programme that the guitar competition is at 1 p.m. and it's nearly three. This is unacceptable. Can't you have a word with someone?'

276

'But I have no influence with the judges, I would not interfere. I'm sure they are doing their best.'

'Well, their best simply isn't good enough. My wife is of a nervous disposition, she's anxious to get home. I'm going to speak to the judges if you won't.'

Roger stomped off and Polly trailed behind. Jan raised his eyebrows and shrugged his shoulders. I was annoyed that Roger should have spoken to Jan like that, but he didn't seem to mind.

'He is an unhappy man,' was all Jan said.

There were hardly any cakes left when we got back. Jan dispersed them to the kids and Bouncer as he packed up the stall.

'This is good. Now we are able to go to the prize-giving.'

Roger came back out of the marquee victorious.

'The judges have seen sense, Rebecca's getting ready, she's on next. She wants you to be there, Trixie.'

Again Jan shrugged and said he wouldn't come in, it might make Rebecca nervous, but he offered to stay with Bouncer.

The tent was very quiet now compared to how busy it had been earlier, and it had a hot smell of canvas and flattened grass. The neat rows of folding chairs were now a bit askew but we tidied the front row and sat down. Rebecca, alone on the stage, looked tiny. The judges sat at a desk, two men and a woman, and when Rebecca was settled, the woman lifted her pencil in the air as a signal for her to start. Rebecca looked across at us and her father called out, 'Off you go now darling!'

The whole thing was a bit anticlimactic. It was all over in about a minute and a half. I wanted her to do it again, this time in slow motion. Now I knew how Olympic athletes must feel, training for four years to run 100 metres in a few seconds.

She played her guitar piece, a piece I'd heard her

play a hundred times in my kitchen. She played faster and a bit jerkier than she usually did, but otherwise she played well. The Atkinses and I applauded enthusiastically, which coerced the few stragglers in the tent into clapping.

Jan and Bouncer were waiting for us when we came out.

'You played very well Rebecca, I heard you,' Jan said.

As soon as we emerged from the tent Polly walked off towards where Roger had parked my car.

'I'm sorry darling,' Roger said, 'I have to take Mummy home now but I promise I'll be back for the prize-giving.' He turned to me. 'I wonder if you wouldn't mind keeping an eye on the girls until I get back, would you Trixie?'

'Of course Roger, no bother.'

When at last the guitar competition was finished and results had been compiled for all the various contests, the prizegiving ceremony was announced. As everyone moved towards the main field I fell into step with Walter and Jenny. They'd had a lovely day they said, as they linked arms and laughed. I noticed how well Jenny looked, she radiated health and happiness, a beautiful-looking woman.

Andy Robertson started the proceedings with a lot of jokes about locals. He was quite witty but I couldn't fully appreciate it as I didn't know who he was talking about. Jan smiled at me and shrugged, he didn't get the in-jokes either. Roger, who made it just on time, was alternately threatening and pleading with Michaela to be quiet and stop whining.

Ailsa Robertson was announced as the winner in the eight-to-twelve-year-old guitar category. Roger's jaw dropped. Rebecca, standing between his legs, threw her head back and looked up at him. I saw Roger put his hands on his daughter's shoulder and squeeze. I had never missed Steven so much in my life. After those few stunned seconds Rebecca took it well. She managed a smile and clapped and congratulated Ailsa when she came past with the trophy. The trophy that should have been Rebecca's. Jan also congratulated Ailsa but he couldn't look at Rebecca.

Next were the field-event prizes and I noticed more Robertsons cropping up although, to be fair, I thought, the name was bound to occur more often, the town was full of them. But I was amazed when Jackie stepped up to collect the award for Personal Best in the Long Jump.

'As you know, ladies and gentlemen,' pronounced Andy, 'this prize goes to the contestant who has the biggest improvement on their previous score, and Jock has a good six inches more than anyone else.'

Even the incomers got that joke.

'I know he had the unfair advantage of being the only one sober, but he was the only one who got his score up and, as I tell you fellas every year, you can't get it up when you're drunk!'

The worse the jokes got, the more the locals cheered. I was getting a bit bored and gagging for a drink, but now he was announcing the dog-show results. A brown Labrador called Vivienne won Best in Show, which was no surprise.

'In the category Dog with the Waggiest Tail the prize goes to Bouncer, owner, Mr Walter McKinnon.'

Jenny turned to me and touched my arm.

'I've a wee confession Trixie. I changed your application form and put Walter's name. It gives the dog a better chance. Don't be annoyed with me.'

'I'm not annoyed, don't be silly!'

And as Walter went up and collected the rosette I tried my hardest not to be annoyed. Was I really so mean-spirited that I was jealous of a sick old man winning Dog with the Waggiest Tail?

But the real kick in the teeth came with the flower show. I didn't win, not even placed. Now that *was* unfair.

'Mrs Betty Robertson, our champion this year and every year as far as I can remember, is a very modest lady. Betty does not seek publicity and has asked the committee if she can collect the rose bowl trophy later in the day.'

Modest? Not brazen enough to lift a prize she knew she didn't deserve, more like. Does not seek publicity! She was so blasé she couldn't even be arsed turning up to collect it! I was robbed, I was gutted, I was publicly humiliated.

The prizegiving over, there was only the raffle to be drawn. No doubt every ticket would belong to a Robertson. Your ticket probably didn't make it into the drum unless you were one of those bastards.

'It's a buff-coloured ticket number 213, ticket 213!'

It was one of mine. I had to pass the trophy table to claim my prize. On my way past I had a strong urge to drop-kick their fucking stupid rose bowl into the loch.

I won a bottle of Old Pulteney malt. It wouldn't go wrong. I was pretty pissed off and I just wanted a drink, but no-one would come with me to the beer tent. Jenny was taking Walter home and Jan had to get organized for the ceilidh. Even Roger wouldn't join me, Michaela was whining to go home.

'Would you mind awfully if I took the girls home now, Trixie? I'll come back and pick you up later if you want.'

Poor Roger, he'd been running around like a blue-arsed fly all day.

'Och no, that's fine Roger, you take the girls home. I think I'll go and check out the beer tent anyway.'

The beer tent was a complete joke. For starters it wasn't even a tent, it was an unhitched horsebox with a steep gradient. Secondly, it only sold one kind of drink: beer. Cans of weak supermarket lager at a pound a go, it wasn't even chilled. But, inasmuch as it was filthy and full of drunks, it had a pub atmosphere. I got a can and a plastic glass and stood outside to get away from the smoke. I felt a tap on my shoulder and turned round. There was nobody there. I turned back to my beer and Kathy, Spider's wife, the madwoman who'd tried to attack me, was pushing her face at me.

'I think I owe you an apology,' she said.

I nearly choked on my lager.

'Eh, hello Kathy.'

'I'm sorry, Trixie. I jumped the gun. I know now that you were the innocent party. It was that filthy red-headed cheuchter nurse.'

Kathy looked as if she was about to start foaming at the mouth.

'Are you here for the ceilidh?' I asked.

Really, I should be directing her to the Inverfaughie Mental Health Awareness Group stall, I thought, she was excellent membership material.

'No, I'm not, I'm just the driver. I've got to go home to the kids. Spider is doing his Master of Ceremonies. He does it for them every year.'

'And will the band turn up this time, d'you think?'

'He's away sorting out the band now, at least that's what he told me. He's probably sniffing out the available fanny.'

Oh, but she was coarse, coarse and obsessive and miles madder than Polly. Kathy had a definite future with IMHAG, she could be chairman of the board.

'There he is!'

I pointed him out as he made his way towards us.

'Hello there Trixie! Can I get you a drink?'

'No thanks Spider, I'm still struggling with the one I've got. I'm not overly fond of this lager.'

'Did I not see you win something at the raffle?'

'Yeah, I won a bottle of Old Pulteney, the only bloody thing I won all day.'

'Huh, tell me about it,' moaned Kathy.

'Well, what are you waiting for? Get it out and give us a dram!'

'Are we allowed to drink whisky here, Spider?'

'Are we allowed to drink whisky? Jesus Christ woman, this is the Highlands!'

I was slightly perturbed at the measures Spider was pouring us from my bottle. I'd intended putting it away and keeping it good, but I supposed he had been pretty free with his whisky that time at his house.

'I saw Jock take the Long Jump Personal Best prize. Good for him!' said Spider.

'Oh that reminds me Spider, I'm glad I met you. I wanted to ask you about Harry. Jackie won't tell me anything. Well that's not strictly true, but he is so bitter he'll only tell me the bad stuff, like when Harry threw him out.'

'Aye well that's Jock for you, bitter and twisted. Harry was decent enough, he never did me any harm. Listen, d'you know where the Portaloo is?'

'It's over behind the coconut shy but they've closed it. It was overflowing, did you not hear the announcement?'

'Och it overflows every year. I'll go anyway, it'll give me something to piss against.'

'Aye, well don't be sniffing around any of your old slappers! I've got my eye on you, Spider,' said Kathy.

'Fuck up,' said Spider with utter contempt as he strolled off.

Kathy turned her attention back to me.

'He's as big a hoormaister as his pal.'

'Who?'

'That Jock or Jackie or whatever he calls himself. You said it yourself, his father threw him out the house for shagging.'

'Really? I didn't know that!'

'Oh aye, he shagged their housemaid, got her pregnant. Spider told me, I think he was bloody jealous.'

'Wait a minute Kathy, run that past me again. Jackie got the maid pregnant?'

'Aye, carrying on right under his father's nose. The woman was married and twice his age but that didn't stop the dirty little fucker.'

The whisky stopped working. Suddenly I didn't feel mellow any more. I felt as if I had been poked with an electric cattle prod. I couldn't wait for Spider to come back, I had to go and find him. He was nearby, laughing with a couple of young American women.

'Spider! Kathy says it was Jackie that got my mum pregnant. Is it true?'

Spider laughed as if I had cracked a joke. Then led me away from the girls.

'Now c'mon Trixie,' he said gently, 'you know it's true.'

Chapter 29

I was crying in the car on the way home but Roger didn't even ask why. I phoned Steven as soon as I got in the door.

'Promise me that you'll never lie to me, will you son?'

'Mum, stop crying, what's wrong?'

'Steven, don't tell me any lies. You're not coming to live with me are you? Just tell me, it's OK, I'll understand, I just don't want you to lie.'

'Mum please, you're scaring me, tell me what's wrong.'

'You're not coming to Inverfaughie are you, Steven?'

'No, I'm not Mum. I'm sorry. Oh Mum please stop crying, has somebody upset you?'

'You know that guy Jackie?'

'Yeah, your friend Jackie. Was it him, what did he say?'

'He's no friend of mine. He's my father and it's what he didn't say that hurts.'

'Mum, have you been drinking?'

'Yes I've been fucking drinking, I'm upset! I didn't tell you because you had your exams but Granny . . . made a mistake when she was young.'

'I know, she got pregnant, that's why they gave you the house.'

'You knew?'

'Nettie told me ages ago.'

'I'm going to strangle that meddling old bag.'

'Calm down, did you say Jackie was your father?'

'Yes, good old Jackie is my father. I thought it was his father but it was him and he didn't tell me. He let me think that Harry was my father, but Harry was my grandfather!'

'You're not making any sense.'

'Och what does it matter? Nobody tells me anything, why bother, it's only me! Who gives a shit?'

'So that means Jackie is my grandfather?'

'That's right, he's lied to you too.'

'Hey, I've got a granddad! Cool!'

I was ready to go when Rebecca chapped the door. I did think about cancelling but that would mean I'd be letting down Jan and the kids, and the Gala Day Ceilidh was the biggest night of the year. More importantly, I wasn't letting that bastard Jackie ruin it for me. Cinderella, I said to myself, you shall go to the ball.

I got done up to the nines in the tasteful understated dress and high heels I'd worn to Mum's funeral. The last time I wore it I had to keep my jacket on to hide my huge arse, but not any more. If I said so myself, I looked terrific. I might not have won any gardening prizes but it had made me a strong contender for Inverfaughie Rear of the Year. As I applied my make-up I kept topped up with wee whiskies any time I started to fade.

'Rebecca tells me you're going to stay on at the ceilidh after the children perform,' Roger said as he drove. 'I hope you don't mind, Trixie, but we'll have to come home. I can't leave Polly on her own too long. I'll give you the car keys when we get there, we can probably get a lift from some of the other parents.'

285

'Don't bother Roger, you take the car, I'm over the limit now anyway. I'll get a taxi or something.'

I couldn't be bothered thinking about the Atkins family's complicated travel arrangements.

Roger got us there early but the place was already quite full. The Calley lounge was reasonably small and it looked like everyone who had been at the gala day had transferred to here. Most of them didn't look like they'd been home. One local, my very own Daddy Cool, was conspicuous by his absence. Not to worry, I knew where to find him and there would be plenty of opportunities for telling him exactly what I thought of him. The ceilidh was neither the time nor the place. I should be concentrating on the kids' show.

'Did Rebecca tell you her good news, Trixie?'

'No, what is it pet? I could do with some good news.'

'I've to play the solo. Jan asked me after the prize-giving this afternoon.'

'Oh that's brilliant! Well, it just shows you, Jan's asked the best guitarist,' then tickling her, I whispered in her ear, 'not the best cup-winner.'

Rebecca giggled and ran away. I was supposed to be sorting out where they should all sit on stage but there wasn't enough room on the wee platform for ten chairs.

'Trixie, I think I can see a solution,' said Roger.

'Good on you Roj,' I said, and left him to it.

As Jan had predicted, the kids were hyper. As people poured into the wee bar and the noise levels rose, the kids got more and more excited. It was difficult to keep them all in the same place. While Jan tuned up the guitars I got them to set their sheet music under their seats. The music stands would have to be passed to them once they were seated.

Spider came over to check with Jan that they were

ready to start on time. They were. The kids' nervousness was infectious, I had the jitters myself now. It was a scary feeling, exciting, this was showbiz.

'Ladies and gentlemen, welcome to another Inverfaughie Gala Day Ceilidh,' said Spider, jauntily swinging his kilt. 'And if it's anything like previous ones there will be an awful lot of sore heads in the village tomorrow!'

Everybody cheered, they didn't need warmed up, they were up for a sesh, the atmosphere was thick with it.

'I'm sure you'll all agree that we've had a super day, the weather didn't let us down and we had the best turnout in years. I know how hard you all worked, so well done one and all!'

Jenny made her way through the closely packed chairs towards me. I could tell by her face that she knew that I knew. Jenny knew everything that went on in this town, word must have got back to her. As she got closer she put on a big wide smile but it didn't get as far as her eyes, they remained shifty.

'What are you doing here? You said you were going to stay in with Walter.' My voice was as cold as I could make it.

'I wasn't going to come, Walter's not up to it but I thought you might need a hand with the kids.'

'You knew, you knew and you didn't tell me.'

'Trixie. It wasn't my place. I told him you'd got the wrong end of the stick. I told Jackie he'd have to tell you and he said he would but . . .'

'You were supposed to be my friend, Jenny. You've lied to me every bit as much as he has.'

'Och I'm sorry Trixie. I'm heartsore, I really am, but I was in a terrible position. I kept hoping he'd tell you, I have to mind my own business in the village.'

'Yeah but everyone in the village knows *my* business! The only one who didn't was me!'

'Och you're upset, you've every right to be, but now that everything is out in the open you and Jackie . . .'

'Hello Jenny, nice to see you!' said Jan, walking up to us. 'I didn't know you were coming.'

Jenny recovered quicker than I did and switched on her smile.

'I'd be missed if I didn't turn out, I always do my party piece. I make a fool of myself every year but what else are parties for?'

'I am looking forward to seeing it. Excuse me ladies, I must go to the stage now.'

'Trixie, I *am* your friend. That's why I came.'

'Leave it, Jenny. Watch the show.'

Spider was on stage waiting for silence.

'Ladies and gentlemen, I'm proud to tell you that we have some of our young folk with us tonight. Don't worry now, they'll be off home safe in their beds before the serious drinking starts! But these youngsters are our standard-bearers, carrying forward the musical traditions of the Highlands, and we want to give them every encouragement. Ladies and gentlemen, please put your hands together for the Inverfaughie Guitar Group!'

I didn't know what to think. Jenny seemed sincerely sorry. After all, she did leave Walter and come to see if I was all right. Maybe she was right, maybe it was for the best, maybe Jackie would stop trying to avoid me now that the truth was out. But I was having to readjust to who I was again. I was almost having to do it on a daily basis. I needed a drink. I didn't want to think about Jenny or Jackie, I just wanted to have a good time, was that too much to ask?

I concentrated on the guitar group, who were absolutely fantastic. I think the audience expected

288

them to umchingaching their way through 'Michael Row the Boat Ashore' or something of that standard, so they were knocked out by the classical repertoire. Without anyone realizing it, Jan had quietly worked wonders with a rowdy bunch of kids.

Hardly anyone talked or went to the bar, instead they listened and clapped every piece. Even I felt proud and all I'd done was bake cakes. Maybe I should take up the guitar.

Roger had done a good job with the chairs as well. I thought he was quite right to put Rebecca's chair out in front, she was the soloist after all. When she played her piece, a traditional lullaby, smoothly and without a hitch, it was well received. I spotted one of the judges applauding, the woman who had held her pencil up, and hoped she was ruing her decision now. Rebecca saw her too and acknowledged the judge's presence with a gracious nod. The whole band joined in to finish off with a toe-tapping arrangement of 'Mairi's Wedding'. After enthusiastic applause, the kids, flushed with success, all clamoured to get off the stage at the same time.

Jenny had brought Mars bars for them and I was kicking myself that I hadn't thought of something nice like that. Everyone was falling over themselves to congratulate the kids, but it was Rebecca who received the greatest acclaim. Roger stood beside her, glowing with pride.

There was a contraflow of kids packing their stuff and ceilidh band setting up. I was glad when the kids left, I was beginning to sober up. Glad to see the back of Roger as well, his constant anxiety had exhausted me. When they went away it meant we had a table to ourselves: me, Jan and my best friend Jenny. While Jan was out at his car I remedied my creeping sobriety. Without a word I left Jenny sitting on her tod and went to the bar. I bought a Coke and took it with me to the toilet.

Safely inside the cubicle I swallowed half the Coke and refilled the glass with whisky from my hip flask. My Coke was now a telltale transparent brown, which I hoped Jan wouldn't notice. There was still some left in the hip flask so I necked it. With the wee charge inside me, I felt a bit better. The lighting and mirrors of the Calley washroom were particularly kind, and as I was washing my hands I took the time to appreciate just how hot I was looking. Fuck them, I thought, fuck them all.

By the time I got back Spider was calling the dances and that snake Jenny had moved in on my date. As I watched her and Jan dance the Gay Gordons I looked forward to getting my hands on him myself. He was a good dancer and that in itself I found quite attractive. The dance floor was packed, the band were great. Apart from the fact that I hated nearly everyone in the room, it was shaping up to be a good night.

True to his word, Jan got the drinks in.

'You are drinking whisky and Coke Trixie, yes?'

While he was away I had a go at Jenny.

'Can you not get someone else to dance with you? Jan asked *me* to the ceilidh tonight.'

'I know he did, I asked him to ask you, he was too shy.'

'Oh, the all-seeing all-knowing Jenny! Is there anything you don't know? Is that why you're here? Not only do you want the credit for him asking me out but, if anything kicks off with me and him, you want a ringside seat?'

'Don't be so stupid Trixie, anyway, he's all yours, I'm not going to dance with him again.'

'No,' I said with my face twisted, 'because it's not your place!'

Jenny shouted to Jan as he struggled towards us, trying not to spill the drinks.

'Oh there you are Jan, Trixie was just saying she's dying for a dance!'

I smiled graciously and accepted Jan's hand onto the dance floor. Over his shoulder I drew her a stinker.

It was a dance I hadn't done before, a waltz, but luckily Jan knew all the steps. When I went to move the wrong way he lightly pressed my back and swept me along. The birling and the whisky were making my head spin, it felt great. I looked across and watched Jenny watching us. How sad was that old woman? She was getting cheap thrills out of this. Well if that's what she was after, I'd put on a show. I turned my attention to Jan and gave him my Princess Di look. I'd had a practice run in the washroom mirror and I reckoned it was still a winner. Jan was a nice man and quite handsome when you got to know him.

'Trixie I was wondering, but I am always asking you favours.'

'I'm always happy to help, Jan,' I said, in Queen of Hearts mode.

'I would like to ask you to Glasgow with us next Saturday, in the minibus, to help with the kids, but perhaps you have had enough of guitars.'

Waltzing was so intimate, I could smell his breath and his aftershave. I could see the flecks of colour in his eyes and each individual eyelash. Our faces were only inches apart. My breasts were pushing into his chest. If it wasn't for our clothes, our groins would be touching.

'I'd love to come to Glasgow, and let me assure you Jan, so far I haven't had *anything like* enough of guitars.'

We were waltzing past Jenny and I wanted her to clock Jan's rapt expression. I shyly flicked my eyes off him just for a second and surveyed her. She didn't look pleased at all, but she seemed to be looking beyond us.

My Princess Di was going down a bomb with Jan, he had a crinkly smile on his face and I wondered if he was trying out a look on me, a Sean Connery maybe.

Lost in each other's eyes, we crashed into another couple. At first I didn't recognize him in the kilt, but it was Jackie, with a woman. I knew from the way she was dressed she was a tourist, but she looked familiar. It was shocking to see him but I was more shocked by the fact that he was obviously having such a good time. I'd never seen him in a kilt before, it was sickening how good he looked. He was laughing with the woman and snuggling up close until he realized it was me he had collided with. I supposed Jan and I must have looked the same.

I instantly pulled away from him and went back to my seat.

'He's here, did you organize that too Jenny?'

'Jackie's here?'

Jenny's eyes scoured the room until she found him.

'This was what I was worried about,' she said.

'I take it then that he doesn't know that I know.'

'I couldn't tell you.'

'What? You don't know if he knows that I know? I thought you knew everything.'

'Well I don't. But I don't think he'd be here if he knew you were.'

'Oh but I am. Aren't I just.'

'Trixie, are you all right? You walked away . . .'

'Oh sorry Jan, I thought the dance was about to finish! I'm fine! I'm absolutely rinky dink! Let's get up for the next one, and the other after that, I've got my dancing feet on now!'

And so we got up for the next one, and the one after that, and the one after that. I made myself highly visible on the dance floor by throwing back my head and laughing any time Jan made a wee joke. Jan was loving it, he thought he was the funniest guy there. The dance after that was a Dashing White Sergeant.

'Jenny, come and join us. Oh please, we need another lady,' said Jan.

'Oh come on,' I said through a sigh. 'You've been sitting on your arse all night.'

Jenny and I gave each other thin smiles and took our places. About halfway round the room we encountered Jackie, again with the woman. Spider made up their threesome. That was where I'd seen her before! She was one of the American women Spider was chatting up at the beer tent. The boys must be hitting on these two women. I looked around and sure enough, sitting at a table on her own, smiling at them, was the other American. She must be Spider's.

Jackie's date, the one we were dancing with, recognized me and nodded in a friendly way. Up close I could see that she wasn't that young. The slim figure and trendy clothes were deceptive, she was a good five years older than me, the dirty old cow. She and her friend probably had a tick list of things to do in Scotland: see *Edinboro*, the *Lack Ness* monster, and *get it on with a guy in a kilt*. I could understand why they found guys in kilts attractive, everything was so accessible. As I smiled at her I had a pornographic image of her getting it from behind with Jackie's kilt pleats spread out across her back.

As our two sets got ready to move on, Jackie was my opposite number. Up to that point when we'd faced another set, we had, as was traditional, politely exchanged heuchs. Then, following Jan's lead, we had ducked under the other set's arms. Not this time, I thought. There was no way I was taking a submissive role this time. Right into Jackie's face I heuched. *Heeeeeuuch!* In time to the music I charged him, he'd

293

have to duck or be smashed. Disappointingly, he ducked, but that was just typical Jackie.

We sat out the next few dances and Jan was very attentive, freshening up my whisky and Coke every so often with more whisky. So's not to embarrass the poor man, Jenny and I were forced to chat to each other.

'That's her over there,' she said pointing to a woman on a man's knee, 'Betty Robertson, the one who won the rose bowl.'

I expected a pensioner but Betty Robertson was in her thirties. She was sprawled on a man's knee like some kind of saloon girl.

'She's a very modest lady, as you can see,' said Jenny.

I had to laugh, this town was full of creeps and weirdos.

The band struck up another Gay Gordons.

'Would either of you ladies like to dance?' said Jan.

'Yes I will Jan, Jenny's already had a Gay Gordons and the poor old thing is knackered.'

I grinned at Jenny as we left the table but she pretended not to notice. I stopped to let another couple make their way onto the floor. It was Betty Robertson and her beau, who took their places directly behind Jan and me. There was quite a crush on the corner when we went into reverse and deary me, it was hardly my fault if I accidentally stepped on Betty Robertson's toes once or twice.

Chapter 30

The band didn't strike up another dance, instead Spider came onstage in a dressing gown to a cacophony of wolf whistles and laughter.

'Now girls, try to control yourselves! I'm not stripping off for you, well, not at the moment and not unless you ask me nicely.'

'Get them off!' shouted Betty Robertson.

'No, ladies and gentlemen, there is a very good reason why I appear before you in a temporary state of undress, one which will become apparent in a few moments. So without further ado, let me introduce our surprise guest of the evening, the one and only Mr Calley Ali Kapoor!'

The inhabitants of Inverfaughie were amazed to see the hotel landlord stand before them, resplendent in borrowed kilt and full Highland dress. As he was a few inches taller than Spider and a good deal wider, the kilt showed more of Ali's brown legs than it was supposed to.

An atmosphere of hysteria swept through the bar, the raucous laughter almost deafening. People were standing on their chairs to get a look at him. I didn't really get the joke, an Asian guy in a kilt wasn't that funny. On cue the band started to play and Ali, unsure of what he was doing, read from his sheet music.

As he sang, Ali's accent filtered through.

> '*Scots, vha hae vi Vallace bled,*
> *Scots, vham Bruce has often led,*
> *Velcome to your gory bed*
> *Or to wictorie!*'

The crowd clapped out the beat, and as the clapping gained momentum, it gathered speed. By the second verse it was out of time with the band. The band had no option but to speed up and Ali had no option but to follow. He was not a naturally gifted singer. With his voice hopping from one note to the next, staring hard at the words, he was struggling. The band raced through the song, playing faster with every verse. His dark skin radiant against the white frill of the tight dress shirt, Ali puffed and strained to keep up. It was becoming mob rule, a rammy, but Ali refused to capitulate. His good-natured exuberance and strong lungs were a match. The speed and volume at which he was forced to sing only enhanced the verve and brio of his performance. When he finished he had earned his applause.

Ali got off stage quickly after that and as he disappeared through the swing doors, a heckler shouted out.

'Hey Spider! Watch him, he'll spill curry all over your good kilt, man!'

This witticism procured belly laughs from the rabble. Spider made a face as if he was worried that this might be a possibility and scooted out after Ali. The cabaret over, Jan turned to us and asked Jenny and me what we wanted to drink.

'It's my round, I'll get them in,' I said.

*   *   *

They were three deep at the bar. After many years' experience of Glasgow's pubs, I automatically clocked everyone round about me. All these people were ahead of me in the informal queue. Anyone who approached the bar after me would be served after me. Already there were people behind me. All around I was catching snippets of conversation. Woven amidst typical bar patter like *just make it doubles* and *who's got the kitty*? I picked out the phrase *Paki bastard* and a woman saying *no harm to them but I wouldn't want one to touch me.* Small town, small minds.

'Now ladies and gentlemen we'll take a wee break from the dancing now with the open spot,' said Spider, fully kilted once more. 'Anyone who wants to do a turn: sing a song, tell a story, take their clothes off – ladies only for that one please – come on up.'

I was getting shoved about in the crush. A guy who'd been served spilled most of his pint just trying to get out. I'd managed to avoid getting soaked but in my high heels, after dancing all night, my feet were killing me. I should have let Jan get them in. A woman was singing now. She was so bad it was difficult to make out what song she was attempting. She bounced around shaking her head and squawking but nobody was paying any attention. There were only two people in front of me now, a fat guy and an old boy.

It was almost inevitable that Jackie would come and stand beside me. He hadn't noticed me and we stood together for several minutes before his eyes travelled round to me and beyond, right through me. I could see his dilemma. He had been sent to the bar, the girls would be expecting drinks, he couldn't go back to the table empty-handed. That meant he'd have to continue standing beside me, fruit of his loins, and pretend not to see me. His bottle went when the fat guy got served and everyone took a step forward, now he was almost pressed against me. This was too close for comfort and Jackie was forced to withdraw, sloping back to his table with his tail between his legs. Tears of rage burned behind my eyes but, fortunately, never put in an appearance.

'Double whisky and diet Coke,' I said the minute the old boy got his change. 'Pineapple and soda and a glass of . . .'

The barman blanked me and turned to serve a girl who had just arrived at the bar.

'Hello? I'm next!' I said. 'Double whisky and diet . . .'

'Sorry,' he said, 'regulars first.'

'Aye that'll be right, I've been here twenty minutes!'

But it was no use, he was ignoring me, taking his time serving the girl. Now *I* had a dilemma. Dignity required me to tell him to stick his drink up his arse but drouth said keep your mouth shut. The guy didn't even apologize when he finally did serve me.

When I put the drinks on the table I was aware of a chemical buzz through my body, a cocktail of adrenaline and whisky.

'Anyone else for a turn?' said Spider.

'Yeah, me!' I shouted from the floor.

I was on the stage with the mic in my hand and talking.

'Right. You want to hear a story?' I asked the audience.

I was wasting my breath, no-one was listening.

'This is a story about a lovely wee town where there are no poofs and hardly any Pakis and life is sweet. And in that lovely wee town lives a lovely man but, ladies and gentlemen, that lovely man is frightened, yes he is, he's very frightened. Och but he's a great guy! The sort of guy you all love, the sort of guy that provides a kilty-shagging service for the tourists, that cripples his wife and kills his alcoholic mother. The sort of guy . . .'

I stopped to savour the change in atmosphere. They were listening now. I couldn't see him anywhere. He wasn't even going to try and stop me. I knew he was there somewhere. Jenny was miming for me to stop. The only noise I could hear was the sound of my own breath through the mic.

'The sort of guy who denies his daughter, oh yes ladies and gentlemen, he shuns his own daughter. A spineless, weak, gutless, sad bastard of a guy. And d'you know who it is, ladies and gentlemen?'

From the floor Jenny burst into song.

'He met me, tea-stained postmistress from 'Fauchie. Dirn nirn nirn! He tried to take me upstairs where I bide.'

People joined in on the second *dirn nirn nirn*, the drummer and accordionist weren't far behind. By the end of the verse they were rocking. The whole pub sang *'Gimme gimme gimme, the Inverfaughie blues,'* but by that time I had been yanked off the stage and into the car park.

I had no idea Jan could be so dominant, and I told him so.

'You have something going on with Jackie? Is he the father of your daughter?'

Crying like a baby I put him straight on the whole story. We sat in the car outside Harrosie, all the while with Jan holding my hand, until I'd got it all off my chest.

'I'm sorry Jan, I've ruined your night.'

'Please don't worry.' He lifted my hand and kissed it. 'Will you be all right?'

He was leaving. In a nice way he was cueing me to get out of the car.

'Yes, thanks Jan, I'll be fine.'

As soon as I got out he spun the car round to head back.

'I hope you feel better tomorrow.'

I stood in the road waving. I watched his car disappear down the hill towards the twinkly lights of Inverfaughie and screamed, 'Here I am! Come and get me! There's not a fucking man amongst you! Inverfaughie bastards!'

I would have screamed more but my voice was hoarse.

Chapter 31

The phone woke me up.

'Well now you know how it feels!' said Steven. 'You woke me last night, don't you remember?'

I pretended I did.

'Mum, we're worried about you. You said last night you're coming back. I've told Dad and we think it's a good idea. You're miserable up there. When are you going to come home?'

'Just as soon as I can get my bags packed and get out of this shit hole.'

That seemed to settle him but he wouldn't get off the phone until I promised I'd call him back later. I lay down again but I couldn't sleep. My head was thumping. I had no idea how I got to bed last night. If I phoned Steven and couldn't remember, what else did I do? Thinking about this brought on a powerful attack of the heebie-jeebies. As soon as I could face it I was going to pour any alcohol in the house down the sink. I still had about half a bottle of Old Pulteney left and it was expensive stuff, but no matter. Look what happened to Rosie, and she was my granny. I did it with the fags, I could do it with drink.

As soon as I'd made the decision I felt better. This was my Last Ever Hangover. Two paracetamol and a sports bottle of Irn Bru later, I began worrying about going back to Glasgow. They didn't allow pets in rented property, and Bouncer was not the most discreet of beasts. Even if I found somewhere that would take us, I'd have to leave him all day when I went to work. They didn't allow dogs in doctors' surgeries either.

It was the combination of the thought of repping again and a surfeit of Irn Bru that made me vomit. As it slowly crept into my consciousness, self-disgust at my performance last night overwhelmed me. I retched and retched till I could retch no more. I felt like bubbling, a good greet would do me the world of good, but I refrained, I didn't deserve it.

As I got washed and dressed other things occurred to me. Rented property in Glasgow didn't usually come with a garden. The phone rang again.

'Trixie! How the hell are you?' said Jenny. 'How's Inverfaughie's very own Jackanory?'

'Terrible. I made a total arse of myself. I said about Rosie dying of the drink, that's the bit I feel worst about.'

'Och you didn't name names, don't be so hard on yourself! If it makes you feel any better it's a bit of an open secret, everything is in a town this size.'

'Jenny, I was an absolute disgrace!'

'Och you weren't the worst.'

'Oh come off it. What's worse than slagging off the whole town to their faces, outing your alkie granny and denouncing your da?'

After a thoughtful silence Jenny replied, 'You're right, I can't think of anything that tops that, but I've got another good one. There was a fight. It's not a proper ceilidh unless there's a good fight. Betty Robertson gubbed that American bit of stuff on the dance floor.'

'Really? Why?'

'Said she was sick of her standing on her toes.'

302

'I wouldn't get sick of standing on her face.'

'Indeed. And there's more good news, guess what?'

'What?'

'I've had an enquiry about your cakes. Ali wants you to supply his high teas.'

'Honestly? A couple of bus loads a day, that's a helluva lot of cakes.'

'Och that's nothing to a master baker the likes of yourself!' And with that she was gone.

I didn't have the chance to tell her that I was supposed to be packing up and moving back to Glasgow. How much could I make from cakes, I wondered. There was the raw materials, the electricity and my time. Maybe I could do tablet as well and Jenny could sell it at the shop. Or maybe not.

I stood and looked out the window. It was another cracking day. Everything looked the way it did yesterday, fresh and wild, beautiful.

'D'you want to move to Glasgow, Bouncer?'

Bouncer was non-committal.

The phone rang for the third time.

'OK Steven, I'm up! I've been up for ages! I've forsworn bevvy. Lips that touch alcohol will never touch mine!'

'I'm glad you are feeling better, Trixie.'

It was Jan. I never expected to hear from him again.

'I called to see if you are well. You sound good.'

'Yes I am, thanks. Or at least better than I was last night. I'm really sorry, Jan. I said some nasty things at the ceilidh, I didn't mean any of it. I'm sorry I let you down.'

'You were angry, you have been hurt, I could see that. You did not let me down. I enjoyed our dancing.'

There was an awkward silence.

'Did you mean it when you said you will come to Glasgow with us for the concert next week?'

'Yes, I will, if you still want me.'

'Yes, I still want you. Of course. I will call you to tell you when the bus will leave.'

'OK.'

I should have told him I was thinking of moving back to Glasgow.

I should start packing, I thought. After I poured all the whisky and wine down the sink, I went upstairs to find my suitcase. I was distracted – from the back window I could see that the garden needed tidying up. It wouldn't take more than an hour or two but weeds sprang up overnight at this time of year, you had to be ever-vigilant to stay on top of it.

Without the suitcase I went into my bedroom and looked out at the loch and the mountains, the islands and the town. This was the view that Mum had loved. This was the life that she had wanted. I watched the ferry come chugging up the loch, rocking the wee boats as it passed, into Inverfaughie. The town looked, as ever, tidy and serene.

I should pack, I thought. Pouring away the drink had finally cleared my head. I should phone Ali and see exactly what he wanted, then I'd know if there would be any profit in it. And the garden needed sorted out before Rebecca came for our walk. From the window I watched a man cycle up from Inverfaughie. He pedalled effortlessly up the steep hill. There were a few things I had to do before I thought about packing.

THE END